THE FIGURE IN THE PHOTOGRAPH

By Kevin Sullivan

The Figure in the Photograph

THE FIGURE IN THE PHOTOGRAPH

KEVIN SULLIVAN

Allison & Busby Limited
11 Wardour Mews
London W1F 8AN
allisonandbusby.com

First published in Great Britain by Allison & Busby in 2020.

A CIP catalogue record for this book is available from
the British Library.

First Edition

ISBN 978-0-7490-2531-1

Typeset in 11.5/16.5 pt Adobe Garamond Pro by
Allison & Busby Ltd.

The paper used for this Allison & Busby publication
has been produced from trees that have been legally sourced
from well-managed and credibly certified forests.

Printed and bound by
CPI Group (UK) Ltd, Croydon, CR0 4YY

For Marija and Katarina
with all my love

CALEDONIAN RAILWAY
Board of Trade (Railway Department),
8 Richmond Terrace, Whitehall, London, SW,
8th August 1898

Sir,

I have the honour to report for the information of the Board of Trade, in compliance with the Order of the 24th March, the result of my enquiry into the incident that occurred at 6.10 a.m. on the 24th March, near Eglinton Street station, Glasgow, on the Caledonian Railway industrial branch line.

A six-wheeled tender, and two four-wheeled carriage beds (unladen), without brake carriage collided with a pedestrian near the junction south of Cathcart Road, where the industrial line crosses the main road ex. Laurieston.

The pedestrian was severely injured as a result of direct contact with the forward wheels on the left side of the tender, and suffered the loss of the right leg and left arm below the elbow. Although help was summoned, death occurred within ten minutes of the incident. A post-mortem found that death was caused by loss of blood.

The constable on traffic duty witnessed the incident and filed a report which was subsequently notarised and has been corroborated by statements given under oath by two independent witnesses. No commercial or criminal liability has been raised.

I have &c.,

H. A. Lancaster, Lieut.-Col., RE

The Assistant Secretary

Railway Department, Board of Trade

CHAPTER ONE

Santiago de Cuba

One week before Christmas in 1897, we entered a hamlet on the way to Cárdenas. Not even a stray dog barked. We noted the silence as we began to move among the houses and shacks. We stopped – but too late. Armed men emerged onto the road, in front of us and behind us. One of them ordered us to dismount. He asked us where we were coming from and where we were going and what our business was. He was about forty, of average height, dressed in black boots, white cotton trousers and a white shirt that might have been washed recently. His grey hair was cropped; he was clean-shaven and his pale face struck me as being scholarly. I guessed he was the commander.

My father explained that we had been commissioned by William Collins, Sons & Co of Glasgow, London and New York to make a record of Cuba's most distinguished buildings.

The commander actually laughed. 'Photographers!'

He asked if we were armed. My father said we were not.

Another man inspected the packs on the horses.

No one was in uniform.

'No weapons,' the man rifling through our saddlebags said.

The commander looked ahead at the village and then, bringing his gaze round to meet ours, he said, 'Follow me.'

We walked behind his horse. My father glanced at me and I glanced at him.

'I am sorry, Juan!' he whispered.

'No, no, it will be fine,' I said.

Behind us our horses neighed in protest at being led by unfamiliar hands. I looked round and saw the beasts surrounded by men bearing carbines and machetes. None of them spoke.

We entered a street made of one-storey mud and thatch houses. There were cooking pots and bits of furniture in the drain that ran down the middle of the street. We had to pick our way through clothes and debris on the packed earth.

At the end of the street was a walled garden about ten yards by ten yards. On three sides the walls were too high to see over; they were thickly covered by creepers from which bright pink blossoms sprouted. The fourth wall was lower, and beyond it I could see fields. Eight human figures lay on the earth along one wall. At first, I thought they were sacks of maize.

They had been bound hand and foot. Each corpse faced skyward.

The commander moved towards the bodies and we followed, putting our hands and then our shirts over our faces to fend off the smell. I looked down at the bodies, first the feet and then the cotton trousers and shirts and finally the faces. Some had pus and other viscous substances coming out of their mouths; some had punctures in their heads; others had punctures in their chests.

'I want you to photograph them,' the commander said.

My father was silent.

'Why?' I asked.

I did not consider if it was prudent to speak. I was simply baffled.

'Because I want people to understand what happens to criminals in Cuba.'

We didn't know which side the dead had been on and which side the living.

My father's voice didn't waver when he said, 'Juan, the Kessler.'

My father was not a cold-blooded man, but neither was he without common sense. Perhaps if they had ordered us to bury the bodies or perform some such task we would have complied less easily. But making photographs offered the slight prospect of safe passage. We set to work.

The Kessler was our tallest tripod, equipped with a hinge and screw that could hold the camera at a perpendicular angle. This way, a photograph of the victims could be taken from above. It required the camera operator to stand on ladders.

'That wall has timber halfway up,' my father said.

The wall adjacent to where the bodies lay had a trellis attached to wooden beams that had been placed among the bricks. The beams offered a makeshift platform on which my father could balance and operate the camera.

Our horses had been brought to the edge of the garden. I set up the tripod and my father brought the Eclipse, our standard portrait camera.

The dead were barefoot; three had beards, all had moustaches, except for the boy at the end, who looked about fourteen. The oldest was perhaps sixty. I guessed that the figure next to the boy, a middle-aged man with cropped grey hair, had been the leader. I might have been quite wrong, yet this group in death appeared to have a kind of hierarchy. One face looked at the blue sky with authority and that was the grey-haired man next to the boy. I wondered if they were father and son. And then I became angry, for the silence around us was the silence of eternity and none of these figures would ever explain or protest or teach or persuade or rob or serve or farm or mend again. My father and I made a portrait of something evil.

And we did this with all the skill and attention to detail that was part of our profession.

They took us to one of the houses and we developed the plates there: three images altogether.

'What are you going to do with these?' I asked the commander, who arrived as the photographs were drying.

I asked him because I wanted to hear his voice. I thought I would be able to tell from his voice if they intended to kill us.

'We'll make sure that people see them,' he said.

Soon after this, they allowed us to continue our journey to Cárdenas.

As we crossed the island, chaos grew and killings multiplied.

The army herded peasants into hamlets to separate them from guerrillas, but the hamlets were more squalid than the worst city slums. Thousands died from typhus and dysentery. The guerrillas burned crops because the planters were allied to the *peninsulares* – and, of course, when the crops were burned it was the peasants who suffered.

* * *

Near El Cristo in the west, we photographed Euphemia and Robert McClellan. Mrs McClellan grinned. Her husband said, 'Effie, a wee bit of gravitas if you please!'

'Och!' she replied.

My father pursed his lips in his amiable way, though the sitters may have missed this as his thick black moustache largely obscured his mouth. He peered again into the viewfinder. His expression was concentrated but good-humoured, as always.

'Are you ready, Señor Camarón?' Mrs McClellan asked in good Castilian. 'My husband wants me to look glum and I can only manage that for a few more seconds!'

When she said this she began to giggle and this caused her husband to begin smiling, and to look away from the camera.

'Effie,' he said, 'Señor Camarón has been very patient, but we have already taken up too much of his time.'

Urgently and earnestly, my father said, 'No, no please, do not think it! We have more time, and Mrs McClellan has a lovely smile!'

It was no more than a statement of fact. My father's habit was to speak truthfully and without calculation.

Mr McClellan composed his features and Mrs McClellan looked at the camera first with mock seriousness and then with an expectant expression. She was no longer laughing, but her eyebrows rose very slightly so that the principal thing that anyone looking at her portrait might have noted was her cheerfulness. My father pressed the shutter.

'Done!' said Mrs McClellan. 'Now, please eat with us. It's well past lunchtime!'

We sat at a table on the edge of a little courtyard that separated the McClellans' residence from their clinic and dispensary.

To me, these people seemed remarkable, very steady and determined. But there was an additional aspect of character that placed them, I thought, at a remove from the planters and officers and merchants we customarily photographed. We had spent much of the morning with Robert and Effie, preparing the backdrop for their portrait and setting up the camera in their dining room. Whatever they did, whether serving coffee or posing for the portrait or discussing their work, they did as though for the first time. They were by turns amused, exasperated and surprised. They provoked and encouraged each other. I thought of two lion cubs meowing and scratching and turning somersaults.

The day became very still. As we drank tea on the veranda and ate pastries and spoke about the war, the silence in the yard and beyond grew more oppressive until Robert said, 'Who's this?'

He spoke easily but he could not keep from his voice a tiny barbed undertone of apprehension.

We looked through the trees to a stretch of plantation and followed the eddying progress of figures moving through the cane. They followed a zigzag path, which we picked out clearly as the tops of the sugar stalks swayed one way and then another.

Two men came out into the open and hurried towards us.

'Who is it?' Effie asked, peering towards a man and a boy. Her voice was less laden with concern than her husband's, but it was not the same voice with which she had joked when they were being photographed.

'Alejandro Reyes from the *huerta*,' Robert said. He stood and moved to the top of the veranda steps.

Effie got up too.

Reyes clattered up the steps and onto the veranda and said, 'Señora McClellan.' (He said *Mac*Lel*lan*, stressing the first and last syllables.) 'Ana Encarni in Las Rosillas is in labour but something is wrong.'

Reyes glanced at us and made a perfunctory bow. Then he twirled his hat between his fingers. Effie went into the house.

Robert turned to us and said, 'Perhaps you can go ahead and make use of the pantry? I'll be back shortly.'

When we had arrived to take a portrait of the McClellans – a gift from prominent townspeople to show the two outsiders that the medical service they provided to the poor of the district was acknowledged and appreciated by the local rich – Robert had shown us the basins and working surface in the little pantry and we had indicated that this would be a suitable place in which to develop the photographs.

Effie returned. She had put on boots and she carried a carpetbag in her left hand and a leather satchel in her right. 'We'll be back before long!' she told us, speaking over her shoulder as she skipped down the steps. The others – her husband, Reyes and the boy – followed her as she plunged into the plantation. The tops of the sugar cane swithered away from us.

My father took the three plates from the camera in the parlour and I went ahead to the pantry and selected enamel trays that would serve our purpose. It was a small room, and when my father joined me there we had barely enough space to move our hands and arms. But we had done this work so often together that we didn't get in each other's way. My father taught me how to develop photographs almost at the same time that he taught me how to read and write.

When the plates were laid out on the working surface and the sodium sulphate and emulsifier had been added to the water, my father closed the door and I separated the negatives from the plates and immersed them in the developing fluid. We worked by the light of an oil lamp that burned through a blue wax filter. In such a small developing space the smell quickly became pervasive. We could not have stayed in this chemical and airless atmosphere for more than a few minutes. I worked quickly, but I was not careless or inattentive. Quite the opposite. In our strange enclosed room by the blue light, separated by a kind of cauterising darkness from the war-torn island beyond, we were wholly absorbed in bringing life to paper.

And life did come. A million facets of the same image sprouted on the page.

Since the trays were not quite large enough to accommodate the entire surface of the paper, the edges were slightly raised, which meant that the outer parts of the image adhered to the paper first. The shapes and shadows moved inward, from the painting on the wall behind the two figures and the edge of the large sideboard, across two bamboo stems on the yellow paper of the backdrop frieze, neatly framing Robert on the right and Effie on the left. I watched the figures appear and marvelled at my father's skill. He had not simply photographed two Europeans in Cuba. He had photographed Robert and Effie McClellan. He had captured their vivacity, their moral purpose. They *looked* like missionaries.

Effie's black hair had been arranged in the Gibson fashion, drawn up loosely and collected at the back. It was profuse and elegantly unruly – like the woman herself, I thought. Robert wore a light linen suit with no watch chain on his waistcoat. His hair had begun to thin but his moustache was as thick and luxuriant as any native-born Cuban.

When the photograph was taken, I had attended to the

expression in Effie's eyes, which was humorous and expectant. I had thought Robert more formal and reserved, but now I saw that his own expression was particular. He had not drawn himself up to strike a pose. He looked *content* – something that few sitters ever managed to achieve.

When we came out of the darkroom even the heavy tropical air seemed fresh. We went to the veranda to wait.

Robert arrived more than an hour later.

'I'm very sorry,' he said, bounding up the steps two at a time. 'We didn't mean to abandon you!'

My father began to protest, earnestly and honestly, that we hadn't felt in the least abandoned but that we should now be on our way.

'That's the other thing,' Robert said. 'It seems there's been trouble between here and the town.' He pulled over a wicker seat and sat between us. 'I think you should really stay with us tonight. It isn't safe on the road now that it's late. We have plenty of room.'

My father glanced out to the yard. He wasn't alarmed by the unspecified 'trouble', just inconvenienced. He looked at me.

'That's very kind of you,' I told Robert, 'but we would be imposing.'

'Och no!' he said, with a sort of friendly indignation. 'Besides, Effie would never let me hear the end of it if I let you go!'

Robert left us again after an hour and soon afterwards returned together with his wife.

She called up to us cheerfully as she crossed the yard in the dark. 'Thank you for staying! I hope you will be comfortable.'

At dinner I found it impossible not to raise the subject of the afternoon's emergency. Neither of them had spoken of it.

'The birth was successful?' I asked.

Effie sighed. 'It was difficult.' She looked down at her potatoes and then she added, 'God's will be done.'

They were both more subdued than they had been earlier in the day, but the conversation at dinner was lively nonetheless. Inevitably, we arrived at the subject of independence.

'Of course it's high time,' Robert said. 'And the Americans will help.'

My father was genuinely puzzled. 'Spain is *already* helping.'

'But the Cubans don't want Spain's help.' Robert was firm.

My father shook his head. 'I haven't met any of these people, the ones who are always said to want separation.' He put his hands out in front of him, palms up. 'That's the truth. The people we meet just want things to be normal again.'

'But normal isn't good enough. Normal is . . .' Robert stopped and glanced at his wife and then continued, 'Normal is the absence of roads and schools and hospitals.'

'We believe,' Effie said, 'that Cubans will benefit from progress, from modern discoveries, modern inventions.'

'But why must these things come from *America*?' My tone was unguarded, perhaps even indignant.

'It doesn't *have* to be America,' Effie said. 'And in this case I think we can agree that the modernisers are Cubans themselves.'

'They've all spent time in the United States,' I said, 'and they receive money from there.'

'That's true,' Robert said, 'and it's logical. The United States has harnessed the energy of its industry and its agriculture for the sake of progress. That's what can happen in Cuba too!'

I wondered in what way Spanish industry had not been harnessed. 'I'm sorry . . . I didn't mean to suggest . . .' But I wasn't at all sure what it was I didn't mean to suggest.

'Ana Encarni in Las Rosillas lost her baby,' Effie said in a tone that was suddenly rather hard. 'We arrived too late. Perhaps something could have been done if it hadn't taken us an hour to reach the *huerta*, or if there was a proper hospital in the town, or if a telegraph line had been carried up into the hills as was promised many years ago. I think these tragedies must end. If the Cubans can run their own affairs better than they have been run until now, then I believe they should have an opportunity to do so.'

'Is it far from here?' I asked. 'The *huerta*?'

'Not far,' Robert said, 'but the track was washed away in the springtime and now it's necessary to go down by the river and then climb up past the *cortijo romero*.' He chuckled. 'If you are in the medical line you have to learn the highways and byways. I think we know every house within fifteen miles of here.'

Effie smiled. 'It has been our privilege to discover a universe in our little corner of God's earth.'

'There are more kinds of personality than there are illnesses,' Robert said.

'I suppose a doctor must be alert,' my father remarked, 'to every shade of emotion.'

Robert nodded. 'I once knew a physician who was so utterly focused on the *science* of illness – the organisms that can be seen beneath a microscope – that when his own child became ill with polio fever he failed to recognise the symptoms!'

'That was a sad case,' Effie said. 'But little could have been done, even if he had diagnosed the infection.'

Robert looked into the middle distance. 'It's the man's reaction afterwards that I find most intriguing. He poured all his energy into the study of polio. I don't think he understood his family any better, but he certainly became an expert on the disease. I hear he's made great strides. They speak of a vaccine soon.'

'And the child?' I asked. 'The doctor's child?'

'Crippled, but otherwise a full recovery.' Robert said. He shook his head slightly. 'Medicine cannot cure all the ills of humanity, but it can help along the way.' Then he added thoughtfully, 'But the best medicine is *empathy*.'

We considered this for several moments. Then Effie said to me in a gentle voice, 'I'm sorry, Juan, I was strident when I spoke of Cuba and Spain. I didn't mean to offend you.'

I raised a hand and replied with some feeling, 'But I'm not at all offended, I respect your opinion, Mrs McClellan!'

She smiled and changed the subject. 'Photography is a very modern art. Isn't it?'

Her cheerfulness seemed to me to illuminate the world around her.

'Have you always specialised in portraits?' Robert asked my father.

'To tell the truth, we *don't* specialise in portraits! We do it because there's a demand.' He looked at Robert and then at Effie and then at me before he added, 'But it's something we do to the very highest standard . . .'

Robert was immediately tactful. 'Your work bears that out, Señor Camarón.'

They had been pleased when we showed them the finished portraits.

When my father explained the commission from William Collins to photograph the island's buildings, Effie was enthusiastic. 'I've a brother in Scotland who's done similar work,' she said. 'He was asked to make photographs of the oldest parts of Glasgow before the buildings were demolished to make way for improvements.'

'I hope the buildings we have documented will last for a long time yet,' my father said. 'Some of them have endured for centuries now.'

'But it must be difficult to do this work in present circumstances?' Robert spoke in a practical, businesslike way – he and Effie were engaged and energetic, but at the root of everything there was pragmatism.

'We have spent almost two years photographing churches and town halls and everything in between,' my father said. 'We have almost completed our work.'

Effie asked about our family. My father explained that he was born in Cuba. His family moved to Spain in 1870, when he was seventeen.

'The time of the first rebellion?' Robert asked.

My father nodded. 'We left soon afterwards . . . there was a question of . . . loyalty.'

'Your family were among the insurgents?'

'My father was a Freemason. A number of that confraternity led the fight against Spanish power.' He added with characteristic candour, '*They* were champions of the progressive ideas you have spoken of – though my father was not *entirely* progressive: he had not freed his slaves. In any case, we left with some urgency. I continued my studies in Madrid.'

Before he decamped from Cuba in the violent autumn of 1870, my grandfather had established a thriving plantation near Poblado de Ceuta, about ten kilometres east of Santiago. His brother, Miguel, made his peace with the authorities and took over the running of the property. On Miguel's death, shortly before we returned to Cuba, the Hacienda de Ceuta devolved to my father, though his cousin in Santiago had acquired the legal right to manage the place.

'You have visited Scotland?' Robert asked. 'Your publisher is from Glasgow.'

'Juan was *born* in Scotland – but we returned to Spain when he was very young.'

Just the two of us had returned. My father's reticence about my mother was the only obdurate, the only *closed* thing about him. She was Scottish and an actress; he had met her at the variety theatre near the Congreso de los Diputados in Madrid. They fell in love.

In Scotland my mother left us.

'Do you remember Glasgow?' Effie asked me.

'I was very young.'

To my astonishment, my father said, 'You were fond of the river.'

'The boats,' Effie said.

'He loved to go across the narrow bridge where the small cutters are moored. We would stand in the middle and Juan would point to the cutters.'

'I don't remember.' To my great embarrassment my voice trailed away into a sort of whisper, as though my inability to recapture this vignette from a faraway city were a painful loss.

The following morning, soon after dawn, we set off. We wanted to photograph the church in El Cristo before continuing to Santiago.

The lower part of the eighteenth-century church tower in El Cristo was slanted; near the top there was a circular gallery: the building looked like a lighthouse that had been disfigured by a powerful wave. My father worked methodically, as always, ensuring that the images conveyed the peculiarity of the structure, but without exaggeration.

He was entranced by buildings. He responded to a well-made facade as other men respond to a poem. When I was about eight years old, I remember in the Puerta Real in Granada my father stopped suddenly in the middle of the road; he was holding my hand; oblivious of the carts and carriages clattering by on either side of us, he said, 'Look at the pediments, Juan!' He pointed up at the facade of a new hotel. 'They are like handwriting!'

My father's general lack of commercial acumen meant that our material resources, which had once been adequate, were systematically depleted. When we sailed from Cádiz for Havana in 1896 our most valuable possessions were the Eclipse and Eastman cameras and the equipment that accompanied them.

Yet with each new departure my father assumed that our fortunes would take a turn for the better. Although he was inclined not to depend upon it – preferring instead to place his confidence in his own work – the plantation legacy promised to deliver us from material uncertainty. But this was not foremost in his thoughts. His life derived meaning from his work, and he believed that the publication of his portfolio on Cuba's architectural heritage would contribute in a significant way to a better understanding of the Spanish world.

When we travelled, he carried the Eclipse and the developing equipment and I carried the Eastman along with the tripods and screens. Our clothes filled a single valise and we each had a satchel with documents and a little money.

* * *

We rode down to Santiago the day the Americans landed at Daiquirí further to the east.

At noon we stopped and rested in the shade of some eucalyptus trees beside a grassy plateau where the narrow path had opened into something like a road. We caught our first sight of the town just after six when we crested a hill on the winding *sendero*. The bay stretched before us: spread around it were steeples and domes. The ocean glittered turquoise as the sun slipped to the west.

'Another hour, I think,' my father said in his hopeful way.

Soon after dark, we were in the townhouse of my father's cousin Paco and his wife, Eleanora. It would have been hard to find a married couple more different from the merry McClellans we had photographed just a day earlier.

Eleanora exuded unhappiness. Her face was long and deeply lined and she looked away when I took her hand as Paco introduced us.

'This is the baby from the photograph,' Paco said, 'but he has certainly grown out of his nursery clothes!'

Eleanora quickly let go of my hand, still avoiding my gaze.

'I am honoured to meet you, Doña Eleanora,' I said.

'Have the horses been stabled?' she asked her husband. 'Did you put them by themselves? There's been tick fever in El Cristo.'

There were two other horses in the stables behind the house, a black mare and a grey stallion with a distinctive brown streak that followed the contour of the head like a cap. I was quite sure we had not brought tick fever or any other contagion with us.

Eleanora led us into a parlour. Since no one had offered to take our things, we carried them with us and placed them behind our seats at the table. A servant brought coffee.

24

'Things are very bad,' Paco said.

'You won't be able to visit the plantation,' Eleanora said, answering a question that my father hadn't asked.

Paco looked at us with evident commiseration. Although he was the same height as his wife he somehow managed to appear shorter. He had pale skin and pale blue eyes. He was nervous and apologetic, whereas his wife was nervous and unfriendly.

'And it's not clear what the situation will be even when the fighting is over,' Eleanora said. 'Your best course would be to head right back the way you came. There's still time to leave the city.'

'I would like to visit the plantation when it becomes possible,' my father said. He spoke very steadily, almost sadly. When he was disappointed by others, my father expressed sadness above all else. 'And Juan and I have work to do here in Santiago. We will photograph the cathedral and the principal buildings.'

Eleanora looked at him with suspicion. She was suspicious, I think, because the only motivation she recognised in anyone was the motivation that governed her own actions – self-interest. And she was contemptuous too. Perhaps she believed that if my father really did care about completing his documentation of Cuban architecture then he was a fool as well as a threat.

This woman's dislike for us was very deep.

'Everything is changing,' she said. 'There is a revolution in Cuba!'

We had been on the island for two years and had travelled from Havana over the course of seven months, so we may have had a deeper acquaintance with the nature and consequences of the upheaval than Doña Eleanora.

'The Spanish cannot hold out against the Americans.' Paco's tone conveyed a species of delicate regret. We were Spanish, while Eleanora and Paco were Cuban.

When we sailed from Cádiz two years earlier this distinction was not well understood, at least in Spain.

'They should have left long ago,' Eleanora said. 'Now we'll take charge of our *own* affairs. Others won't steal what rightly belongs to us.'

I understood, and I think my father understood, that Eleanora was not speaking about Spaniards in general but about two Spaniards in particular.

My father, though inclined to be accommodating, was sensible. 'We would like to stay with you,' he told Eleanora and then, turning to Paco, he added, 'I had understood from our correspondence that you would offer us the hospitality that one member of a family is entitled to expect from another.'

He waited.

'There is a room across the hall that you can have,' Eleanora said at last.

I feared that they were not going to offer us any food, but in this at least my pessimism was unfounded.

Over dinner, Paco spoke with enthusiasm about how things would change for the better when the Spanish left.

'With American capital we can start to mechanise. This is what I've always argued!'

'But you have *Spanish* capital,' I said. I was still smarting at the way we had been received and I did not think we would be with this disagreeable couple for very long – so I was inclined to be blunt.

'What would *you* know about that?' Eleanora asked.

Precisely nothing, as it happened. Either Eleanora had a sixth sense that allowed her to identify and exploit whatever weakness existed in other people, or she simply assumed ignorance, stupidity, culpability and a whole host of other failings and by this scattershot approach hit her target in due course. She had hit the target first time in this case.

'Better that you don't express opinions when you don't have the facts at your disposal,' she said.

'The Americans are nearer,' Paco said. His role seemed to be that of a fireman, running after his wife and dousing the flames she ignited. 'They understand us better. They understand our needs.'

'But you're Spanish!' I persisted.

'We are Cuban,' Paco said.

Just the saying of it seemed to make him grow. He gave the impression of a man who in the face of overwhelming difficulty had championed a sacred principle. Yet all he had done was state the obvious and invest it with a kind of metaphysical import.

'Then, my father is Cuban too,' I said. 'He was born here.'

Eleanor spoke with a kind of finality. 'But he chose to make his life elsewhere.'

I recognised that whatever criteria my father might not meet would be pressed into service in the matter of the right to inherit property.

'Well, I'm back here now,' he remarked amiably.

CHAPTER TWO

We woke up next morning amid the screams and crashes of artillery shells.

Eleanora and Paco were in the parlour. The table had been turned on its side and placed over one of the two large windows. The explosions continued for more than an hour. Then there was a lull, when we heard people shouting in the street. Then the bombardment began again. The nearest impact seemed to be two or three streets away.

'The brewery,' Paco said. 'It's being used as a headquarters for the troops on this side of the town.'

The shooting dwindled after eleven and by noon it had stopped completely.

'I want to see what's happening,' my father said.

Paco looked at him with genuine mystification. 'You can't go out! They'll kill you.'

'We heard voices earlier,' my father observed reasonably. 'I want to see what's going on.'

Eleanora waited in silence. She very much wanted us both to go out and have our heads blown off.

Minutes later we scuttled into the street. We stood for several moments with our backs against the wall of the house. We did this instinctively. If a shell had exploded in the street we would simply have presented ourselves for slaughter. Standing by the wall was not rational. Yet it seemed somehow prudent.

After a second or two, my father pushed himself forward and began to walk away from the house. I followed.

It was deathly still. At the end of the street my father advanced beyond the shelter of a high wall and abruptly retreated, crashing into me.

He mumbled an apology but the sound of his voice was subsumed in a larger sound that was familiar yet strange. As we steadied ourselves we beheld a riderless horse galloping past. It bolted at a rate I would not have imagined possible. It passed us like a demon spirit.

When the horse had disappeared we could still hear the sound of hooves and the sound that the terrified animal made as it gulped air.

There was a crack; the packed earth beneath us shivered, and my father was pushed against me a second time. I lost my balance and we fell together. Then I heard a louder crack, the roar of an artillery shell exploding. I felt something dig into my shin. I thought my father had kicked me. I looked down and saw that there was a cut several inches long. It took me moments to understand that I could only see the cut because my trousers had been torn. Blood flowed over the linen and onto my shoe.

'Can you stand?' my father asked. He began to help me up. My foot felt odd, with the trouser leg torn away. The blood trickling steadily onto my shoe tickled the skin of my ankle. The cut was deep, as though someone had methodically made a long incision with a razor.

'You should not have gone out,' Paco told us when we were readmitted to the house.

Eleanor looked down at my bleeding foot. 'Get water and linen,' she instructed the servant.

I stayed in our ground-floor room for two days. At the end of the second day I was able to get up and limp about without reopening the wound. I felt light-headed.

The bombardment continued as it had begun, with sporadic outbursts of shelling and intermittent periods of calm, during which we heard people tentatively emerge from cover in order to fetch water or forage for food.

'I would like to photograph the cathedral,' my father said, pacing up and down.

Later that day I hobbled into the parlour and we listened to the shelling. Just before evening it reached a new intensity.

The next day there was a lull.

'We have no food,' Paco said, joining my father and me in the parlour in the middle of the morning. 'We *must* go out and see what we can find.'

This transformed my father's irrational desire to view the facade of the cathedral and check that it had not been defaced by artillery into a rational need to preserve our well-being.

'You stay here,' he told me.

I moved ahead of him to the door. 'I need to know if my foot's good enough for a proper walk.'

It was a great relief to be outside again. We were hungry for news as well as food. Several times we were passed by military carts and columns of soldiers.

Some makeshift stalls had been set up in an arcade next to the market. There were provisions, all at hugely inflated prices. Paco ordered supplies and got two boys to bring them to the house with the promise of payment when they arrived.

There were shell craters in the deserted cathedral square. My father walked backward into the middle of the square so that he could see the whole facade. He looked at it as though in a trance. I hobbled over and took him by the arm.

'We'll come back,' I said.

He glanced at me, distracted, and then looked at the facade again.

When he saw that we had planted ourselves in the middle of the square for no good reason, Paco hurried away.

'It's a great jumble,' my father remarked sadly.

He was referring to the facade. Between the heavy towers, the central arch looked like a sunken valley. This was not the most elegant example of island rococo.

But his discernment was not what struck me in those few moments of silence before we hurried away. What struck me was my father's absolute serenity in the midst of danger. When he gazed at the facade he was *absorbed* by its geometry. He understood what the builders had tried to do. His eye roved over the surface in search of redeeming features. The silence that surrounded us then was the tip of the great, tender silence that enveloped my father when he captured the poetry of buildings.

Beautiful buildings must be photographed with respect.

Ugly buildings must be photographed with love.

My father's gift was to identify and celebrate what even the least successful builder had sought to achieve.

The stillness in the square was shattered by the startling crack of small-arms fire. We had become accustomed to the sound of artillery explosions, a sort of crump when far away and a raucous cacophony when close at hand. This new sound was on a more human – and a more immediately threatening – scale. It was short and sharp. It seemed to me to have an almost *vindictive* quality. We heard five or six shots and then to our alarm we saw on the other side of the square little puffs of dust where the bullets had landed in the earth.

Paco was already fifty yards away.

'We were fired at!' I told him excitedly when we caught up. 'There are sharpshooters *in* the town!'

He was pleased. 'Then they were *our* people!' We ran in order to keep up with him. 'They are rising!' he shouted.

The Americans fought hard to capture Santiago, and the Spanish fought harder to defend it. The battle outside the town, to the north-west by San Juan Heights, was bitter and bloody. The wounded were brought to the field hospital next to the brewery.

The Americans might have been stopped if the war at sea had gone better for Spain, but the imperial fleet was harried up and down the coast, its vessels picked off; the last to be sunk was the *Cristóbal Colón*.

This was the point at which the *revolucionarios* raised their standard inside Santiago. *Militares* and *irregulares* traded fire across rooftops and fought in the streets.

Two days after we had ventured to the market and the cathedral square, we saw men and boys race along the street waving the Cuban flag. And soon after that there was the sound of a fusillade. One of the flag-bearers staggered back the way he had come. He was holding his head and his shirt was bloodied.

On the fourth day, Eleanora announced that a neighbour had told her an artillery shell had hit the lower part of the cathedral facade.

I went to our room to find my father preparing the camera and tripod.

'You can't go out now!' I said.

'I must.'

'Why must you?'

'It could be destroyed!' He had nearly completed his preparations.

'I'll take the tripod,' I said.

He looked at me in a manner so striking that I took a step backward. I remember everything that happened that day. I remember that the expression on my father's face as I proposed to accompany him was clear and uncomplicated.

He said, 'Juan, I will go alone.'

His footfall on the lobby floorboards was heavy because he carried the tripod as well as the camera.

'I'm going to join you when I've bandaged my leg,' I said.

'No. Stay here.'

He hurried away. I noticed, perhaps for the first time, that he had begun to stoop.

Quickly, I swabbed the wound in iodine and applied a dressing which I secured with a bandage. The most time-consuming part of this was the bandage. If I ran a needle and thread from top to bottom it remained in place longer than if I fastened it with pins.

I left the house more than a quarter of an hour after my father. I stepped into the silence, looking first one way and then the other. The street was empty.

I took two steps forward. The torn skin on my leg adjusted to movement with a dull ache. This was a great improvement. I believed I could walk to the square without limping. I struck out, keeping close to the side of the street, ready to step into a doorway if the shelling started again.

Far in the distance, I heard shooting. As I passed the last doorway I realised that something was not quite right. There was a flash of colour and movement and in an instant a man stood in front of me blocking my way. He must have stepped from the doorway with extraordinary speed. I heard a sound and turned to see another man behind, very close. He held a machete.

'What are you doing?' the man blocking my path asked.

'Get out of my way.'

'You're not giving orders here any more,' he said.

'Get out of my way!'

I had hardly completed the sentence before I felt the point of the machete in my back. I stepped forward but the man in front didn't move. The machete followed me. The man in front reached forward. I tried to move to one side but he got hold of my shirt. I could smell his breath.

I felt a kind of detached fury. Detached because this was not the disaster I had hurried from the house to meet.

The man behind pressed the machete into my back while his partner felt for the money pouch he guessed was somewhere inside my clothing. It was round my neck and tucked to one side of my shirt. He found it without difficulty and began to pull it over my head.

I learned to box in Granada. I was, to my own surprise, rather good at it. Later, when I studied in Madrid, I encountered an old Jesuit who had lived in Japan and he introduced me to the novel art of judo. I became rather good at that too.

So, I spun round to disarm the man with the machete, but before I could lay a hand on him I was hit on the side of the head by a club. I remember seeing the man with the machete step away from me, and then I fell to the ground. I may also have heard the sound of raised voices. Men who do violence to other men often find it necessary to accompany this violence with anger. They may have cursed me as they hurried away with my silver.

I do not believe I lay on the ground for very long. I do not know. When I reached the square a group of *irregulares* occupied a corner on the side furthest from the cathedral.

In the middle of the square was the body of my father.

A knot of bystanders had gathered. Someone had closed his eyes.

The tripod lay beside him, and about three feet away, the camera. The camera had toppled backward when he was shot. The distance between it and the tripod suggested that they had been separated by the fall, and the camera had bounced once or twice before coming to rest.

I knelt and placed my hand on my father's heart and felt the shocking unnaturalness of his collapsed ribs. One side of his shirt was saturated in blood and there was blood beneath him on the earth.

His body lay as lifeless as the camera and the tripod and the cathedral stones. A soft Caribbean breeze ruffled his black hair.

I may have knelt beside him for a minute or ten minutes. I heard a voice I recognised. 'What's happened!' Paco was breathless. 'I got here as soon as I heard,' he said, looking down at my father. 'I was at home.'

He took charge.

Regulations to stop the spread of typhus required summary burial. We carried my father's body to a cart that Paco had found and I followed the cart to the cemetery. I put the tripod beside him on the cart and carried the camera with me. One of the lenses was cracked.

CHAPTER THREE

The next morning, I took the broken plates from the Eclipse across the courtyard to the hut by the stables. Some time before, we had established a developing room there. When I opened the door, the early morning smell of charcoal and tree bark was replaced by the sharp odour of polysulphide. I breathed the air as though its chemical residue were incense. What I did next – the steady application of the photographer's craft – was a kind of homage to my father. I worked mechanically, in a daze.

I placed the plates on the developing board and slowly separated the glass from the wooden frame. One of the plates was broken into three pieces. The other was sheared away in a serrated pattern along the edges, with the central part of the glass still intact.

I watched the first shapes form under the viscous fluid, the tops of the cathedral and the complicated arrangement of neo-classical colonnades, then the doors and the railings on the street. There were figures in the square, men moving from right to left. They moved at a crouch and such was the skill and clarity of my father's work that I saw quite unmistakably that three of them were holding carbines. My eye roved across the surface of the image, following the clear lines etched on the front of the building and then withdrawing into the foreground between the camera and the cathedral.

A single figure captured my attention. When I spotted him, standing far to the right almost off camera together with two men bearing rifles, I was so stunned that I stepped back from the developing table and knocked against the shelf behind me, hitting it hard enough to rattle the bottles and tin boxes that were stacked there.

My father had not been a chance victim of the battle for Santiago.

My father had been executed.

This I knew for a certainty.

He did not die because he had risked everything to create a final portrait. He was put to death for the sake of a legacy, a sugar plantation east of Santiago.

Because standing with two *irregulares* was his cousin Paco.

Paco, who had told me he had hurried from home when news reached him that my father had been shot. Paco, who had feigned shock and sorrow when he beheld my father lying dead on the cobblestones.

When my father took his last photographs, Paco was on a corner of the square with two armed men.

I placed the second plate in the solution and watched as the outline of the cathedral began to appear. I scanned the foreground figure by figure, but the spot where Paco and the soldiers had stood was part of the section that had been sheared off when the camera fell over. The fragment that had survived tapered away at the bottom in a jagged 'v'. There were no more than half a dozen figures, but I recognised one of them.

One of the soldiers who had been with Paco was moving behind the parapet that bordered a terrace on the east side of the cathedral, his rifle raised.

From behind that parapet there was a clear firing line to the middle of the square.

My father had photographed his own assassin.

This was a logical leap, but I knew it was true because I knew that Paco had lied.

The man on the terrace was hatless, about forty, with thick black hair pushed back over a high forehead. He had a thick moustache and his lips were slightly apart in the manner of someone fully engaged in a moment and in a situation that is fraught with possibility and peril. I imagined that he moved across the terrace quickly, and that – despite the fact that this particular precaution is meaningless in a place where rifles are being fired and artillery shells are exploding – he tried to move quietly, almost on tiptoe.

Did it never occur to him that shooting a photographer from the building he is photographing is to invite detection?

I heard the sound of voices from the main house. I placed the two photographs on the drying line, put the lamp out and opened the door.

As I stepped into the courtyard, Paco and Eleanora emerged from the kitchen at the back of the house and began to move towards the stables.

I remember the expression on Eleanora's face when she saw me. She had tried the previous day to display the normal sadness of bereavement. Now, there was simple dislike.

'You were in the square when my father died!' I told Paco.

He was walking across the courtyard in front of Eleanora. He looked at me as though I were a child whose persistence has become tiresome, but he didn't reply. Eleanora spoke for both of them.

'You should not have come to Santiago.'

Paco hurried into the stable. Eleanora stopped and glared.

'Your father should not have come. He had no business here. *You* have no business here.'

She had to shout this final sentence because there was an ear-splitting crash in the road outside and smoke billowed over the wall. Moments later, pieces of shattered brick scattered into the garden. There was another crash and then another and we heard Paco shouting at the horses. The sound of frantic whinnying was like a weird accompaniment to the sound of artillery, and this was joined by the short sharp report of rifle fire.

'Go in the house,' Eleanora said dismissively and I looked down and saw that she was holding a pistol in her right hand. She began to move towards the stables.

I remained where I was, contemplating the high-pitched complaint of terrified horses and the clatter of shells and bullets. Then I followed her into the stables.

The horses had started to kick the gates of their stalls hard enough to make the wood crack. Eleanora was reaching up with both hands trying to calm the black stallion. She had put her pistol on the high saddle frame near the entrance.

I remember the expression on Paco's face. It was surprised, as though he had not expected to die in this manner, in this place. I remember the smell of horses and cordite and dust. I remember Eleanora lying on the floor, her dress up above her knees, which were pale and misshapen. The horses continued with their desperate protests. The bullets seemed almost to grow out of the artillery bombardment. I do not remember lifting the gun from the saddle stand. I remember the smell of dust and blood.

CHAPTER FOUR

Death is more than the absence of life. Death is dynamic. It moves among the living, stepping nimbly, examining the personalities and weaknesses, the fears and antagonisms of mortal beings. It lashes out as a jungle creature, changing the alchemy of the world.

I remember the ascendancy of noise, the indescribable clamour of impact after impact as the guns on the edge of the city rained down fire upon the depleted forces of imperial Spain. I knew it was the end of our world. I could not see beyond the garden wall but I understood the nature of the cataclysm that enveloped Paco and Eleanora's house. We had reached the stage of a contest where one of the protagonists has already secured victory and is pummelling the defeated opponent, to snuff out resistance but also to make a show of superior power.

I stumbled from the stable, almost falling over the brick border of the path. I ran to the house and went inside. In the spot where I had been, between the stable and the house, there was a kind of thunderclap but infinitely louder than any natural sound. I felt a gust, as though a chemical wind propelled me forward with enormous force. I do not know if I threw myself onto the wooden floor or if I was thrown there, but one moment I was upright and the next I lay with my face down and I could smell sulphur and dust. I leapt to my feet as though the force that had followed me into the house were a pursuing demon.

What are demons? Magical phenomena, insubstantial elements of the natural world that take on material form through the energy of our imaginations. What is the logic, the rationale of flight? Whether I perished in the American bombardment of Santiago or whether I survived was surely a matter of chance; I might have been killed inside the house as easily as outside the house. It made as much sense to stand still and upright in the hallway as it did to race frantically among the rooms.

Yet, the demons that pursue us do so from far away and from close at hand, from long ago and from this very second. They may be no more than spectral figments but they are near impossible to escape.

I moved with the greatest of speed and at the same time – this is something that I have considered as if it were a puzzle constructed by one of the ancients and never solved – I displayed something very close to a clinical presence of mind.

In the room where my father and I had slept, I collected the valise that contained the portfolio of images produced since we had arrived from Cádiz – my father's testament to the distinctive and extraordinary buildings of colonial Cuba. The weight of the valise and the feel of the handle in my palm were unfamiliar. It had always been carried by my father. There was a duplicate set, which my father had sometimes used as a reference when preparing the accompanying text, and I know that he had been studying images from this set while I was recuperating from the effects of my wound, but I did not trouble to find it – in the bedroom where we had slept, or in the dining room, where my father had occasionally sat and worked. I had the pristine set, the one that was ready to be sent to William Collins.

I hurried back out into the hall and climbed the stairs. Smoke was billowing into the house from the yard; there were bursts of sound from the lane behind the house and the street in front. As I climbed, my nostrils were assailed by a new sensation, something related to but different from the dust that enveloped me from the yard outside. This was an acrid smoke from near at hand, hot and suffocating. As though my senses were out of time, I understood long after I should have done so that the house was on fire. To my right, along the corridor opposite Paco and Eleanora's room, I saw the oscillating tips of flame. At the top of the stairs I shouted but no one replied. I believed the house was empty. This was a convenient belief. Afterwards I wondered if I should have run along the corridor to see if there might have been a living soul there, unconscious from fright or overwhelmed by the toxic fumes. Instead, I stepped into Paco and Eleanora's room.

There was a great mahogany bed: I think I had never seen such a monstrous piece of furniture. My thoughts were sharp and calculating. I grasped at once that the bed could only have been constructed in situ; it certainly could not have been carried upstairs – it was too large and too heavy for the stairs to bear the weight. If it had been constructed in situ it could have been fashioned in a manner that accommodated the requirements of the two people who slept in it – one in particular. I cannot exactly reconstruct my train of thought. I do not know what prompted me to hurry round the bed and kneel down beside it. Yet I imagined Eleanora expending volumes of attention and energy to securing her own material well-being; there was no desk in the room, no trunk. I knew by some primordial instinct that the wealth of this household, perhaps its secrets too, lay beneath the bed.

A chintz cloth separated the lower and upper mattresses and hung down over the frame as far as the red tiles, the lower border defined by a row of tassles. I lifted the cover and looked beneath. Set a little way in, fixed to the wooden underside of the bed, was a strongbox.

I stood up, cast around for a suitable implement and settled at once on a long brass candlestick that stood by the door. I lifted this considerable weight and moved back to the side of the bed, where I pulled the cover away with such violence that I tore the material. I knelt down and realised at once that I would not be able to swing the candlestick like a hammer. However, in the limited space and by lying on my back I was able to employ it as a battering ram. It required just half a dozen blows before the strongbox came loose and clattered onto the tiles. It was the size of a desk drawer. I dragged it out and lifted it, pleased to find that it was no heavier than the Kessler tripod.

With the valise and the strongbox, I fled the burning house.

Señor Melchior da Costa was the sort of notary who might have been born into his profession. It was very difficult to imagine Señor da Costa as anything other than the principal in a gloomy office whose eight or nine denizens spent their waking hours copying property titles. He was examining the title to my father's estate, which I had extracted from Eleanora and Paco's strongbox, and the corresponding title that one of his minions had first of all identified and then copied in a sub office of the land registry.

In ordinary times, this might have taken three weeks; in the far from ordinary summer and autumn of 1898 it had taken three months, but it had been completed. The revolution had not prevented me from escaping a monumental piece of fraud – and the much vaunted 'liberation' of Cuba had resulted in such little real change that the land registry and every other department of administration, after a period of disruption, had resumed their functions almost as though nothing momentous had happened. Cuba had thrown off the shackles of Spain and embraced the United States as its new overlord, but Señor da Costa and his minions behaved as they had always done, moving through a world of matching documents.

The title in the strongbox showed that Paco had no claim to the plantation: it had been inherited exclusively by my father, and Paco's right to manage the property had ceased when his own father had died.

Having established my inheritance, I had instructed Señor da Costa to arrange the sale of the plantation. He had done this quickly, securing a very satisfactory price.

'Well, Señor Camarón.' He had an oddly sceptical way of speaking, as though he could not quite bring himself to believe whatever it was he was saying. 'I have divided the funds as per your instructions. As you will see in the summary that has been prepared for you' – he pointed to the two sheets of copperplate that lay on the polished table in front of me – 'the larger sum has been deposited with the Banco Urquijo in Madrid. You may draw on this with absolute freedom when you return to Spain, though, of course, outside Spain, you may be obliged to wait for several days. The remainder has been placed with the British Linen Bank in Glasgow.' As he said this, his eyebrows rose above the tortoiseshell frames of his thick lenses.

In the two months that I had been dealing with Señor da Costa, an engagement that had necessitated perhaps half a dozen visits to his office, I had begun to like him. His round face was expressive in a way that his tone of voice – always stately and utterly inimical to any sort of dramatic flurry – was not. His raised eyebrows communicated a degree of curiosity regarding the decision of a Spanish photographer in Cuba to deposit part of his inheritance with a provincial bank in Scotland. I do not believe he would have been curious if he had not also been sympathetic.

'My mother was Scottish.'

'Ah,' Señor da Costa said with such a remarkable absence of emotion that the single syllable communicated precisely nothing, but his eyebrows remained raised, from which I deduced that I should elaborate this explanation.

'I do not remember her,' I said. 'We were separated when I was still a child. In my father's papers I discovered a document indicating a connection about which I knew nothing.'

'A connection?'

'My mother's family are from the Isle of Bute, on the River Clyde, near Glasgow. It transpires that my father was the owner of property there . . . and as the result of his death . . .'

'I see.' Señor da Costa's eyebrows lowered and so did the corners of his mouth as he pursed his lips. His head tilted slightly to one side and then righted itself. 'I am sorry that you have – if you will forgive me – come into such good fortune by way of such a sad loss.'

He considered this and so did I. Then his eyebrows lifted. 'Do you propose to live in Scotland, or will you sell your property there?'

'I will sell the property – but in the meantime, I will conclude my father's business. His publisher, William Collins, Sons & Co is in Glasgow. They have already taken delivery of my father's portfolio and have expressed their satisfaction with the work we have produced.'

'We have an association in Glasgow,' Señor da Costa said. 'An association of long standing.'

'In Glasgow,' I said, redundantly. Señor da Costa's habit of pausing between short sentences had caused me to fill what I perceived as a vacuum.

'Our firm and' – he pronounced the name with considerable care – 'Mackintosh & Co have traded for a very long time – more than fifty years, I believe.'

After this piece of information had been imparted, Señor da Costa asked if he could be of further service.

CHAPTER FIVE

Edward Morton was a man of about my own height, maybe a decade older. He wore a plain black suit that was well cut. He had jet black hair and a reserved manner.

'Thank you for offering accommodation,' I said.

'Señor da Costa's letter was fortuitous. I would very much like to know more about the situation in Cuba.'

This frankness was characteristic: Morton spoke in a matter-of-fact way that seemed to leave little room for social niceties. He had formerly been a chief clerk at Mackintosh & Co but had struck out on his own, among other things starting a company that had patented a new kind of typewriter. With the system in use until then, the typist could not see the letter as it was printed: Morton had developed a model that made the letters immediately visible. The newly popular 'TopTap' was in the process of making him very wealthy.

Morton had been asked, following Señor da Costa's introduction to his former employer, to offer me hospitality on my arrival in Glasgow.

'We want to sell our machines in America,' he said. 'Now the Spaniards are out of Havana, there may be opportunities for us, and Cuba could be the back door to the United States.'

I did not want to dwell on what had happened in Cuba, but I was happy enough to oblige him with whatever insights I might have.

'Do the Americans have a clear idea of what must now be done?' he asked after I had been settled into a comfortable room on the second floor of his home on the very southern edge of the city. 'Do they have the vision to make sure that the new Cuba is better than the old?'

Like so many people, he assumed that the new dispensation had a fighting chance of being better than what was there before.

I sighed. 'Human nature doesn't change,' I said. 'The Americans will encounter the very same problems that confounded Madrid.'

'I believe people can be improved.'

I was distracted, testing the shadow of memory to see if it stretched from Santiago to Scotland, to see if I could free myself from what I had done and what I had failed to do. I wanted to move from beneath the weight of vengeance and shame. I wanted to give a reasonable account of myself in a new country with new people.

I had stopped listening.

'Will you make photographs while you are here?' Morton repeated.

'I hadn't thought about it,' I said truthfully.

* * *

I was in Scotland to resolve the matter of my father's property on the Isle of Bute. Through the documents I rescued from the house in Santiago, I had traced a Mr Tristan MacKenzie, a solicitor with offices in the centre of Glasgow. When I called on Mr MacKenzie, I was informed that he was in the fifth month of a six-month visit to his brother in Cape Town. It was for this reason that I stayed with Morton for several weeks rather than several days.

There was a housekeeper, Mrs Simpson, and there were two girls, Molly and Lizzie, who had recently come from a village in Ulster. A butler, tall, middle-aged and with the bearing of a wrestler, appeared to operate in a separate jurisdiction from Mrs Simpson and her girls. His name was Hans. I was unable to determine whether he and Mrs Simpson were lovers, since they spoke in a kind of code when I was within earshot, or whether they simply wanted to deny an unwelcome guest any useful intelligence about the household.

The day after I arrived, Morton handed me two newspapers and asked me to review the long descriptions of the war in Cuba that were prominent in each. 'Our accounts are about events among the *besiegers*,' he said. 'You can tell me what it was like to be *besieged*.'

The newspaper articles reflected a familiar belief that following their liberation from Spain, the people of Cuba could be compensated for all the blood that had been spilt. The island could be redeemed with judicious and generous American assistance.

I thought this to be utterly misguided. The war was fought because people like Morton believed that the world could be improved – and, with enormous reserves of self-confidence, they assumed that *they* were the chosen ones manifestly qualified to do the improving.

'It was fought to spread values,' I told him. 'That's what the Cuban revolutionaries always said – progress, modernisation, the growth of trade. I believe them.'

'But why would you object?'

'All of those things were coming anyway.'

'From Spain?' he asked incredulously.

'Perhaps not,' I said, 'but when you go to war in defence of values, the first casualties are those very same values.'

He didn't grasp this. 'You cannot make countries better,' I continued. 'Perhaps they can make themselves better. Others cannot do it for them.'

In the following days, he asked me in the minutest detail about what it was like to be in a city under American attack – the disposition of troops, the kind of injuries I had seen, the relative strength of infantry on both sides.

It took me an unconscionable period of time before I realised that Morton's interest was not exclusively limited to the typewriter market. As I learned in due course, his company had developed a mechanism that could increase the efficiency of automatic rifles: he was keen to sell his product in the Americas.

One day, we sat smoking. He puffed on a cigar and I on a cigarette. I had taken to smoking Myrtle Groves because I liked the picture on the tin. It showed an ivy-clad house nestling in a forest. The tobacco was sharper and less flavoured than a Spanish cigarette. Perhaps acquiring a taste for Myrtle Groves was part of my effort to acquire a taste for the world beyond Spain. It didn't last very long. In due course I returned to my pipe.

'Have you decided, then?' Morton asked. 'Will you go back to taking photographs?'

I exhaled thin smoke.

'The last images I developed were the ones my father took immediately before he was killed.'

I felt as I said this that I was on the verge of betraying a sacred trust. I was disinclined to speak about my father's death, particularly to someone whose company I was beginning to dislike. Yet, perhaps this had to be spoken about.

Morton watched through thick cigar smoke and waited.

'I developed two plates,' I said, looking down at the ash on the end of my cigarette, and then, after pausing for a moment, I told him about the clear photographic evidence that my father's cousin had been at the scene when my father was shot.

I told him about Paco's untruthful assurance that he had not been there and about the sharpshooter on the roof of the cathedral, the man who had found a position from which to raise his rifle and point it at my father.

Morton continued to look at me steadily. 'Do you have the photographs?'

I went up to my room and brought back the two images. I placed them in front of him on the dining table.

After a close inspection, during which he began to nod at first very slightly and then more decisively, he said, 'Yes, I see. I see how you could piece together the narrative.'

I hadn't thought of it as a narrative, but that is what it was.

'The armed men disperse. One of them goes to the roof. He points his weapon.' Then, to my astonishment he added, 'And the witnesses had been moved away.'

'I beg your pardon?'

He glanced up at me. 'The witnesses,' he said, pointing to a small group of people in the first photograph, three girls with shawls over their heads and two old women. They stood fifty yards from my father, to his left, near the road that led off the square towards the district where Paco and Eleanora's house was.

And in the second picture where the girls had stood there now stood a man I'd later observed among the bystanders when I knelt down and cradled the lifeless body of my father. This man had remarked – to me and to everyone – that my father had had no business taking photographs in the middle of a great battle.

I had looked at these images a hundred times. I had not seen this change in the configuration of people in the square. I had not seen it because I had not understood the photographs as part of a story, as a fragment of unfolding events.

Perhaps I had looked with too much emotion and with too little detachment. I had been so preoccupied with the killer at the centre of the image I had not grasped the scope of the conspiracy. My father's assassins were on all sides, working consciously and systematically, and the camera exposed them.

I sat back and lit another cigarette.

'Can you make use of this?' Morton asked.

I did not at first understand what he meant.

'Can you make use of this,' he asked again, 'to bring these people to justice?'

Justice had been meted out to Paco and Eleanora – whether barbaric or righteous I did not know.

I had tried at the start of the American occupation to engage the authorities over the identity of the man on the roof – but this was quixotic. The man was woven into the fabric of a revolution that had triumphed. His marksmanship was submerged in the legend of liberation.

'No,' I said.

Morton nodded again. Then he said, 'Imagine what you could do with your camera!'

I looked up from the pictures on the table. 'Events can be understood through photographs?'

We were both silent. Then I said, 'But I could hardly photograph city squares in the expectation that some sort of crime would be committed!'

'Of course not. But if you took two or three photographs, let's say, and you compared them, it would be interesting to see just how much you could learn about a given scene.' He puffed on his cigar. 'It's a different way of looking at the world!'

CHAPTER SIX

The next morning at nine o'clock I set up the Eclipse at the window of my bedroom and adjusted the angle to encompass both sides of the street stretching south-west as far as the first junction. About a third of the line of sight was obscured by trees, though since they had only just begun to bud it was possible to make out windows and pavements through the branches. The bedroom's bay window meant that I was able to view the scene almost head on, with very little obscured. I was looking at the facades of perhaps twenty houses (later, when I had developed my method, I would not have been so vague about numbers).

I took the first picture at a quarter past nine (in the six months since the equipment had last been used, the metal grooves that held the plates in place had slightly altered their shape and I had to adjust them with the use of a screwdriver so that the plates fitted neatly; this required several minutes of finicky handiwork).

I took the next picture at a quarter past eleven, another after two hours and the fourth picture two hours after that.

By the late afternoon I had established myself in one of the storerooms behind the kitchen engulfed in the familiar and evocative fumes of developing fluid.

The process of developing – after the time that had elapsed since I'd last done this – felt entirely natural and *right*.

I hung the pictures up and when they were dry I took them through to the dining room and placed them on the table. I did not have a notebook. I did not have the faintest idea how I planned to proceed. I had no method, no technique, just a curious sense of excitement that I might discover something about the street, about the *world*, something that could only be discovered through photographs.

The houses were laid out in two lines moving at an obtuse angle so that those in the foreground were an inch apart on the photograph, those at the furthest end of the street about four inches apart. The focus was clear. I was pleased by this. I had not lost the basic skills of composition and execution.

I looked at one image and then at the next and on through the sequence.

I approached this exercise as if it were one of those picture tests that appear in the popular papers, where the viewer is invited to compare two apparently identical drawings and identify ten differences hidden in the detail.

The four pictures looked identical.

But of course, they were different.

In two pictures, for example, there were birds flying. Three birds in one and a whole flock in the other, silhouetted against the white sky. In one picture a dog strolled along the pavement. In another a pigeon had perched on the upstairs windowsill of the second house from Morton's.

There were differences too in the configuration of the garden gates. The gate of the house diagonally opposite Morton's drew my attention. It was closed in the first three pictures and open in the last. Therefore, I could conclude that someone had entered or left the house in the last three hours.

A small and apparently useless observation, yet it showed that logical conclusions could be reached from photographic comparison. I began to compare the images more rigorously.

'What have you found?' Morton asked when he returned to the house on the day of my first experiment.

I was still in the dining room. 'Your neighbour across the road has had a visitor,' I said, pointing to the three images of the gate closed, and one of the gate open. 'Or he has gone out.'

He looked closely at the photographs.

'See this,' I said, using a pencil to identify a carriage that appeared in all four photographs. In the first, it was stationed outside the house next to Morton's and it was facing towards the city. In the next, it was in the middle of the road, again pointing towards the city. In the third, it was parked outside the house again, now facing north, and in the fourth, it was at the very far end of the street and moving away from the city. The cab itself was indistinguishable from any other of the same design but we could tell it was the same vehicle because the cabbie, sitting on his high chair, had a piece of paper folded into the band of his trilby.

'That's Robertson's man,' Morton said. 'He makes a note of the miles so that Robertson can pace his horses. Terrible skinflint. He'll hold onto the beasts long after they should be put out to pasture.'

'So, your neighbour went out at a quarter past eleven,' I said, 'and returned at a quarter past three.'

'Let's confirm that, shall we!'

I raised my hand to object, but Morton appeared oblivious to any difficulty.

'Bring the photographs,' he said and disappeared through the dining room door.

I picked up the pictures and followed him out.

'Perhaps he'll feel this an intrusion,' I said as we crossed the lobby. 'He may believe he has been spied upon.'

'He's a man of science. He can have no objection.'

This struck me as being rather cavalier.

I was right.

'Damn your impertinence!' Robertson spluttered after we laid out the photographs on his hall table and explained what I had done.

'I do apologise—' I began.

'Don't apologise,' Morton interjected. 'We've done nothing to apologise about.' He turned to his neighbour and seemed to straighten up – whether to assert his dignity or in preparation for physical combat I did not know. 'We have engaged in a scientific experiment.'

But as he said this, he began to edge away from the irate Robertson towards the door. I scooped up the photographs and did likewise.

Robertson glared at us, but he remained standing in the same position.

Morton opened the door and we slipped out.

'I have caused you a great deal of trouble,' I said as we walked back to the house.

'No trouble,' Morton said. 'Never liked the man.'

Inside, I put the photographs again on the kitchen table and we began to study them.

'This is a powerful tool,' Morton said.

Over the following days, I photographed Morton's street from the bay window of my bedroom many times. We learned several things. We learned, for example, that the northern section of the street received more visits than the southern section, from goods vehicles – haberdashers, window-cleaners, poultry suppliers. This seemed at odds with the social geography of the district. The whole street was prosperous, but the level of prosperity could generally be said to rise following a trajectory from north to south, so one would have expected commercial suppliers to gravitate to the southern, slightly better heeled part. Then we observed that those vendors who were photographed outside the more affluent addresses appeared early in the morning, too early for their presence to diminish the daytime gentility of the area, and we concluded that those who were *not* observed may have called on the same addresses later in the day, but at the back, in this way ensuring that decorum was maintained.

I experimented with different intervals of time between photographs – four hours, three and a half hours, all the way down to half an hour. In due course I concluded that the optimal timing was every forty-five minutes to an hour. I concluded too that it was in the nature of the exercise to make the intervals always the same. There was no logic to this – five photographs taken at different intervals in the course of a day might yield useful information just as much as five photographs taken at fixed intervals, but since I was developing a system of comparison I settled very early on the principle of minimising the scope for variables of any sort and this included variables in the length of time between photographs.

I could not afford to use up plates at the rate required for serial photography so I set about designing a method whereby the same plate could be used for six different pictures, by exposing the lens only to a portion of the plate rather than to the whole plate. This was a delicate manoeuvre which required a reconfiguration of lens and plate to a precise and fixed surface area and the most satisfactory way of doing this was to have small notches made in a steel rule and then to push the plate in front of the lens till it found the notch and stopped. When I drew the specifications for this mechanism it occurred to me that it could be combined with a timing device. This would allow me to choose the scene, focus the lens and then leave the camera to operate automatically for a number of hours.

'I can help you there!' Morton said, and soon after this we travelled to his typewriter factory. The manufacturing was done on the first two storeys of a three-storey office building on the main street of Rutherglen, a town south of Glasgow, about three miles from Morton's house. The offices were in half a dozen rooms located in various parts of the third floor. In one of the smaller rooms we met the technical director.

Mr Caruso was a short man in his fifties with a small hopeful face dominated by an outsized moustache. He was balding but had refused to bow to the vagaries of this condition: strands of long hair had been oiled and carefully patted down in order to hide his skull from view. The surfeit of hair on his face and the paucity of hair on the top of his head gave him an odd appearance, as though his features had been arranged in the wrong order. This oddness was compounded by Mr Caruso's somewhat bulging eyes. He looked rather like a puppet in a permanent state of surprise.

But if his appearance was odd his manner was brisk and encouraging. I explained the principle of serial photography and I showed him my drawing of a device that could move the photographic plates at fixed intervals. He listened carefully, nodded, looked at the drawings, nodded some more and then he said simply, 'This can be done.'

Downstairs in the factory, as we discussed the specific requirements of the automatic camera, Mr Caruso conducted us from the department that assembled letter frames (with the distinctive and hugely successful front-strike) and keyboards, to the one that fitted the frames and keyboards into the different styles of casing, to the women sitting at a long table on the first floor who connected the roller carriage and ribbon platen and inserted these into the finished machine.

'I believe the platen cylinder will serve for the regular movement of the plate,' Mr Caruso told me, 'if we can connect it satisfactorily with the clock mechanism.'

At no point in the course of our hour-long encounter did Mr Caruso express any doubts about the viability of the machine. Nor did he express scepticism about the use to which the automatic camera was to be put. His thoughts seemed to move in absolute harmony with his mechanical perception of – as far as I could see – just about everything. His daily preoccupation was with the rigorous pursuit of precision.

'We can have something ready to show you in a week or two,' he said. His measured voice seemed to me to be at one with the hum of productive enterprise that filled the building.

But I didn't receive this intimation of a timeframe in the same measured way. I was impatient. My odd camera was pointing to something new and worthwhile. I had begun to look upon serial photography with that peculiar fascination that gripped my father when he studied the merits and demerits of a rococo pediment.

In my room later that day I took out a batch of six photographs and laid them on the bed. I examined each in turn, comparing the sky and the trees and the windowsills and the asphalt and the paving stones. My eye roved from one image to the next and I noted that it was impossible to concentrate on the myriad details – the shadows changing with the hour, the pattern made by a carriage wheel, the footfall of a woman as she stepped from the pavement onto the road – and the more I became attuned to the detail, the harder it was to make straightforward comparison.

I went downstairs where I found Mrs Simpson in the kitchen kneading dough. She had placed a piece of greaseproof paper across the surface of the huge table in the centre of the room to protect the dough from the crevices and whorls in the wood.

I apologised for interrupting her. She nodded brusquely. 'What is it, sir?'

'May I have a piece of that paper?'

I don't believe I could have made a less expected request.

'The paper, sir?'

'Not a very large piece.' I pointed to the paper on the table. 'Perhaps about twice that much. And also, if you wouldn't mind, may I trouble you for a pair of scissors.'

She opened her mouth and then closed it again. Then she wiped her hands on a cloth and moved to a small sideboard next to the pantry door where she found a pair of scissors. The paper was stored in a roll at the bottom of the sideboard opposite.

'Perhaps I can help you with that,' I said. The roll looked heavy.

'That's quite alright, sir!' she said with shrill courtesy, as though I had made an indecent proposal.

She didn't lift the roll of paper out of the sideboard but twisted it instead so that she was able to measure out a portion, which she sheared off with a knife.

Back in the room I took a pencil and traced a rectangle around one of the photographs and cut it out of the paper. Then I made thirty-five duplicate rectangles and cut them out. I divided each into six boxes of the same size, three in one row and three in the row below, and I cut out the top left box in six of the rectangles, then the top centre box in the next six and so on till I had thirty-six rectangles – each with a box cut out – that could be used to block all but the selected box in six different images. Instead of comparing whole photographs I now had the means to compare subdivisions of the photographs.

I pulled a chair over to the bed, sat opposite the pictures, placed the six pieces of paper in turn over each of them, blocking out five sixths of the image each time, and proceeded to note down every single observable difference in the exposed sixth.

Using this method, I was able to learn infinitely more about things that had transpired on the street during the period in which the photographs were taken.

Hours later, I was still making notes about the first batch of photographs.

In the ten days before Mr Caruso sent word that my timing mechanism was ready, I worked every day on the photographs. As I examined them in minute detail I entered into a visible and yet thoroughly opaque world. It was filled with things that could be seen but which would almost never be registered. The comings and goings of wood pigeons and tradesmen, alley cats and neighbours are fragments of a picture that changes by the second, that forms and then dissolves.

It took me several days to make my first discovery and this concerned Mr Robertson next door. I had imagined that his fury when we showed him the first photographs was prompted by an understandable belief that his privacy (and that of any other citizen) was threatened by the intrusion of a hidden camera. It was a matter of principle.

But it wasn't. It was a matter of domestic infidelity.

Mr Robertson was in the habit of accompanying his wife every day to the Episcopalian church on the other side of the park, where Mrs Robertson's brother was the curate. Mrs Robertson was active in the management of a school attached to the church. The photographs revealed that rather than go on to the railway station and from there to his office in the city, Mr Robertson regularly returned to the house. His carriage appeared in several images and he himself was captured in one photograph, walking down the garden path and glancing backward and up, waving furtively to a figure at the window on the third floor, a figure Morton identified as that of the Robertsons' recently arrived Irish scullery maid.

And so, at the very beginning of my experiment with serial photography I was obliged to confront the ethical dilemma that it entailed.

Was I to be a peeping Tom? Was I to devote my energy and whatever skill I might possess to the surreptitious observation of men and women who had no idea they were being observed? Was I to be *a spy*, a secret watcher, a voyeur?

Yet, I had chanced upon a way of studying the human psyche, the human predicament. The people in my images were like the spheres of life that can be observed through a scientist's microscope. I did not sit in judgement over Mr Robertson. I certainly did not intend to make any use of the photographic evidence that he was engaged in an affair with his servant. The picture of this man that the camera uncovered added to the portrait of the street.

It wasn't a portrait of perfection. It was a portrait of humanity with all its weaknesses and defects.

CHAPTER SEVEN

When I stepped from the carriage in Rutherglen outside the offices of the TopTap typewriter company I saw a large crowd gathered round a group of policemen on the pavement of the next block.

I asked the commissionaire what had happened.

'Someone's been murdered.'

As is the way with certain people when they have something shocking to impart, the commissionaire looked at me carefully to see how I would respond to his dramatic news. I was not a stranger to murder: I experienced a moment of irritation because of his attentiveness, but I smothered this.

'In the street?' I asked.

'In the back of the dance hall.'

The crowd had gathered below a sign advertising the Caribbean Ballroom.

'Have they caught the fellow who did it?'

'He got clean away!'

I climbed to the third floor.

Mr Caruso came from behind his desk and shook me warmly by the hand. 'Mr Camarón,' he said. 'It was a delicate task you set us, but I think we've risen to the challenge!'

He ushered me through to a small room next to his office. 'Here it is,' he announced, with a sort of proprietorial tenderness. To my surprise and relief the Eclipse was sitting, quite intact, separately from the timing mechanism.

Relief because, having surrendered the camera to Mr Caruso and having granted him permission to make whatever structural adjustments might be necessary to fit the timer, I had allowed a seed of uncertainty to grow that the typewriter manufacturer – untrained in the science of photography – might damage the camera in the process of joining it to an extraneous device.

I must have betrayed my feelings because Mr Caruso chuckled and said, 'The camera is entirely unchanged, Mr Camarón! The other elements have been altered in order to accommodate it.' He lifted up a plate, which, I could see, had been divided by means of lead strips into six separate sections, and slid it behind the viewfinder in the normal way. Four sturdy clips had been affixed to the end of the plate and it was by means of these that the timer was attached to the other side of the camera, with an arm stretching from the timer to the plate, which I saw to be the mechanism that moved the plate at fixed intervals.

'The timer is an ordinary carriage clock with the casing removed,' Mr Caruso explained.

When he had fitted the plate to the camera and the timer to

the plate, he lifted the composite device onto its side, revealing a normal clock face.

'It is done like this,' he said, turning the minute hand from twelve o'clock to one minute past and then waiting for a few seconds until we heard a distinctive click. He then turned the minute hand to two minutes past and waited a second time until we heard the click. He took out his pocket watch and waited. 'This plate is a dummy,' he told me, 'so we're not making a photograph, but I have prepared two genuine plates. This is simply for the purposes of demonstration – to establish the principle, as it were.'

As he finished speaking, we heard the whirr of the camera shutter. He glanced at his watch and said, 'One minute precisely.'

The plate slid eight inches to the right, moved by the arm attached to the timer: this was effected without even the tiniest sound.

I glanced from the machine to Mr Caruso. He was looking at the camera with a half-smile.

'The mechanism is ingenious,' I said.

'It is very simple.' He spoke softly. 'The most effective machines are simple.'

Seconds passed and we heard the distinctive whirr of the shutter closing.

'Now!' Mr Caruso said, suddenly full of life. 'Shall we give it a spin?'

I willingly agreed.

'May I propose that we set up the camera in my office?' he said. 'It has a view of the street below.'

It was soon after nine o'clock when we had mounted the

equipment on its tripod and primed it to take six photographs. The company premises occupied the corner of a block that was a window's breadth deeper into the street than the blocks running west. This meant that the side window of Mr Caruso's office gave an unobstructed view of the street.

'Shall we set it for half past nine and then for each half-past the hour after that?' Mr Caruso asked.

I agreed and waited for him to set the timer, but he simply stood and looked at it and then, after a few seconds, as if surprised by my lack of activity, he indicated with a flick of his hand and an expectant expression that I should be the one to begin the experiment. I turned the hand of the clock to half past nine and then to half past ten, repeating the procedure until half past two, each time waiting for the click to indicate that the appropriate groove on the plate had been identified and selected.

Mr Caruso looked at his watch and said, 'Well, Mr Camarón, I have other work to attend to. I do very much hope we will both have something to celebrate when you come back after half past two.'

I went down the stairs and out into the street wondering how I might spend the next five hours. There was still a crowd outside the dance hall, though it was smaller than when I had arrived at the office half an hour earlier. I walked in that direction for no more reason than that it was as satisfactory as walking in the opposite direction.

And as I started to walk, I had for the very first time the odd sensation that I was moving through a composition of my own making. I was walking among the shapes and shadows of the scene I would study in the minutest detail hours from now.

At the centre of the crowd, the body of the murder victim lay on a canvas stretcher, waiting, I gathered, to be taken to the mortuary. It had not been covered. The victim was a young woman. Her shoes had been removed and her toes, enshrouded in thick black stockings, protruded from the hem of her grey skirt.

The toes were not side by side, but appeared to rest on the stretcher at a strange angle. I remembered the shape that was made by Eleanora's corpse.

The memory was accompanied by a feeling of nausea.

I crossed the road, moving away from the crowd. I was almost grateful for the distraction of having to thread my way between carts and out of the path of a speeding tram. On the opposite side of the street, I stopped and got my breath back and willed myself to feel normal again.

The town folded me into itself. I listened to the noise of traffic and the grunts and yelps and rising voices of people on the crowded pavement. I wanted to submerge myself deep in this river of humanity, far from Santiago, far from the events that killed my father and his cousin and his cousin's wife.

The clicking camera on the third storey of the office block in Rutherglen was to be my distraction, the busy street my camouflage.

At twenty-five minutes past two, I returned to the office.

Mr Caruso looked up from his desk and gestured for me to take a seat. I spent several minutes looking at the hairs pasted across the top of his bald head as his pen scratched busily across the columns of a ledger book and he bowed over his work in the manner of a short-sighted schoolboy, eyes close to the page, his free hand encircling his writing hand as though to shield his work from prying eyes.

The seconds ticked away and at half past the hour I heard, above the sound of Mr Caruso's scratching, the distinctive click and then the whirr of the shutter. I stood and moved to the camera. Mr Caruso threw down his pen and came and stood beside me.

As I had done that morning, and for just as little reason, I waited for him to act, and he indicated that it was for me, the photographer, to attend to the camera. I took another step forward and detached the plate and placed it in the satchel I had brought for that purpose.

Mr Caruso helped me disassemble the equipment and fold up the tripod.

'Well!' he said with evident satisfaction. 'I believe we have done what we set out to do. I remain at your service, Mr Camarón.'

We shook hands and moments later I stood outside the building waiting for the commissionaire to hail me a cab.

On the way back to Morton's I hardly noticed the carriages and carts, the groups of children in the park playing in the balmy afternoon. I felt as though I were carrying a newborn child in the satchel on my knee.

At the house I informed Mrs Simpson that under no circumstances was she to come into the cubbyhole behind the kitchen, where I had assembled my developing materials.

By six o'clock I was in possession of six images of the same section of the main street in Rutherglen, made on the half hour every hour since half past nine that morning. I took the photographs up to my room, spread them out on the bed and set to work with my greaseproof frames and my notebook.

Hans brought supper on a tray. I was still making notes when Morton returned to the house shortly before midnight.

I had by then found something that would end the life of Arabella Threadmyre.

A twenty-five-year-old laundrywoman from the West End of Glasgow, Arabella Threadmyre did not appear in the photographs. She existed, though, in the shadows and spaces and shapes that were recorded by my camera. She existed in her very *absence* from the images.

Morton appeared to be drunk. He knocked loudly and when I opened the door, he strode in and said, 'What have you found? Does the thing work? Was Caruso any good?'

I pointed to the first of the six pictures.

'Look in the middle of the road, travelling south,' I said. I placed my index finger at the point where a tall vehicle with a semi-circular advertisement framed an illustration of neatly piled linen.

'A laundry van.'

'Now, look outside the Caribbean Ballroom. What do you see?'

'A policeman.'

'Here, in the second picture, in the lane moving north.' I pointed.

'The laundry van.'

'The same van at half past nine and at half past ten' – I pointed to the next photograph – 'and at half past eleven.' In the third image the van was travelling south again. 'In the first three photographs there's a policeman outside the ballroom. Now, look at half past twelve.' I pointed to the pavement in front of the ballroom.

'No policeman.'

And what do you see . . . ?'

'The van is parked outside.' He looked up at me and asked rather irritably, 'But what does it mean?'

'Perhaps nothing at all. Yet, it seems to me the driver of this van moved up and down the street in front of the ballroom, but only stopped outside when the policeman had gone.'

'Why was the policeman there?'

'Because a young woman was hacked to death with a pickaxe just behind the dance floor. The details are in the evening paper.'

CHAPTER EIGHT

The following day, I visited the police station in Rutherglen together with Morton.

I disliked his insistence that he accompany me – indeed, I disliked his proprietorial approach to the timing device. He had contributed key ideas to the invention, but I felt he couldn't rightly claim it as his own. However, as he was a man who had patented a new and successful kind of typewriter, and since my serial photography device had been crafted by one of his workmen in one of his factories, he did appear to have a strong claim if he chose to press it. I did not know whether to view him as a patron or a thief-in-waiting. And at the root of everything, I had not changed my initial impression. I didn't particularly like Edward Morton. I had decided not to remain his lodger much longer.

At the same time, had I come alone to the police station, a

foreigner with an odd and likely useless piece of information – I would not be given a hearing.

We were shown into a room adjacent to the main office on the ground floor. The woman who escorted us bore a certain resemblance to the corpse I had seen outside the dance hall. The living woman was about twenty-five and dressed in a white blouse and a slate grey skirt. I tried to imagine what she would look like if she smiled, but I could not.

Sergeant Garvey was similarly dour.

As Morton explained why we had come, the sergeant watched us both, revealing not a glimmer of interest or, I thought, comprehension. He was about forty; his black hair, oiled and brushed back, had begun to retreat and was visibly thinning. His brown eyes were inexpressive; his thick moustache failed to obscure thin lips and bad teeth and his skin was pockmarked.

'So,' Morton concluded, 'we believe that these photographs may possibly be of use in your investigation.'

We waited for the sergeant to respond but instead of saying anything he looked first at Morton, then at me, then at Morton again. Finally, he asked, 'What is it that you want?'

I was by now more accustomed to Morton's way of speaking English, but he adjusted his normal register when he spoke to the policeman and I found parts of the exchange impenetrable. Garvey's responses were barely comprehensible.

'We want you to look at the photographs,' Morton told him.

I removed the six images from the satchel and placed them in front of the sergeant.

Ostentatiously, he did not allow his gaze to fall on the pictures, but kept it on the two of us.

'This is of no use to me,' he said. 'I don't know why you

brought this here. Go and offer your pictures to the newspapers. They've no place in a police station.'

He stood and picked up the photographs and tossed them over to the other side of the desk so that I had to scoop them up or they would have slid onto the floor.

The woman who had escorted us into the interview ignored us as we walked through the outer office. On the pavement outside, I glared at the passing traffic.

'What a . . .' I began, but I couldn't think of a suitably descriptive word to describe the policeman's effrontery.

'I should have made enquiries in advance,' Morton said. 'We weren't properly introduced.'

Morton signalled to his carriage.

'Did you notice anything odd about the sergeant?' he asked.

'Yes, he is an ignorant fool.'

'When you shook hands,' Morton continued. His tone wasn't angry, like mine; it was thoughtful.

I began to calm down. I *had* noticed something, but I hadn't thought anything of it.

'His grip was tight and then loose and then tight again,' I said.

The carriage, which had been parked on the other side of the road, pulled up next to us.

'I gather, then, that you are not acquainted with that particular confraternity?'

My grandfather was a Mason. My father – by choice and avocation – was not. I often thought that things might have gone more easily for him if he had taken advantage of his own father's connections. I hadn't thought anything of this when I shook Sergeant Garvey by the hand, but I saw it now. I believe we would have received a more agreeable hearing if we'd been able to reciprocate whatever signal was embedded in his odd grip.

'Well,' Morton said, recovering his sunny disposition. 'We'll go over his head!'

'Over his head?'

'The chief constable.'

'You know him?'

'We have friends in common.' He looked at me and then added in his characteristically sardonic way, 'Not friends of the handshaking variety, but friends in high places nonetheless.'

We visited the chief constable at his home the following morning. It was ten o'clock and he was at breakfast: we were invited to join him in the dining room. At the end of a long table, a high arched window behind him, he sat by himself, his silhouette creating – I thought – the impression of a bullfrog. He had a large head and massive sloping shoulders beneath which was a round torso. A cloth covered just one end of the table, where breakfast was laid. The rest of the polished oak surface gleamed beneath a low chandelier.

Chief Constable McGregor took a mouthful of something when he saw us and then put down his fork and wiped his lips. He stood up and came round to meet us, moving slowly, so that we covered a good deal more of the distance than he did. He had a thick moustache that dropped on either side of bulbous red lips (a morsel of food rested snugly at the corner of his mouth, wedged there by strands of the walrus moustache).

He extended his hand lugubriously. His grip was limp and unremarkable.

Morton named two city councillors whose acquaintance he and the chief shared. At this, the man's face became less reserved.

A servant had followed us in and he placed three cups and saucers and a teapot on the table.

'You fellows up for eating?' McGregor asked. His words seemed to burble up from somewhere in the recesses of his enormous chest, emerging from his mouth with the same carelessness as the morsel of sausage on his lower lip.

We said we were not up for eating.

'Tea, then.'

McGregor lit a cheroot and the servant poured tea.

I placed the photographs on the table.

'Tommy Auchenleck's an awful man,' McGregor said through a plume of white smoke that made him narrow his eyes.

Tommy Auchenleck was one of the councillors whose name had opened the door to the chief constable's home.

'Incorrigible!' Morton said.

McGregor's expression appeared to be suspended for a few seconds – eyes narrowed, cigar hand resting, elbow on the table – then his features crumbled into a grin; his cheeks became redder and a loud peal of laughter rumbled up from the capacious chest and out over the breakfast debris.

Morton explained that we had spoken to the sergeant at Rutherglen police station and had not been satisfied with our reception.

'We believe these photographs may be of some assistance in solving the murder,' I said, passing the photographs across the table.

I had not made such an explicit claim before. I wondered

if I was overstating the case. But I certainly didn't want to be dismissed again without a hearing.

McGregor looked at me as he accepted the photographs and I experienced an upsurge of indignation. There was an insolence, I thought, in his casual scrutiny, the insolence of an office-holder in the presence of a citizen who requires his help.

'So it looks as though the laundryman's up to no good,' McGregor said when we had talked him through the sequence of images. 'Is he the killer?'

He had understood the principle, but imperfectly. He seemed to think the photographs were some kind of magic. Yet he remained remarkably unaffected, speaking in a tone of mild interest. If serial photography could really catch killers, one might have expected a policeman to express more excitement.

'We can't arrive at that conclusion,' I said.

'So, what's the use of this then?'

'Well, you could have the officer investigating the murder track down the owner of this van,' Morton said. 'It might come to nothing, or it might come to something.'

'It might come to something,' McGregor repeated in a tone of voice that was just short of a sneer. 'Or it might not.'

He looked down at the photographs and then at the two of us. After a moment's thought he said, 'I suppose I'd better keep these.'

'Give my regards to that awful man,' McGregor told Morton as we took our leave.

Two days later Morton arrived home in the early evening with a copy of the *Evening Citizen*.

'There, on the front page,' he said.

There on the front page was an item that read as follows:

RUTHERGLEN MURDER SOLVED

Police Catch Killer from Caribbean Ballroom
Woman Confesses, Husband Arrested Too

Mrs Threadmyre of the Chequers Laundry on Great Western Road has told police she took the life of Mary Boyle at the Caribbean Ballroom, Rutherglen, on Tuesday last. Arabella Threadmyre acted in a jealous rage when she learned of Miss Boyle's liaison with Mr Threadmyre.

Police located the Threadmyres after a witness reported seeing a van from the laundry outside the ballroom on the day of the murder.

Sergeant Alfred Garvey told the Evening Citizen *that when confronted by investigating officers Mr and Mrs Threadmyre broke down and confessed. Sergeant Garvey, at once feared by criminals and admired by his peers, is well known as an officer who favours the modern, scientific approach to crime detection.*

Arabella Threadmyre told police she had gone to the dance hall, where Mary Boyle was a bookkeeper, to warn the young woman to stay away from her husband. When Miss Boyle rebuffed her, Mrs Threadmyre attacked her rival with a mallet and then with an axe, both of which had been left by workmen on the backstairs of the premises where the interview between the two women took place.

Returning to her home above the Chequers Laundry, Mrs Threadmyre told her husband what she had done. After this, Thaddeus Threadmyre, whose company laundered linen from the dance hall premises, went to the scene of the crime

and tried to locate a hatpin belonging to his wife, which she
believed she had lost during the execution of the homicide. He
had intended to remove this piece of incriminating evidence.

'We're the witness!' Morton said. 'And not a word about
our camera!'

I read the piece a second time.

'They caught the killer,' I said. 'I suppose that's what matters.'

It was *my* camera.

More details appeared in the papers over the next few
days. Most of the reports praised Sergeant Garvey's inspired
detective work that had led to the arrest of the 'she-witch of
the South Side'.

CHAPTER NINE

During this period, I made serial photographs of several streets; I did not uncover crimes or capture instances of egregious human frailty, but I honed my method of extracting – through the disciplined application of minute comparison – insights about the people who were captured in the images. I learned to tell, for example, a great deal about a man's personality by the looks he drew from others. He might have his back to the camera but his face and his soul were reflected in the expressions of the men and women and children photographed reacting to him. Every picture tells a story, and when you look closely the story may be more detailed and more surprising than at first glance.

As a result of her confession, Arabella Threadmyre's trial was swift, and the sentence was never in doubt. She was remanded in Duke Street Prison ahead of her execution. Arabella refused to appeal, though her husband begged her to. The newspapers made much of what they described as the guilty woman's 'death wish'.

Thaddeus Threadmyre was sentenced to twenty years' hard labour for trying first to help Arabella cover up her crime and then withholding information from the police. In the papers he was portrayed as a man who had strayed (and in view of Arabella's violent nature who could blame him? the papers seemed to suggest) and who had lost his lover, his wife and his liberty because of one peccadillo.

'There's a gentleman to see you,' Mrs Simpson told me when I returned to the house one afternoon.

She spoke in her clipped brogue and in her customary tone (so inexpressive of any feeling as to be almost aggressively remote). And yet there was an edge to her voice that made me wonder about the waiting gentleman. She returned to the kitchen and left me to deal with the caller.

Mrs Simpson, I thought when I recognised my visitor, had the measure of Alfred Garvey. He was no gentleman.

'Mr Camarón!' he said, advancing to meet me and shaking my hand firmly (and without anything in the way of a special sign).

I was baffled by his changed manner.

'I understand you have business on the Isle of Bute,' he began.

I disliked the notion of this man snooping into my affairs. I waited for him to continue.

He softened his expression, apparently in an effort to appear more agreeable. This made him look awkward, almost childish.

'I came first of all to thank you for your contribution in the case of Arabella.'

The doomed woman's celebrity meant that she could now be referred to by her Christian name alone.

I remained silent.

'I wanted to ask for your assistance in another case.'

This was unexpected! I was surprised by Garvey's clumsy attempt to ingratiate – but more surprised by my instant curiosity about the prospect of using serial photography to solve another crime.

'The Gorbals,' Morton said, somewhat sourly, when I recounted Garvey's visit and the request he had made. 'Far from salubrious.'

'The nature of the assignment is such that I will spend some nights there.'

Morton gave me a frank look and – not in the least to my surprise – came straight to the point. 'I was willing to have you here, and if you go, you do so of your own volition – but I will be patenting the timer.'

I felt a curious sense of release. The subject had been hanging over us.

'I believe I may have a claim to this idea,' I said.

'Ideas don't matter. My man devised the mechanism . . .' He paused and then continued, still speaking in an even tone, 'But I'm not stealing your method. Go and help in the Gorbals – that's your prerogative. I won't insist that you return the timer we made for you. Use it if you like. I will make money from it and I suspect you never will.'

These were the terms on which I left the house where Señor da Costa had arranged for me to stay in Glasgow.

CHAPTER TEN

James MacKay spoke with a sonorous intonation. His manner was confident and he carried himself with a sort of lumbering gravitas appropriate to a distinguished professor in his sixties.

'Señor Camarón!' he boomed, walking round his desk and advancing towards me.

His handshake was firm. He indicated an armchair on one side of an empty fireplace.

'You had a rough crossing?' he asked solicitously.

'It was some weeks ago. I am well recovered.'

His office was large and comfortable, lined with medical texts and dominated by a huge desk covered with papers. It was not, however, the papers or the books around the walls that drew the attention. On the desk, floating in formaldehyde in a sealed glass, was a human hand.

He caught me staring at it.

'It belonged to a Lascar sailor,' he said, smiling. The expression of surprise on my face may have bordered on shock. 'He died of a rare complaint, which was diagnosed through a swelling in the knuckles of the thumb.' He sat down opposite me and added, 'I don't have it there as a paperweight. I'll present it at a lecture tomorrow and after that it will be returned to the medical faculty museum.'

I looked from the Lascar's hand to the professor's face.

'We are immensely grateful that you've agreed to help us,' he began. Then he suddenly turned in his chair and called through the open door, 'Harriet! Bring us a pot of tea!'

When he raised his voice, the boom turned into a kind of detonation and I found myself sitting far back in the seat I'd just taken, as if to let the force of the professor's voice pass in front of me.

Professor MacKay had a thick, neatly trimmed grey beard and sparse grey hair brushed back from a high forehead. A flimsy pince-nez perched at the end of his nose with the cord dangling down one side.

'Oh!' he said, standing up almost as soon as he had sat down. 'I've a letter for you!'

He fetched an envelope from his desk and handed it to me.

'I'll see about the tea,' he said, stepping heavily towards the door. He called his secretary's name again and demanded to know why it should always take such an unconscionably long time to produce a pot of tea.

I recognised the writing on the outside of the envelope.

Dear Juan,
I am writing to you care of Professor MacKay as we have learned through a friend of Robert who is a journalist in

Glasgow that you are assisting the professor with your new system of photography. Your work on the recent murder case has been extraordinary! Robert and I were struck by your talent, Juan, and by your understanding of people.

I have taken the liberty of alerting my niece Marjorie Jane Macgregor that you are in Glasgow. Professor MacKay will let her know where you are staying. Please do not think this a presumption, Juan. Marjorie is a bright girl – and a friendly face in a new city will surely be a boon. She is about the same age as you. Her mother and father have recently gone to the Lord.

Isn't it remarkable that your travels have taken you to Glasgow! I know that you will be able to do great work there, and wherever the spirit moves you. I know too that your father would be proud of you.

Please write and tell us your impressions of the city and its people. We are happy to wander the face of the earth and we place our hope in a Providence that is higher than human affection – but a little of our hearts remains where you are now!

Robert sends his very best wishes.

May God bless and protect you.

Effie McClellan

Professor MacKay came back into his office followed by Harriet carrying a tray.

'Robert McClellan was one of my brightest students,' the professor said as tea was served on a little table between the two armchairs. 'You met him through your regular line of work, I understand?'

'My father and I were in Cuba to produce a photographic inventory of the island's architecture. We also made portraits. We stayed with Mr and Mrs McClellan just before we arrived in Santiago, and they sat for a photograph.'

'That was quite a place!' Professor MacKay said, holding out a plate on which there were small brown pastries.

I took a pastry.

'The disturbances,' he continued, 'they were severe in Santiago?'

'The town was cut off.'

He nodded. 'Was there water?'

'Not enough, particularly towards the end.'

'There were medical facilities?'

'They were overstretched.'

He nodded again and seemed to make a calculation.

'Insufficient water could conceivably slow down the spread of cholera. There was typhus, I understand. That would have spread quickly in the climate. Was food a problem?'

I had been quizzed many times about conditions inside Santiago. Morton and others had wanted to know what the siege had been like, but the professor's curiosity was remarkably systematic. He asked about things he understood.

'The authorities had reserves of maize and these were distributed. Fear was a greater problem than hunger.'

He nodded again, lifted his cup and saucer and took a sip of tea.

'Fear,' he said. 'Contagious.'

He thought for a moment and then he added, 'The district we are going to visit is just south of the river. The murders took place a block or two from one of the main bridges. A year ago in the very same district there was an outbreak of bubonic plague.' He waited for me to show surprise. When I did so, he nodded and said, 'Exactly! In the heart of a modern metropolis – plague! The same that ravaged Charles the Second's London!'

'At least we didn't have plague in Santiago,' I said.

'For that you should be truly grateful. We have plenty of scourges, but that one is particularly loathsome. And now there's a new killer in the same district,' he continued, 'and there isn't a soul who's not afraid.'

He put his cup and saucer on the table and placed his large hands on his knees.

'Well, my colleagues in the police have told me of the originality of your method, and I'm bound to say that we need originality in the present case, because none of the conventional approaches has worked.'

He reached into his pocket and took out a large blue handkerchief with which he dabbed his lips before stuffing it back into his pocket.

'There have been four killings since the first one, in November last year, all within a quarter of a mile of one another. The murders have taken place on one of the main roads into the centre of the city – we don't know how the fellow has managed to escape detection. He has killed in the middle of the night and he has killed in the middle of the day; it's as though he has performed these murders in plain view – yet no one has seen him. The results of his work command attention, though. The bodies have been dismembered, the arms and legs amputated and taken away.'

His face brightened. 'You'll dine with us this evening, I hope.'

Perhaps only a pathologist could have jumped as easily from murder to dinner.

'That's very kind of you.'

'Good!' He rubbed his hands with a kind of relish as though pleased to return to the intriguing puzzle of the serial murders. 'Now, the man we're after has been back at the scene of the crime. Fortunately, he wasn't able to complete his work this time.'

'He was disturbed?'

He nodded. 'A girl called Edie Hamilton, eighteen years old from a village near the city, an assistant in a haberdasher's in the Saltmarket. She was coming home, at seven o'clock three days ago; it was still light. She was grabbed from behind just as she entered the close where she lives.'

'The close?'

He looked at me as if he had just remembered that I suffered from some sort of disability. 'In Glasgow we call the entrance to a tenement a "close".'

'Was she able to defend herself?'

'She managed to scream; her neighbour on the ground floor opened his door and the assailant fled. When the neighbour and the girl plucked up the courage to venture out into the street, the man had made good his escape. We have one or two likely suspects, but we don't quite have proof.'

'The victims are male and female?'

He nodded. 'Most of them young. The first, Maggie McAllister, was in her early twenties; the next, Brendan Gillespie was just nineteen. He was the youngest – Edie Hamilton would have gained that distinction if the fellow had had his way. The third victim, Willie McGonagall – I don't know exactly how old, but I believe he was in his twenties; he was about to be married. Then came Bessie Armstrong, murdered at the end of March, and' – he paused for a moment, searching for the name – 'Harold . . . no . . . Henry . . . no . . . *Hector* MacKinnon, a month later.'

He was about to add something, but his attention was distracted by a soft knock at the door.

A man of about thirty entered. He had pale skin and a blonde moustache; his thick light hair was parted in the middle. A pair of dark brown eyes darted between the professor and me as the new arrival walked towards us. Tall and neatly dressed, he wore a dark suit with a new white collar and a grey tie.

'This is Sergeant Macarthur,' the professor said.

I stood. Sergeant Macarthur presented a cold hand, rather tentatively.

'Shall we visit the scene of the crime?' the professor asked.

Travelling from the university to the district where the murders had been committed was like travelling from the earth to the moon.

We crossed the city in the professor's brougham, MacKay and I inside and Macarthur in front with the driver. It was just before eleven and the scene displayed an early summer exuberance; we passed through a large park where there were small boys with caps and slingshots, girls in white smocks and buttoned-up boots, men in cotton suits, women pushing prams, and matrons wearing straw hats to fend off the weak sun that wafted through a pervasive patina of soot and smoke.

As we entered the main thoroughfare into the city from the west, an endless array of carts and drays contended with tramcars and broughams and omnibuses and every kind of vehicle that can be placed on wheels. All around, I heard snatches of the singsong dialect that seemed as much a part of these streets as the soot and the noise. The vowels were throttled before they were properly made, and some of the consonants – the 'r's and 'm's and 'g's in particular – appeared to enjoy a kind of ascendancy over every other sound. Morton and Professor MacKay spoke with a modified version of the same patois. I could understand them. Sergeant Macarthur spoke a less modified version.

Crossing the river, it was only possible to catch glimpses of black oily water: the river was as clogged with ships as the city centre was clogged with carriages.

The buildings were uniformly black. Around the university the black buildings were townhouses with richly embellished facades and mansard roofs. In the city centre there were stone palaces housing banks and shipping companies and department stores. Now, as the brougham emerged from the bridge in a sea of carts and clattering omnibuses and trams, we entered a broad canyon with plain facades and serried ranks of windows.

'This is the place!' Professor MacKay said, as though we had just arrived at a particularly agreeable tearoom.

We climbed down onto the pavement outside a four-storey building that was so black it almost glittered in the fragile sunlight. From a distance it might have looked as though it were made of Italian marble. Close up, there was a marked absence of renaissance luxury, however. The building had all the hallmarks of a slum.

'This is the bad end of the street,' Macarthur explained.

A figure dressed in black, with a black helmet shading a face that was framed in thick black whiskers and bisected by a thick black moustache, emerged from the darkness of the close, advanced towards us and saluted.

'Thur wullnae be tha' much tae see the day,' the constable said apologetically.

I glanced along the facade. Windows had opened and people were leaning out to observe us; there were men in shirtsleeves, collarless and with their braces hanging down over waistbands, and women covered up in shawls so as not to expose the flimsiness of their indoor clothes. A small band of children began to form on the pavement about twenty yards from where we stood, like a band of braves appraising a vulnerable wagon train in a Wild West show.

'Let's take a look inside,' Professor MacKay said, still speaking as though we were tourists on an outing.

The exasperated expression on the constable's face suggested that this was the very thing he had hoped would not be proposed. He glanced at Macarthur, but when he didn't receive any comfort there, he restored his expression to one of earnest discipline, turned and began to lead us into the darkness.

'It was just here,' the constable announced when we were halfway into the close.

We stood at the bottom of a set of broad stone stairs. Smells of excreta, stale vegetables and ash were distilled in the enclosed dark.

'What is it?' a voice called out from the floor above.

'Shh,' someone else said.

The door beside us opened and almost as quickly closed again.

'The girl was seized here,' the constable said, standing with his back to the steps.

'The fellow may have intended to do his awful business over there,' the professor suggested, pointing to a passageway that led past the stairs to a backcourt. There was a wooden gate at

94

the end. It stood ajar, and we could see into the pale daylight, a scrubby patch of ash at the end of which were iron rubbish boxes. Sheets and clothes hung on lines near the boxes.

'Is the girl here?' I asked.

'She's away hame tae her ain,' the constable said, his tone rising with mild disbelief, as though something so obvious should not have had to be said out loud.

'She's gone back to her village,' Macarthur translated.

'Let's see the other places.' The professor turned and strode towards the light.

As we came out onto the street, Macarthur and the constable hung back and engaged in a hurried altercation. The professor and I stood by the brougham waiting for the two policemen to join us. The professor had not been taciturn before, but now, it seemed to me, he waited nervously for the men to finish their conversation. He showed no inclination to make small talk. I examined his brougham. It was well sprung and its polished wood and brass bespoke wealth and power. It was a rich man's vehicle parked in a poor man's street. I glanced along the road at tradesmen's drays with exhausted animals harnessed to them. The professor's two black ponies were sleek and well fed; they snorted impatiently, as though they too were out of place here and anxious to leave.

A tram clattered towards us from the south. The passengers looked at us with curiosity and at the street with a kind of fascination, as though they were aboard a ship sailing from one prosperous island to another across an ocean of poverty.

'He wasn't told we wanted to see the whole area,' Macarthur reported when he had finished conferring with the policeman. 'He thinks we've already attracted too much attention, says he should send for another constable. The police station is just a few blocks away. They can have an extra man here in five minutes.'

'What do *you* think?' MacKay asked.

Macarthur shrugged. 'Perhaps we can send your driver up to the cross. He can wait for us there. It's busier and he'll attract less attention. We might as well press on.'

MacKay instructed the driver to move to the junction six blocks to the north, just before the river. We began to follow the same route, with the constable in the lead.

The children who had gathered on the pavement were aged between about two and twelve. They were mostly boys, but in among them were three or four girls with long straggly hair that was continually being scratched. The boys mostly had their hair cropped. All but one of the children were barefoot. The one who had shoes looked to be the oldest. As we approached, the constable made a path for us through the middle of the group. The children retreated grudgingly, leaving just enough room for us to pass in single file.

'Is it aboot the murders?' the boy with shoes asked the constable.

'You be quiet,' the constable barked.

The boy said something under his breath and scowled.

We hurried to the next close but one. The brougham had disappeared in the distance.

'Maggie McAllister, 28th November,' Macarthur said. 'She let the murderer into the family apartment; the father was at work, the mother was marketing.'

'The ground floor?' I asked.

'No, the second storey.' He pointed to a window above the entrance. The curtains were drawn.

Just at that moment, a grimy window not two yards away

96

opened noisily and a man put his head out. 'Are you for the rent?' he asked in a voice that tried to be defiant but sounded merely nervous. He was middle-aged, with a round red face and thinning red hair. He wore a singlet; the lower part of his body was obscured by the wall.

The constable stepped towards him threateningly.

'No, it's no' the rent,' Macarthur said. 'It disnae concern you.'

The man's expression changed from apprehension to relief. He closed the window.

'The next was on 25th December,' Macarthur continued, 'and it happened over there.' He pointed to a close on the other side of the road.

Outside the close, I looked first north and then south. One thing impressed me: the long straight line of this street was very well suited to serial photography.

'Did the murder take place inside or outside?'

'In the close,' the constable said. 'It was early. Nobody saw a thing.'

I tried to imagine the first people encountering a bleeding corpse, absent arms and legs, on Christmas morning.

'Brendan Gillespie was a lamplighter,' Macarthur said. 'He was leaving for his morning round.'

We emerged from the close as another tram passed. The passengers looked at us as though we were fish in a tank. The constable led us back to the other side of the road, holding up his hand to stop a cart that was piled high with barrels. They must have been empty or the carter would not have been able to come to a halt in time. He sat up on his bench, his whip swaying in front of him like a fishing line, looking stonily at the policeman and his well-dressed charges.

We were disrupting the life of this place. My father used to say that he and I were at home anywhere. Perhaps that was true. The first time I heard the singsong intonation of the granadinos, when we arrived after five days on the road from Madrid, I thought the words coming out of people's mouths were not Spanish. It was as though we had moved to a different world. 'We'll get used to it,' my father said. And we did. The manners of the people were exotic, and the buildings around the Puerta Real and the Plaza Nueva were like those in Madrid but on a miniature scale. There were fewer streets, they were cleaner, and the people who moved among them seemed to me less numerous and less desperate. It was as though we had come from a metropolis to a village, but a village with the furniture and facades of a metropolis.

Our position had always been awkward: we were gentlemen who worked with our hands. We made portraits of granadinos in Andalusian costume. My father was meticulous, fussing over every last mantilla fold. 'People will see *them* through *us*,' he told me. 'We must show them at their best!'

Most people saw *us* as a couple of Madrileños with magic mahogany boxes. In Cuba, too, the moment we opened our mouths we were asked when we had arrived. Every vowel identified us as incomers and for many by then incomers were poor or powerful – problematic either way.

'Willie McGonagall, late January this year,' Macarthur said. He had taken a notebook out of his inside pocket. He examined it. 'The thirtieth.'

This time, the location was not a close but an entrance broad enough to take a horse and cart. The constable led us through to a small courtyard behind a public house. The courtyard was surrounded by windows. There was one small alcove created by the wall of a shed in which there were dustbins. I stepped into the alcove and shuddered. I was hidden from view, save for the aperture directly in front of me. As long as no one passed, the murderer would have been able to kill here unmolested. Yet we were within earshot of voices from the public house.

'What time of day?' the professor asked.

'The body was found at three in the afternoon.'

MacKay looked up at the surrounding windows. 'And no one saw anything?'

'People come and go, to empty the rubbish. The carter brings in ale for the public house. They take it through the cellar door there.' Macarthur pointed to a half wooden door at the bottom of the building opposite the shed for the rubbish bins. We all looked. 'But no one saw anything untoward, until the corpse was found.'

'There must have been a great deal of blood,' I said, looking at the narrow space between the wall and the rubbish bins.

Macarthur consulted his notebook again. 'As a matter of fact there was very little.'

The professor took a step forward. 'Either it was soaked up by the cinders there, or the killer used a tourniquet. Dashed cool if he did.'

'Could it be one of their own, sir?' the constable asked.

Macarthur gave him a sharp look. The constable was clearly not expected to participate in the deliberations of his betters. 'Maybe,' he said, answering, it seemed to me, because he didn't want to leave the hypothesis floating in the air. 'But why wouldn't they give him up to us? He's killing *them*.'

'One of their own?' I asked.

'Fenians.'

I looked at the professor.

'Irish,' he explained.

'Jews too around here,' Macarthur added, 'and Italians. Not many of *us* left in these parts.' He looked at me in a manner I had long ago come to recognise. It was designed to indicate that whatever I might say or do, my foreignness would count against me in the end.

The remaining two murders had been committed at the end of March and April, and the bodies had been found near the steps of a bank facing the busy crossing where Professor MacKay's brougham waited for us. One corpse was discovered at four o'clock in the afternoon, wrapped in a canvas bag and still warm. The other was spotted by a police constable at midnight. It was wrapped in a black blanket.

Our escort led us along two blocks in which the quality of the shops on either side of the road improved. This was apparently the 'good' end of the street. News of our presence had spread; the band of children who had greeted us at our first stop was nothing compared to the crowd that had assembled by the time we arrived at the bank. The constable made a path for us and we edged forward until we faced five long and imposing steps leading up to a stone portico and a mahogany entrance with two glass-filled doors. On either side of the top step was a steel accordion gate that could be pulled across the entrance when the bank was closed.

A commissionaire hurried down the steps and complained to the constable that our crowd was deterring customers from entering the bank. Together the constable and the commissionaire began to shoo away the onlookers, so that after thirty seconds we stood on our own on one side of the steps and the onlookers gawked from the other side. A stout lady in a black coat too heavy for the season emerged from the bank and climbed down the steps apparently oblivious of the large number of people watching her. Another lady, pushing a pram, made her way to the bottom of the steps and began to turn the pram preparatory to dragging it up to the entrance. Two boys broke away from the crowd and took a wheel each and helped carry the pram up, in hopes of a halfpenny, no doubt, and at the very least seizing the chance to be at the centre of the scene that was the focus of universal interest.

'The victims?' I asked Macarthur.

When I spoke, even though I had asked my question in an undertone, all eyes in the crowd fixed upon me.

Macarthur glanced at his notebook. 'Bessie Armstrong was a laundress; she lived two closes from the end of Crown Street; Hector MacKinnon was a Highlander, a schoolteacher, and he' – Macarthur looked across the square. He began to point to the close next to a dry-salter and the entire crowd followed, bodies turning, necks craning – 'he lived on the first floor, where the curtains are drawn.'

'A Highlander?' I asked.

'From Oban,' he said.

'Not Irish then?'

Macarthur and MacKay looked at me with the same expression, somewhere between surprise and irritation. I did not have an opportunity to enquire further because, just after I had spoken, a portly man in a light grey suit hurried down the steps and came towards us.

He was the first individual with whom we had had contact since entering this district who very clearly could not be brought into line with a sharp word from our accompanying constable. He was, in manner, dress and tone of voice, one of *us*. I was depressed by the clarity of this. We were interlopers in a blighted land.

The professor extended his hand and the man in the grey suit shook it. The professor introduced Sergeant Macarthur and me, and the man gave us each a handshake, very deliberate and courtly.

'Archibald Presser,' he said. 'My compliments.' He glanced at the bystanders. 'I'm afraid this is not the attention we would choose to attract in ideal circumstances.'

'Let's talk inside,' the professor said, beginning to climb the steps.

As we made our way into the bank, the constable and commissionaire announced to the crowd that there was nothing further to see.

We entered an atrium: in the centre was a polished wooden bench and around this was a mahogany counter through which a narrow entrance led onto a stairway. Perhaps twenty people could have fitted into the public area, but now there were just two. Half a dozen clerks sat behind the counter facing the public and half a dozen more sat at separate desks. Mr Presser ushered us through the opening and up the stairs to his office. The stairs creaked.

On one wall of the bank manager's office was a huge circular window that looked onto the intersection and, a block past that, to the masts and funnels of the ships on the river.

'What a remarkable view!' I said.

The window offered an ideal vantage point for the camera.

Mr Presser's manner was more like that of an undertaker than a bank manager. He didn't seem inclined to smile and his pale blue eyes betrayed no tendency to glimmer, sparkle or otherwise indicate emotion. As tea was served by a young clerk in an ill-fitting suit, Mr Presser told us that business had been badly affected by the dreadful crime perpetrated not once but twice on his very doorstep.

'We've even had customers closing their accounts!'

He looked at me and then at Professor MacKay and then at Macarthur giving us each a grim second or two of his attention and then he continued, 'Of course, we will help in the investigation in any way we can. It's better for the bank that the culprit is found sooner rather than later.'

'There is a way in which you and the bank *can* render an invaluable service, Mr Presser,' I began.

I was impatient to get the use of this man's office and, on impulse, I dived right in to the business at hand.

To my surprise, the professor dived in beside me (and in doing so he pronounced my name in the Scottish way – whether to diminish my status as an outsider or simply as an oversight, I could not tell).

'Mr Cameron is visiting us from the Americas,' he explained to Mr Presser, who was looking at me with earnest curiosity. 'He is a pioneer in a photographic technique that has helped to solve some very difficult cases.'

'Sir,' I carried on quickly, competing for Mr Presser's attention. 'Would it be possible for me to place my camera in your office?'

He seemed about to reply, but no words formed. Then

he noted that Macarthur had not touched his tea, and he leant forward and lifted the cup and saucer and insisted that Macarthur should drink it while it was hot.

'And how on earth would that help you with your investigations?' he asked at last.

'I have developed a camera which is capable of recording the same scene repeatedly, at fixed intervals over an extended period. The device can monitor everything that happens in a particular place.'

I saw no flicker of comprehension in his undertaker's eyes.

'You see, sir, if the camera had been set up at your window, recording everything that happens in the intersection outside' – Mr Presser looked through his window, and so did the professor and the sergeant – 'we might have been able to catch sight of the murderer. But even if we had not been fortunate enough to do that we would at least have been able to examine the images of the same scene with a view to identifying any events that might be tiny clues.'

His brow wrinkled. 'But you might as well put a constable on watch,' he said reasonably. 'If that's the way you catch a criminal, by sitting at the window waiting for him to come and commit a crime.'

'The camera makes a record,' I said. 'That's the difference, Mr Presser. You see, a constable might not notice anything out of the ordinary, but the camera doesn't forget. It makes a record, and by studying the record we can identify individuals that might otherwise appear entirely uninteresting but who, in reality, hold the key to what actually happened.'

'You see, this crime is very particular,' the professor continued. 'All of the murders have taken place either in

Crown Street or in the square outside your bank. This means that in the likelihood – and I am afraid that in light of the failed attempt on the life of Edie Hamilton that likelihood must be very strong – in the likelihood that the killer strikes again, he will strike either here or in Crown Street. What Mr Cameron proposes to do, and I second this proposal, is to establish one camera overlooking the intersection, and another that will take in as much as possible of the street itself.'

'And then you just sit back and wait for another murder?' Mr Presser asked, not with an air of scepticism or dismissal, but rather with honest incredulity.

The professor smiled. 'No, we don't sit back! We examine the plates every day and we try to establish whether there are any clues, any strange or inexplicable phenomena in the photographic record. Mr Cameron has been able to catch a murderer using exactly this technique.'

Mr Presser sipped his tea and asked, 'How large is the equipment?'

'Not large, sir. It will fit into this space.' I stood up and walked to the window and indicated a square on the floor, two feet by two feet.

'It will be a distraction to the staff, knowing that they are being photographed when they come to work.'

'Sir!' I said, unable to keep a note of horror out of my voice. 'What we have discussed must remain among only those of us who are now in this room. None of your staff must know!'

'Secrecy is paramount,' the professor added reassuringly. 'If the killer should discover what we are doing he will take steps to elude us. That is precisely why this office offers such remarkable advantages. From here you can see everything that happens in the square outside, but you cannot be seen.'

Mr Presser furrowed his brow again. 'Under normal circumstances I would of course have to seek approval . . . but I can see the need for discretion . . . you are the representative of the police in this affair?' he said, turning to Macarthur.

'I am.'

Mr Presser nodded. 'You will not object if I request a written explanation, duly signed and attested, outlining the scheme and assuming full responsibility for it.'

'I will draw it up right away, sir,' Macarthur said.

'And I will attest,' Professor MacKay added. 'I am a Justice of the Peace.'

'Now,' Mr Presser asked, still uncertain, 'how does this camera work? Is it going to fill my office with some sort of infernal chemical odour?'

CHAPTER ELEVEN

'Till this evening then,' the professor said, climbing into his brougham.

Macarthur and I boarded a cab and crossed the river, turning right on the opposite bank and travelling two blocks to a one-storey building about a hundred yards from the water's edge. Macarthur paid the cabbie and we went inside.

The lobby smelt of disinfectant. A short, wizened man of about fifty came round from behind a long counter and said, 'Sergeant Macarthur, you've brought me a live one!'

This was delivered in a tone that was more exploratory than comic. The little man looked at me with the calculating air of a dishonest shopkeeper sizing up a new customer. He had a lined face and small glittering eyes, his grey head was balding and his scalp was as wrinkled as his face. He wore a white coat indicating an indeterminate medical status. His manner and appearance raised a whole series of questions and at the same time seemed to suggest that any question would receive an unsatisfactory response.

'That's enough, Billy,' Macarthur said sharply. 'This is Mr Cameron.'

Billy continued to look at me appraisingly and then extended a hand. His grip was claw-like.

'You'd better follow me, then,' he said.

He led us into a large cold room arranged to facilitate the examination of corpses. There were three steel tables. None, I was relieved to note, had a cadaver on it. Taking up the entire surface of the far wall was an iron cabinet in three tiers, each of which had five doors. I wondered how many of the dead might be in residence.

Billy waited for us to join him just inside the door. He scratched the back of his ear and then looked at me, still appraising.

'I have everything that you need here, Mr Cameron.'

He walked across the room and round the first of the tables and opened a door next to the iron coffins. 'We photograph the dead, Mr Cameron, before we dissect them.'

The walls of the small developing room were black. I saw two trays on a trestle table and smelt the familiar acrid scent of sodium sulphide.

'You'll make sure that everything in here is ready for Mr Cameron to use,' Macarthur instructed Billy. 'He's to come and go as he pleases.'

'Just you let me know when to expect you, Mr Cameron,' Billy said, still looking at me with disconcerting interest. 'Everything will be ready.'

He led us back through the dissecting room and along a tiled corridor to a door at the back of the building.

The temperature was at least ten degrees lower than outside. 'It has to be like this,' Billy said, seeing me shiver, 'for the bodies.'

We crossed the courtyard behind the mortuary and stepped into a long narrow crowded lane. On the cobbles on either side were upturned boxes and rickety tables covered with food, clothes and trinkets. There was a powerful smell of sweat and decay, a contrast to the antiseptic odour of the mortuary.

'Billy's not to know what you are doing,' Macarthur told me, speaking above the guttural jagged accents that surrounded us. 'He's been told that you are here to photograph police stations.'

We made our way slowly through the crush of bodies. I looked from one face to another, physically different but all with the preoccupied expression of people for whom the greatest daily challenge is to fend off want.

When we emerged onto the main road I could see the river to our right and a bridge parallel to the one we had crossed twenty minutes earlier.

Across the bridge, past a forest of masts and funnels on either side, we came to a street made of ancient tenements. Where there was glass in the windows it was thick with grime, so thick that in some cases the windows were almost indistinguishable from the black stone around them. Where there was no glass there was paper, or rags, or nothing at all. The closes were so dank and dirty that the odour of stale food and human waste emanated onto the road in a permanent miasma.

Above one entrance was a sign advertising the sale of spirits. A man wearing only trousers and nothing else – no jacket or shirt or shoes – lay on the pavement looking up at us in a stupor.

There were no tramlines here. I saw two women pushing prams piled high with what I took to be laundry, though when we got closer I saw that one of the prams was loaded with a kind of linoleum. The women were young but they looked old. They wore woollen shawls despite the season; their hair was braided into long pigtails. They scrutinised us with expressions that combined aggression with shrewdness.

We walked two blocks in silence before Macarthur said, 'When we get there, let me do the talking.'

After another block we turned into a smaller road and began to head past tenements towards the west again.

We came to a church, with a school building attached to it. There was a small courtyard between the church and the school and I could hear the sound of children in the playground at the other end of the courtyard. They were being led in some sort of game by a tall thin schoolmaster. The church filled its allotted space in the city's grid with neo-Gothic extravagance, all stained glass and statues. The central arch reached as high as the tops of the tenements.

'They have no money to put shoes on their feet; everything goes to the priests,' Macarthur remarked sourly.

I glanced at the sergeant.

'They?'

'The Fenians.'

The church, then, was a Catholic one. Remarkably, there were at least three more churches within two blocks. I supposed they belonged to competing denominations.

'You said one of the victims was Scottish?' I remembered the odd look that the professor and the sergeant had given me when we discussed the background of the victims.

'A Highlander.'

'Doesn't that mean the motive cannot simply be hatred of Fenians?'

He gave me the same odd look.

'I don't understand,' I said.

'They don't have to be Irish to be Papist! Some of the Highlanders didn't turn.'

'Didn't turn?'

He snorted. 'In the time of the Reformers – they didn't turn to the Protestant faith.'

I remembered the way Paco had declared himself Cuban. He had flared up like a fighting cock. Macarthur was the opposite. There was a coolness about his assertion, a logic in his categorising of Highlanders and Fenians. I did not believe he bore ill will towards these people. He simply bracketed them so that he knew where he stood.

He pointed to a building across the next intersection and said, 'That's the place. It's just been refurbished. I believe you'll find it better on the inside than it looks from here.'

The old stone facade had once been painted white, but the white had turned a brownish grey. Across this indeterminate muddy colour was painted in black letters between the windows on the second storey and the windows on the third, *Simpson's Hotel. Lodging and Ale.*

When we reached the corner, I looked to the north and saw that we were a block behind the point where we had arrived earlier for our initial tour of inspection. The location was perfect. Running down the middle of the facade from the third floor to the pavement was a series of bay windows.

Inside the hotel there was a small lobby with a reception desk next to a broad wooden stairway with an iron banister. On either side of the stairway and on either side of the reception there were large china pots with aspidistra. I smelt plaster and paint.

The man standing behind the desk had black hair that came over his ears but stopped in a horseshoe line around the top of his skull, like a tonsure. The skin on his head and face was very pale and his cheeks and chin delineated the shape of a pair of coal tongs.

'Are you William Gibson?' Macarthur asked.

The man looked doubtful.

'You the police?'

Macarthur allowed his hands to float out from his body, palms up, as though to indicate the absurdity of this man presuming to enter into some sort of conversational joust.

The man shrugged. 'I'm Gibson.'

'This is Mr Cameron.'

Gibson turned the register round on the scarred surface of the desk. *Cameron* had been written, with a defective nib, on the top line of a new page.

'Sign here,' he said. Then, looking first at me and then at Macarthur, he added, 'You know we're not officially open? You'll not have proper service till next week. We're doing this as a favour' – he glanced at Macarthur, and then looked at me again – 'for the police. You'll be our only guest for a wee while.'

He stepped round to the outside of the desk. 'I'll show you to your room, Mr Cameron.'

When he walked out into the lobby, Gibson's appearance seemed somehow to grow larger. He had the broad shoulders of a prize fighter and he walked towards the stairs with the deliberate gait of someone with a capacity to impose himself physically on his surroundings.

On the first floor he advanced along a corridor that was uncarpeted and echoed to the sound of his shoes. Macarthur stopped outside a room at the top of the stairs but Gibson continued, and stopped several doors further on. The sergeant touched my arm indicating that I should wait with him.

'It's *this* room,' Macarthur said. 'Number 8. It was requested in particular.'

'It's not ready,' Gibson said. There was a trace of defiance in his tone and it betrayed him. He was not telling the truth. He began to unlock the door further along the corridor.

'This is the room we're going to have,' Macarthur said.

'You have to pay extra for that room.'

'Come here.' Macarthur flashed a smile and spoke in a voice that was emollient and amused, as though agreement between them was possible.

Gibson hesitated and then walked slowly back to where Macarthur and I were standing. When he reached the outside of room number 8 he stopped and after a few seconds of indecision he began to open his mouth to speak. He glanced unhappily down at the bare boards as he chose the words with which to begin bargaining.

But no words came.

One moment Macarthur was standing perfectly still, his hands by his side, and the next Gibson was pinned against the door with Macarthur's wrist serving as a kind of vice against the other man's throat.

Macarthur's expression didn't change, but Gibson's did. He looked surprised.

Surprise was quickly replaced by panic. Gibson tried to scream but the sound that emanated from his constricted windpipe was more of a gurgle than a scream. His eyes began to pop out of his head; his pale face turned red.

'You are going to give Mr Cameron room number 8,' Macarthur whispered.

He reduced the pressure on Gibson's windpipe enough for the head to nod in acquiescence. Macarthur seemed to consider for a few seconds the possibility of inflicting more pain, but he released his grip.

Gibson maintained sufficient courage to glare angrily, first at Macarthur and then at me. He muttered something as he fumbled for the key. When he found it and put it in the lock his hand trembled.

The door opened. Macarthur took the key. Gibson stepped aside and let the sergeant enter. I could think of nothing to do or say that would mend things. I followed Macarthur. Gibson hurried back down the stairs.

We walked to the bay window.

'We have had five murders,' Macarthur told me calmly by way of explaining the fracas I had just witnessed. 'If your camera can help us end that I'll do whatever needs to be done.'

He might have been apologising for the scene with Gibson. Or he might have been serving notice of the kind of behaviour I should expect from him.

I stepped forward to observe the view. There was more than

enough space in the bay for the camera. The road stretched north for seven blocks. I could see the entrance to the close where Maggie McAllister was dismembered and then the entrances, diminishing in perspective but not in clarity, all the way to the cross where my camera in the bank would continue the record.

'It's ideal,' I said.

When we returned to the lobby, Gibson was back behind his desk. I watched from the bottom of the stairs as the sergeant spoke to him.

'The room has to be paid for in advance, one week,' Gibson whispered. I could not tell whether he spoke sotto voce because he was ashamed and angry or because he was physically unable to speak in a normal voice as a result of Macarthur's assault.

The sergeant removed a handful of notes from the inside pocket of his jacket. 'This is for the room,' he said. Then he extracted an additional note. 'And this is for you.'

Gibson accepted the money meekly, looking down at the counter.

CHAPTER TWELVE

Macarthur called at the hotel shortly before six and we walked together to the river, where a long line of cabs waited in front of an elegant Georgian terrace. We climbed the steps near the middle of the terrace: a commissionaire saluted and held open a frosted glass door.

Inside, there was a low hum of male voices, and a smell of cigar smoke and cologne. I followed Macarthur up a broad staircase to the first floor where we entered a grand dining room with floor-to-ceiling windows overlooking the river. The room was already full, and here the buzz of male voices that served as an undercurrent in the lobby below became a bona fide cacophony. The sound was boisterous and confident and tinged with alcohol.

Professor MacKay waved to us from a table in the corner. He was with a man of about fifty, stout but not fat, with a drooping moustache and pale skin, ruddy cheeks and sad brown eyes. The man reminded me of those planters in the Sierra Maestra who lost everything in the war of independence. He had the same newly forlorn air about him.

'Juan,' the professor said in his booming voice, 'allow me to introduce my friend William Harrison.'

Harrison extended his hand, looking at me with curiosity. Unlike Billy Fraser, whose frank scrutiny had been predatory, Harrison's examination of my face and clothes was subtle and reticent.

I sat down and immediately a waiter filled my glass from a carafe of wine.

'I had intended to order a Rioja,' the professor continued, still speaking to me, 'and then I thought: why would the fellow come all the way to Scotland for a vintage he can drink at home!'

Macarthur's glass was filled after mine.

'A good Chianti,' the professor said. 'It will bring Juan into the circle of companionship!' He beamed and raised his glass. 'Here's to a successful endeavour!'

The wine was very good indeed.

'Is the hotel satisfactory?' MacKay asked.

'It's ideal for the purpose,' I said, 'like the bank.'

'Capital!'

MacKay was renowned in medical circles for his work on analysing body tissue. When I met him that morning he had conveyed a natural authority. Now, however, his manner was unsteady, his bonhomie excessive.

Harrison, by contrast, was subdued, albeit convivially. There was about him a gentle intelligence that infused the few words he spoke. He and his sister ran a chemist shop on the square where Mr Presser's bank was located, but they were preparing to retire to South Africa.

'I have a friend in the Western Cape. Now that the insurrection appears to have run out of steam, we are thinking of buying a vineyard there.'

I recognised the same wistful optimism that was my father's characteristic approach to great changes in life.

'He's going into the wine trade,' the professor joked. 'I think that deserves just about universal approbation!'

Macarthur laughed politely. He was the junior of the three men, in age and social status.

We were served mussels, barley soup and lamb. The first carafe was followed by a second and then a third.

'How long did you spend in Cuba, Mr Cameron?' Harrison asked.

'We were there for two years,' I told him. Then to MacKay: 'The McClellans were very kind when we met them.'

'You remember Robert McClellan?' the professor asked Harrison. 'Brightest student I ever had and he upped and off and went to Cuba!'

'Alan Fletcher's brother-in-law?'

'That's the one.' Turning to me: 'How are they faring there in the tropics? Are they winning souls?'

It wasn't clear to me whether the question was ironic or not.

'My father and I were with them only very briefly,' I said. 'I believe they are very highly thought of in the district. I know that they provide an invaluable service to many, including the poorest people there.'

'Robert McClellan was destined to be a surgeon – and not just a sawbones,' MacKay said dismissively. 'He could have made enormous advances, but what's he doing instead? Running a country practice!'

'They seemed to me to be very content, very purposeful,' I said.

'You developed your timing device in Cuba?' Harrison asked.

I glanced at the professor and then at Macarthur. The professor chuckled. 'Mr Harrison has our confidence, Juan.'

'I should like to understand the technique,' Harrison said. 'Did you set out to invent such a device or did it happen by chance?'

The detailed and laborious process of developing serial photography was my refuge from brooding on what happened in Santiago, but of course I did not say this. I told them the idea had originated in Glasgow; they were pleased by this. I recounted the first experiment – the one that had upset Morton's neighbour – and then the surprising results of the images in Rutherglen.

'It was Jack here who heard the true story about the Threadmyre case,' the professor told Harrison. 'The sergeant who worked on the case felt that Juan would be able to help us.'

Macarthur had not until then taken much part in the conversation. He was out of place in this prosperous dining room filled with prosperous and – I guessed – powerful men. 'Sergeant Garvey and I have been friends since school,' he explained for Harrison's benefit.

I glossed over Garvey's initial recalcitrance. I had no doubt that he had been leant upon by his superiors. I explained that when the police had arrived to question Thaddeus Threadmyre – because his cart had appeared in the photographs – he had tried to cover up for Arabella and in doing so had trapped himself in a web of inconsistencies. A confession followed.

'But hadn't there been witnesses?' Harrison asked.

'Yes,' I said, 'and this, I believe, is the key to serial photography. People had *seen* the laundry cart – it had been driving up and down the street all morning and it had stood outside the ballroom – but they had not *recorded* it. We remember only a fraction of what we see, and only that fraction that attracts our particular interest at the time. The virtue of the camera is that it records *everything*, interesting or not, and this can be studied afterwards.'

When dinner was over we moved to an adjoining room where armchairs were arranged around tables next to a long and well-stocked bar. I wondered which was our host: MacKay or Harrison.

MacKay's comments became more acid as he drank. He spoke with vehemence about a subject on which he was an authority.

'The epidemic was a scandal!' he said.

Harrison had mentioned the outbreak of plague in the city.

'It was Professor MacKay who identified one of the sources of infection,' Macarthur told me, his steady policeman's voice acting as a counterweight to MacKay's volatile indignation. I had thought of MacKay as the patron and Macarthur as the client, but the sergeant was now coming to the professor's aid.

'What was the source?' I asked.

'The first case was not far from here,' Macarthur said. 'An old woman and her granddaughter. They died within two days of each other. That meant two wakes in quick succession.'

'Wakes?'

'Friends and relatives keep watch.'

'They don't simply keep watch,' MacKay interjected. 'They send the spirit off into the great beyond with all the fun of the fair!'

'The Irish have music on these occasions,' Harrison explained, 'and plenty of alcohol.'

'People eat and drink and congregate,' MacKay continued. 'The next people to fall victim were mourners who'd been at the first wakes. Then, when they succumbed, there were more wakes: that's how the pestilence was spreading.'

MacKay shrugged sullenly and emptied his glass. 'Those people live in the very depths of hell waiting for their next affliction.'

'The symptoms of plague are similar to those of cholera?' I asked.

'Not in the least,' the professor said, and with drunken relish he described the grotesque and hideously painful torment experienced by plague victims before they are released by death.

When we emerged onto the waterfront, the long summer twilight had not quite ended. The noise of the city and the river had subsided so that the cool air was strangely still. A boy from the club was sent to fetch the professor's brougham. We crossed the road and stood on the pavement overlooking the embankment. Music could be heard from several of the clubs and men and women walked back and forth on both sides of the road. At first I thought nothing of this and then I realised that the encounters that were taking place were of a specific kind. I felt my elbow being lightly tapped and I turned to see two pretty girls smiling at me.

'D'ye have the time, sir?' one of them asked.

'Away with ye!' the professor said, raising his voice and speaking in a suddenly vicious tone. He raised his stick and Macarthur intervened quickly, placing himself between the professor and the girls and speaking to the girls in an aside that was confidential and instantly effective.

The pair withdrew, leaving a miasma of cheap scent.

MacKay opened his mouth and I thought he was going to call something after them, but Macarthur again intervened.

'Here's your carriage, Professor!' he said, and, taking MacKay by the arm, he stepped out onto the road and they walked towards the approaching brougham.

'Let me walk you back to your hotel, Mr Cameron,' Harrison said. 'It's late and you're not on your home turf.'

I realised that I was rather drunk. I nodded and allowed Harrison to guide me along the embankment towards the bridge that led by way of the square onto Crown Street.

'But this will take you well out of your way,' I said.

He laughed. 'It's not very late and I know my road. Let me accompany you, Mr Cameron, you are our guest.'

We had not gone more than a hundred yards before we were accosted again by the same two girls. 'The fine weather brings them out like flowers in bloom,' Harrison whispered as they approached.

'Take us for a drink,' the taller one said.

'Off you go now!' Harrison growled.

As they passed us, the tall one said, suddenly spiteful, 'You can tell Jamie MacKay he needn't be so high and mighty! He's worse than the rest of you.'

Harrison quickened his pace and as we crossed the road he remarked distractedly, 'We have in this city, Mr Cameron, some of the greatest engineering works on the face of the earth, but the human heart cannot be tamed.'

'I'm not sure I understand.'

He glanced at me. 'You were in Cuba when the Americans came.'

I nodded.

'I have associates who were part of that struggle.'

He looked at me again. The walk through the quiet, cool, shadowy streets was beginning to clear my head.

'They became involved because they wished to see progress,' he continued. 'They wished to lift the people of Cuba out of penury.'

This language echoed in my befuddled brain.

'And such work is needed, not just in places like Cuba that have seized their independence. It is needed here too. We have learned how to gird the world with shipping lanes; we have connected continents with the telegraph line, but we haven't learned how to liberate the human soul.'

'To liberate the human soul?'

'From all that afflicts us. If I were a religious man I would call it sin, but as I am not religious I will settle for words like passion and lust and avarice.'

At dinner I had wondered which was our host – MacKay or Harrison. I concluded now that it was Harrison. Throughout the evening, MacKay had been expansive while Harrison had been affable but quiet, but he had not shown much deference towards the professor.

I remembered the way Robert McClellan had spoken of Cuban independence. The same language of improvement and progress.

When we reached the entrance to Simpson's Hotel, Harrison shook my hand and said, 'I'm feeling sober again! Thank you for your company this evening, Mr Cameron. I think you know that if you need any assistance – anything at all – I am at your service. You know where to find me.'

CHAPTER THIRTEEN

When I entered the hotel, I found Gibson on the sofa in the lobby smoking a cigarette. He was without his jacket and his checked waistcoat was unbuttoned.

I saw out of the corner of my eye a figure moving near the door. A young woman had been sitting on a high stool in the corner. She was about average height, dressed in the drab grey of a kitchen hand. Her hair had been let down so that she looked unkempt and at the same time pretty.

Gibson stood up and came towards me.

'Can I get you anything, Mr Cameron?' He held out the heavy room key.

I said there was nothing I needed and made my way up the stairs, trying hard to climb in a steady and inconspicuous manner. The fact that I had to concentrate on this simply pointed up its impossibility. I staggered and steadied myself on the banister and then, to pretend that I was perfectly sober, I climbed the stairs two at a time, achieving in this way a stimulating sense that I was flying.

I did not trip on the stairs or on the carpet in the corridor. But outside my door I realised that the key was not in my hand. I felt in my jacket pockets and my trouser pockets but could not locate it.

'Shall I open for you, Mr Cameron?' a voice beside me said.

Gibson had the key. I gazed at it in his hand.

'You dropped it, sir.'

He unlocked the door. I stepped inside and turned to take the key.

'Goodnight then, sir,' he said.

I locked the door and threw off my clothes and fell into bed and slept.

Later, I woke with a tremendous thirst. I lit a candle and drank from the covered pitcher on the dressing table. Then I unlocked the door and went out. The flame flickered in the darkness as I padded to the lavatory at the end of the corridor. Returning to my room I thought I heard a noise on the floor above, a footfall that matched my own as I moved along the corridor. But in an empty building every sound echoes: I concluded that I'd heard no more than the echo of my own steps. I glanced down from the top of the stairs and saw a faint light in the lobby, the refracted glow of a lamp in the street.

In the morning I was wakened by the sound of hammering at the door.

'Mr Cameron,' Gibson said, inflecting his voice on the first syllable of both words, 'it's after eight o'clock! Sergeant Macarthur's here to collect you!'

'We promised Mr Presser we'd arrive at the same time every morning,' Macarthur said when I climbed into the cab. 'We promised we wouldn't get in his way or give his staff any reason to be curious.'

'We'll only be a little late,' I said.

'Señor Camarón,' he replied, making a show of the Spanish pronunciation, 'in these parts we place great store by punctuality, and, no' – he took his watch out of his waistcoat and flicked it open – 'we will *not* be a *little* late. We'll be a full fifteen minutes late!'

We travelled a block in silence and then he said in a more emollient tone, 'I had wanted to take this opportunity to discuss a different matter.'

'What was that?'

'You must be on your guard when you are using the developing facilities.'

'On my guard?'

The cab stopped outside the bank.

'Just a minute!' Macarthur shouted through the open window to the cabbie.

'We arranged to have you make your photographs in Billy Fraser's developing room because there isn't anywhere nearby that is quite so convenient, and the premises are owned by the corporation – so there's no additional cost.'

He hesitated for a moment.

'Will ye be long?' the cabbie shouted down.

Macarthur seemed glad of the interruption.

'We'll be as long as we have to be!' he shouted up, in a tone that discouraged further discussion.

He seemed to be seeking exactly the right words. 'Fraser works for the corporation and he works for us sometimes. But the fact is that he's been in trouble with the police in the past.'

'I see.'

He shook his head, 'No, that alone wouldn't merit concern on your part or mine. But after we'd arranged for you to have the use of the mortuary, Billy became a figure of interest in the present case.'

'A figure of interest?'

'He was seen in Crown Street, heading south and apparently in great haste, the morning Edie Hamilton was attacked. He was nearby just moments after the girl was accosted.'

'But if you think he's mixed up in this business why on earth don't we move our operation somewhere else, whatever the inconvenience!'

He raised his hand. 'If we moved you somewhere else, Billy would become suspicious.'

'But he'll quickly gather what I'm here to do!'

'Not if you stay on your guard.'

'He'll see my photographs!'

'Not if you don't show them to him. That is what I wanted to emphasise.'

He opened the door and began to climb out. 'We've already kept Mr Presser long enough.'

The bank manager watched intently as I carefully removed the plates. A pot of tea was brought. I drank and felt less hungover.

'You can't take photographs at night, am I right?' Mr Presser asked.

'You are right.'

'The plates are glass?'

'With an emulsified surface.'

I lifted one out of the straw-packed box and handed it to him. He held it gingerly, as if it might surreptitiously record his image.

'People think cameras are heavy,' I said, 'but the camera is no more than the weight of a carriage clock. It's the plates that give it extra weight.'

He returned the plate and I placed it directly behind the lens, which I had mounted on the main frame. I stepped back and crouched and aligned the camera with the square outside.

'You can't have the window open,' Mr Presser said very firmly. He had obviously been thinking about this, and he laid down the prohibition anticipating that it might put a spanner in the works.

I nodded and said, 'I understand.'

'Is that a problem?' Macarthur asked.

'I took the liberty of examining the window when we were here yesterday and the quality of the glass is good enough. So, what I propose to do is to use the window glass as the final lens. I've done something similar in the past and achieved satisfactory results.'

I pressed the viewfinder up against the pane and invited each of them to look through the aperture. They did.

'By Jove!' Macarthur said. 'I see what you mean! That's remarkable!'

It was.

From Mr Presser's office, my camera was able to record two hundred square yards of a bustling intersection. Every detail was clear. I looked through the viewfinder again. There were half a dozen men, five of them in bowler hats and one in a flat cap, standing under the streetlights at the centre of the cross. There were as many boys, all with caps. Two of the boys were smoking. A policeman stood with his hands behind his back watching the traffic. Three omnibuses and two trams moved slowly north towards the river, and two trams moved past them in the opposite direction on the other side of the island where the men and boys were gathered. The omnibuses and trams were surrounded by carts and broughams and cabs: pedestrians scurried among the vehicles. On the north-east side of the square, pedestrians walked past a stationer's shop, a lawyer's office, a public bar, and Harrison's pharmacy. On the north-west side there were considerably fewer people on the pavement; a woman with a gaggle of children around her moved past another bar and a shoe shop and a dry-salter. A group of workmen and two women pushing prams walked in the opposite direction.

I had installed, as the primary lens, a new German glass that considerably enlarged the foreground of the picture, so that I was even able to capture the top of the commissionaire's military cap standing immediately below the window at the bottom of the bank steps. On either side of the commissionaire there were women and boys walking to and fro and a handful of men in bowler hats. Altogether there were perhaps fifty people in the frame, every detail clear, from the gloves on the hands of a matron with a small child to the polished boots of the policeman in the middle of the cross.

I set the timer to activate at forty-five-minute intervals and stood back.

'When will you begin?' Mr Presser asked.

I waited a few seconds till I heard the first click and the whirr of the shutter.

'There,' I said. Mr Presser looked at me with an expression that sought greater elaboration. 'It has already begun.'

'There's been a visitor for you,' Gibson told me when I returned to the hotel. 'A lady . . . said you might be expecting her . . . a *well-spoken* lady,' he continued. 'She left this.'

He held out a small, cream-coloured envelope.

Dear Mr Camarón, I read when I was back in my room, *My aunt, Euphemia McClellan, has written to tell me that you are visiting Glasgow. I understand that you met my aunt and uncle in Cuba during the recent conflict. Professor MacKay, who is an acquaintance of my uncle, kindly let me know where you are staying. I took the liberty of calling on you today. If I can offer you any assistance during your stay I will be very happy to do so.*

Marjorie Jane Macgregor concluded her note by giving the name and address of a shop in the city centre.

I spent the next twenty minutes preparing the camera in the alcove and after I had released the catch and started the timer I went downstairs to have breakfast.

Soon after ten o'clock I left the hotel and struck out towards the south. The further I walked the newer the tenements were. The buildings were better proportioned; three storeys instead of four and the facades were ornamented. The tiled closes, as far as I could tell, were odourless. Children in the streets wore shoes and they had footballs and steel hoops to play with. Two little girls walking with a matronly gait pushed prams that were almost as high as themselves.

I passed shops and department stores and public houses. Throngs of people milled in the sunlight. After about a mile, at the end of the main thoroughfare I came to a monumental gateway. I walked between the giant gateposts and began to ascend a leafy avenue into a park.

Beneath the pervasive smell of coal dust was an aroma of blossoms. I followed a route that described a giant arc and led to a boating pond. I stopped to watch two small boys launch a wooden yacht into the pond. It moved sluggishly at first and then the wind caught its little sails and it began to skim across the surface. The boys gawked and the smaller one ran round the pond to meet the vessel when it docked on the far shore.

I took a seat. I could hear the boys shouting to one another excitedly in their singsong accent. They were dressed in grey shorts and white shirts; the youngest had a crown of black curls that seemed to rise up from his head like some kind of exotic pot plant.

The women who walked through the park wore lilac and lemon and the palest pink; a small number were all in white. The air was so engrained with particles of coal that to wear white denoted, I thought, either a generous laundry regime or a whimsical refusal to accept the practical constraints of life in a factory city.

Poorer women wore darker colours. Two large matrons passed me where I sat by the pond, resplendent in tent-like dresses that were a shade of chestnut. There were, too, women in mourning black.

It was peaceful. The benches and well-tended lawns and the ornate bandstand in the distance testified to prosperity and decorum.

When I left the pond, the two boys were still running from one side to the other, racing their little yacht. I climbed to the top of the hill at the centre of the park where there was a flagpole. The city was spread out beneath me like a survey map. To the east the countryside reached into the tenements and factories, making a meandering border of greensward and woodland where the industrial black came to a sudden end and the natural world began. All across the north and north-east there were factory chimneys and rows and rows of elevated roofs. In the west I could see the tower of the university planted in a carpet of treetops. Closer to hand and stretching to the west were the tips of cranes along the river, the steel mesh of lifting equipment leavened by wooden masts and a hundred painted funnels. Between the flagpole and the city, spread out like a dark stain south of the river, was the district around Crown Street, where a maniac was at large.

I walked back down the hill towards the sound of carts and cabs and omnibuses clattering over cobbles. Just outside the gates, trams were stopping and I wondered which one would take me back the way I had come.

'Are you going into town, Mr Camarón?' a voice beside me asked.

I turned to see a tall and well-dressed woman of about forty. She looked at me with an intelligent expression, her eyes twinkling since I was clearly confused – about selecting a tram and about how she knew me by name.

'I'm Jeanie Harrison,' she said, extending a gloved hand. 'You dined with my brother yesterday evening and he described you down to a T. I'm afraid you are rather conspicuous among us drab Glaswegians, Mr Cameron!'

It was as though they had a convention by which they used the foreign pronunciation in the first instance and then proceeded to the more comfortable local version of my name.

'How do you do,' I said, still rather mystified at being recognised and greeted by chance in such an unfamiliar place.

Jeanie pointed to the second tram. 'This one goes past your hotel, if that is where you were heading,' she said helpfully.

We moved together to the tram in the indeterminate way that people do when it is not yet clear whether they are moving as one or as two separate and independent entities. I let Jeanie climb aboard first and followed her into the downstairs cabin. It was almost full, but there were two seats free near the front. She walked quickly and took the window seat and then resolved my dilemma by turning and saying, 'Mr Cameron, please come and sit down before this seat is taken.'

I did as she proposed.

'I'm going back to the shop,' she explained, 'so we are going the same way, I think.'

She asked me my impressions of Glasgow. Her accent was clear and easy to understand, and she spoke in a relaxed and friendly way. She had been visiting the allotment she maintained near the Queen's Park. 'We have our medicaments from the industrial chemists nowadays,' she said, 'but a number of herbs are still thoroughly efficacious.'

I was happy to share with her some of my thoughts about the city and its people.

'You are right to see the great contrasts,' she said as we moved past the intricately decorated sandstone terraces leading away from the park. 'There is tremendous prosperity but there is terrible deprivation too, and I think one day we will have to reckon with the evils that surround us.'

'Is it just William and you in the shop?' I asked.

Her face clouded briefly and she said, 'Just the two of us, yes.' After a moment, she added, 'We have worked together since our father died. My husband had his own business before he passed on.'

'I'm sorry,' I said.

She looked out of the window as we crossed a large junction which separated poor streets from prosperous ones.

'But William tells me you were in Cuba,' she said after a pause. 'Tell me now, is it really the case that poverty is less visible in a warm climate?'

'It is!' I was so taken by Jeanie Harrison's intelligence and confidence that I became rather garrulous. 'When we were in the Caribbean,' I said, 'we saw less poverty – though we knew perfectly well that it was all around us. You see, there's not much difference between a rich man's sandals and a poor man's sandals.'

'But a rich man's winter coat and a poor man's – there is no mistaking the difference *there*!' she said slowly. It was as though she had deliberately and systematically discerned my own way of thinking.

As I had no reason to go back to the hotel immediately I decided to stay on the tram till it reached the city centre. I stood up to let Jeanie leave her seat as we approached the square between Crown Street and the river. We were jostled by the crush, but Jeanie's height and athletic build appeared to give her a kind of matronly dominance and she began to forge a path for herself through the sea of bodies.

'It's been a pleasure meeting you, Mr Cameron,' she said over her shoulder. 'Please come and see us at the shop if there is anything we can do to be of assistance.'

I left the tram two stops later, after it had crossed the river.

CHAPTER FOURTEEN

The scent of coal mixed with the scent of manure. Where people spoke to one another they were obliged to shout above the noise of cartwheels and screeching klaxons, the roar of horses' hooves and the shrill insistent sound of policemen's whistles; above everything, like the filigree decoration on a railway station roof, was the raucous cawing of a million pigeons. The human voice inhabited this space like a fugitive seeking shelter in the eddies and whirls of an ocean of sound.

I had not consciously intended to call on Marjorie Jane Macgregor, but when I reached the top of a hill that gently climbed past the main station I found myself on the street she had identified in her note.

The window of Fletcher & Co was filled with portraits. The interior was large, about the size of three rooms. The walls were covered with framed photographs.

At the far corner was a table piled high with invoices and payment stubs and ledgers, pens and ink and envelopes. Behind the table sat a girl who looked about the same age as me. A bell above me tinkled as the door closed. The girl looked up.

She watched me with a measured expression. If I had stopped to examine the photographs, I guessed that she would have allowed me to do this undisturbed. At the same time, she indicated with a half-smile that if I were to make an enquiry I would not be rebuffed.

I advanced through the gallery and when I reached the desk I said, 'Good afternoon; I am looking for Miss Macgregor.'

She smiled and stood up and walked round the desk extending her hand.

'You must be Señor Camarón.'

'Miss Macgregor? Thank you for your note!' I said, a little breathlessly. 'It was very kind of you to call on me.'

She was strikingly pretty.

'You work in a photographic gallery,' I remarked, making a statement that in its utter redundancy struck me as being monumentally foolish.

'I do,' she replied, glancing around as if to check that there were indeed photographs on the walls.

'I'm a photographer,' I said.

'I know,' she replied.

Clearly the conversation was taking a stilted turn and just as clearly this was entirely due to my want of social finesse.

'I happened to be in this part of town,' I blundered on. 'Perhaps this is not a convenient time . . .'

For what? I wondered desperately.

'. . . to call . . .' I added by way of finishing the sentence, and then, deciding that it wasn't properly finished, I attached the words 'on you' to the end.

She smiled.

'This is the *ideal* time! It's midday.'

She asked me to wait and disappeared through a narrow door behind the desk. An older woman appeared and looked at me in the appraising way that older women have, not discourteous but nonetheless thorough.

'Good afternoon,' she said.

'I'll be with you in a moment, Mr Cameron,' Miss Macgregor called, pronouncing my name in the Scottish way and popping her head round the door. Her head disappeared again.

I retreated from the desk, behind which the woman had taken a seat, and loitered in front of the photographs.

The solid burghers in the framed portraits stared back at me with the bafflement of people who are prosperous enough to have their photograph taken but are not entirely sure how they wish to look. I could have studied these portraits for a long time. They were well made, and in several, I could see, the photographer had got beyond the financial means and the bafflement to find an element of the sitter's personality.

I felt the woman's eyes boring into the back of my head and this prompted me to keep on the move. When I had got to the end of the wall by the door, I crossed over and began to work my way along the other side.

The pictures here were different. They documented not the material well-being and moral righteousness of the city's elite, but the squalor and misery of men and women who stared into the camera from backcourts and alleyways and rubbish-strewn gutters. The subjects were not 'types' but real people, not 'the poor' but human beings who were poor, who lived and breathed.

There were portraits of buildings too. And they belonged to my father's school. The pictures of facades and interiors of closes were done in such a way that the builder's intent could be seen, even when the reality was a distortion of the intent. Thus, a slum tenement was depicted in a way that highlighted the faux turrets and castellated roofline; a factory was shown in profile, revealing a whimsical resemblance to a renaissance palace.

Miss Macgregor emerged from the back room. She wore a black skirt and a dark blouse with a black embroidered jacket. Her sensible black boots were designed for walking through muddy streets.

Outside, I said, 'Perhaps I could take you to lunch?'

'I was rather hoping you would!' She glanced at me and smiled. 'Otherwise I'll have to wait till dinnertime before I have anything to eat!'

I let her decide in which direction we were to proceed and she began to lead me back to the city centre.

'My aunt wrote to say that you were coming. She said you are a photographer, but she didn't say what you would be doing in Glasgow. Are you here on business, Mr Cameron?'

'Please call me Juan.'

'Juan.'

'Yes, sort of business. I'm carrying out an experiment.'

My own response surprised me. I was in Glasgow to arrange the publication of my father's book and, when Mr MacKenzie, the lawyer, returned from Cape Town, to view and then sell my property on the Isle of Bute.

'It's just over here,' she said, pointing to the other side of the road and indicating that we should wait for a gap in the traffic. 'What sort of experiment?'

'I've developed a particular type of camera that takes photographs by itself at regular intervals.'

'Come!' she said.

I thought at first that she was expressing surprise or scepticism about what I had just said (some people refuse to believe that it is possible to get a machine to obey the dictates of an alarm clock), but in fact she was indicating that we should take advantage of an opportunity that had opened up to cross the road. She skipped away from the kerb and I skipped after her. I was accustomed to traffic as dense and dangerous as this, yet my wits appeared to have deserted me. Conducting a conversation and crossing the road at the same time had apparently overtaxed my normal faculties.

In the middle of the street and in the very heart of my own sudden confusion I sensed that something profound had just happened. For the smallest fraction of a moment I seemed to step outside my own consciousness. I was entranced by the very step and manner of the woman I was following.

'What kind of photographs?' she asked when we had reached the other side. Her tone made no allowance for the thirty seconds that had elapsed as we dodged between a tramcar and an omnibus on one side and a handful of heavily laden carts on the other.

'Street scenes.'

'Really!'

'Yes,' I said, pleased that I seemed to have made an impression.

'But what is the advantage of taking photographs at regular intervals?'

I didn't have a chance to explain just then because as soon as she had asked the question she said, 'Here's the place! I hope you're hungry!'

We left the pavement through an entrance that was tucked between the offices of a bank on one side and those of a shipping company on the other. Inside, we climbed a flight of wooden stairs. As we ascended, the sounds of a large number of voices began to be heard. A smell of turnips and potatoes and beef pervaded the air.

At the top of the stairs was a large room filled with oblong tables, most of which were taken. Miss Macgregor looked around with the eye of someone familiar to this place and said, 'There's a couple of seats!' She pointed. 'By the window!'

A girl appeared soon after we had sat down. Miss Macgregor asked for Scotch broth and mutton pie and I said I would have the same.

'You were going to tell me,' she said brightly after the girl had gone.

'About what?' I asked, with equal brightness but with a confusion that was beginning to disconcert.

'About the advantage of taking photographs at regular intervals.'

Over Scotch broth and mutton pie I explained the technique. She asked the sort of perceptive questions that I had decided she was bound to ask. Only at one juncture was there a momentarily unnerving descent from the high plane of empathy, and this was when I asked if I could call her Marjorie and she said, 'I wish you wouldn't,' and I said, 'Oh.' And she said, 'People call me Jane, and for reasons I can't quite explain I prefer that.'

I preferred it too, except that having been given permission to address her in this familiar way I found that in the whole course of the rest of the meal the occasion to address her by any name at all did not arise.

'The photographs,' I said. 'The photographs in your shop. They are remarkable. They are real portraits, of the city, of its people.'

I didn't know why I spoke in this peculiar way, as if I could only communicate ideas through a series of little word pictures.

'They are my uncle's work,' Jane said.

I noticed that some strands of her long hair had come loose; they created a little bouquet of wisps on her forehead.

'Some years ago,' she went on, 'the corporation undertook to clear a large part of the poorest districts and build new homes. Cholera was on the rise, and conditions in the worst slums were unspeakable. My uncle was commissioned to document the old buildings before they were demolished. Of course, he would never have considered photographing buildings without also making a record of the people who lived in them.'

We were silent for a moment and then I said, 'In her letter your aunt told me about your bereavement. I'm sorry.'

I remembered the odd language Effie McClellan used. *Her mother and father have recently gone to the Lord.*

She nodded and pursed her lips and then she asked mischievously, 'What else did my aunt say about me?'

'Well, she told me you were . . .' I tried to remember the exact word. What was it? 'A *bright* girl.'

She broke into peals of laughter. 'My aunt is very kind.' She paused, still laughing, and then she said, 'I think she is right! I will accept this as a very great and true compliment! I am content to be thus described. Bright! Tell me, Juan. Do you agree?'

She leant very slightly towards me when she spoke.

'I do!' I said. My face felt flushed.

Later, when we were drinking thick bitter coffee, Jane said, 'My aunt told me about your father and what a gentle man he was. She told me what happened.'

I did not know how to respond.

'My parents died very suddenly and unexpectedly,' she continued. 'There isn't much that can be said to lessen the sadness, but I think it's best to be straightforward. It must have been difficult for you too.'

I wanted to explain, but I didn't really know where to begin.

'I shouldn't have mentioned this,' she said. She looked at me with an expression of such simple regret that before I knew it I had reached across the table and touched her wrist.

'I very much appreciate your thoughtfulness,' I said. Perhaps I should have added something, but for now there was nothing.

Then, in a bolt from the opposite end of the universe, it occurred to me that I was being utterly self-centred.

'And your parents?' I said. 'Was it in the . . .'

My words trailed away. I do not know why, but I had a sudden conviction that it would offend norms of social propriety to suggest that someone's parents had died of plague.

She smiled. Then she looked at me steadily and spoke gently.

'They didn't die of plague, though in a way they too were victims of the epidemic. We always travelled to Rothesay for two or three weeks in the summer. It's just an hour's sail down the river. There are such beautiful walks in the hills. You can see the other islands and the lochs from the house that we used to rent. Last year we stayed an extra week and though it wasn't said, we certainly weren't encouraged to return to Glasgow at the height of the panic caused by the sickness. I thought then that we were like those Florentines in the stories of Boccaccio.'

I very much wished that I knew what she was talking about. And at the same time I wondered why the name of the town – Rothesay – was familiar.

'*The Decameron*,' she prompted. 'The stories told among a group of travellers who stayed outside Florence because of the plague.'

'Ah,' I said.

'It was on the second day of our extra week that my mother and father were killed.'

'What happened?'

'They went out in the buggy early in the morning. I preferred to stay at home and read a book.' Her expression was suddenly troubled, but it passed and she carried on speaking in her gentle way. 'They went off to Ettrick Bay on the west of the island. It was one of their favourite places. I can imagine what they were like on their last morning. They loved each other's company. They used to make each other laugh. I can imagine them laughing as they rode over those beautiful hills and down towards the sea.

'Then something happened that positively defies belief. One of the wheels became fixed in the tramline – there's a tram that connects Rothesay with Ettrick Bay – and when my father tried to jerk the carriage out, the wheel sheared away and my parents were thrown from the buggy. My father died at once. My mother died as they carried her to the doctor.

'The thing I often think about is just how absurd it was that they travelled to such a beautiful place only to be snared by a tramline.'

She sipped her coffee and studied the tablecloth.

'I'm so sorry,' I said.

She looked at me indulgently as I considered how inadequate and foolish words sometimes are.

'The very same week,' she said, 'seven people were killed in a railway accident just a few blocks from here. Such tragedies are a part of our existence, I suppose.' She sipped more coffee. 'There was another case very close to your hotel,' she added. 'A man died last spring. He had been crossing the railway tracks on the main road, but not fast enough. The engine wheels cut off his legs.'

I considered this macabre detail coming from the lips of such a beautiful woman. Then her expression changed completely to one of consternation and she said, 'Oh dear! I am talking about the most horrible things! You must think me a monster!'

'Not at all!' I said, and for the hundredth time in the space of an hour I wondered why I was entirely incapable of making the simplest observation in this girl's company that did not make me appear either fatuous or dim.

When we walked back to the shop she said, 'This afternoon we are expecting a German collector. I am to interpret.'

'You speak German!'

Again this capacity to state the obvious.

'*Ja!*' she replied, glancing at me and starting to laugh. '*Und auch Französisch!*'

She saw my confusion and said, 'I'm sorry, I didn't mean to mock you.'

For the briefest moment her fingers touched the material of my jacket. A spark began at the point of contact and travelled all the way to my heart.

At the entrance to the shop, she invited me to afternoon tea at the Fletchers' on the day after next. I readily accepted.

'I can't think where I've heard the name of this town,' I said as I was leaving. 'The town where you spent the summer to be away from the plague.'

'Rothesay?'

I nodded.

'It's on the Isle of Bute.'

CHAPTER FIFTEEN

I extracted the plates from the apparatus in the hotel after the final photograph had been taken at eight. I had fifteen negatives spread over three plates – three squares on the third plate were unused. I put the plates carefully into the satchel and packed the camera lens in its box and put it in the satchel next to the plates. The tripod and frame I dismantled and placed in a long toolbox that I left on the bed. I closed the door and locked it. Downstairs I heard Gibson and the girl laughing in the kitchen. He hurried out as I crossed the lobby.

'Is there anything I can do for you, Mr Cameron?'

When I first arrived I'd been struck by Gibson's paleness and his rather saturnine manner. Now he seemed changed. I wondered if he'd taken laudanum. He betrayed that odd, leisurely, jarring *happiness*.

I thanked him and said there was nothing I needed done.

Walking along Crown Street I shuddered at the memory of Professor MacKay's description of plague. Spread by vermin, it manifests itself through swelling glands and fever. Two or three days of agony are ended by asphyxiation. It had incubated just a handful of streets away.

When I reached the mortuary, Billy was at his post in the lobby, sucking on his pipe. He greeted me by cocking his right eyebrow. The rest of his body, from the top of his scalp on down, remained perfectly immobile.

Then he seemed to topple from his perch. 'This way, sir. The room is at your disposal. I will show you where everything is.'

In the darkroom he had laid out the developing trays and chemicals.

'If I may be of assistance?' he said.

'I'll work alone, thank you.'

He looked at me appraisingly and shrugged. He withdrew and closed the door behind him.

I removed my jacket and rolled up my sleeves. When I placed the first of the negatives in the tray, I quickly determined that the solution had been treated with sulphate. I thought this might leave a yellow tint, which could diminish clarity, particularly if the scene was illuminated by bright sunlight as had been the case that afternoon, so before I immersed the paper I added a thimbleful of potassium to the first wash and waited till I was certain the surface had been completely and evenly treated.

I took the first of the plates and with a scalpel separated the rectangle covering a portion of the surface from the right. There was a faint line on the back, where the paper-clamp behind the lens had left a mark. I put the oblong into the solution and watched the image of Crown Street at half past nine on the morning of 22nd June 1899 begin to emerge, staining the surface of the paper with tenements and carts and men and women and dogs and gutters and lamp posts. The whole process from insertion to removal took fifty seconds, timed against my pocket watch.

I held the dripping picture, fingers on the periphery. I found that I was very slowly and very gently shaking my head. I felt that I had in my hands what was needed in order to solve a crime as ancient as mankind.

At a quarter past nine Crown Street had been alive with incident. A tram, visibly crowded, trundled in the distance towards the river, while closer to the hotel and on the other side of the road another tram, this one with fewer passengers, had stopped. A woman in a black shirt and jacket and hat was climbing aboard. A boy with a hoop stood outside the grocer's shop two doors from the hotel. He looked to the south, his face puckered up because of the sun. The hoop carried significance; I wondered if this little fellow had strayed into the neighbourhood of the hotel from the better-heeled district to the south. Behind him a man raised a cigarette to – or drew it away from – his lips as he marched towards the river. He was looking to one side, as if checking to see if it was safe to cross the road. A girl of about five in a white petticoat had just run out of the close where the lamplighter Brendan Gillespie was murdered. This little girl, all golden curls and energy, was surely as far removed – mentally if not physically – from the atrocity as it was possible to imagine. About twenty yards from her, three men stood beneath a streetlamp talking: one wore a bowler hat; another held a cap in his left hand. I could see the whiskers on two of the men and the moustache on one; the third had his back slightly at an angle to the camera.

I looked with an all-seeing eye upon the intricacies of creation.

I counted sixty-seven individual figures, fourteen vehicles and seventeen animals.

It took me more than half an hour to develop the remaining fourteen pictures, as I had to change the solution after every second image. When I had begun to work, the cubicle had been chilly; when I finished it was airless and hot. I opened the door and stepped out into the mortuary like a swimmer shooting up from the deep in search of oxygen. I inhaled and then put a hand involuntarily up to my mouth.

I was not alone. Or perhaps I was. I couldn't just at that point determine what the proper terminology might be. The room was occupied by a body other than mine, but it was not a living body.

A corpse lay on the middle table. It was covered, but I could see from the contours of the shroud that it was female.

I hurried to the double door and let myself out into the corridor. There was no one there and no one in the lobby. I walked out to the front of the building.

Stepping into the street, I looked up and down. Carts trundled over the cobbles heading towards the bridge. On the other side of the road a woman dawdled slowly past, pushing a pram and nearer at hand, coming towards me from the direction of the street market, I saw Billy Fraser.

'You're finished!' he said genially. I noticed that he had a slight limp.

'There's a body in the mortuary,' I remarked.

'Yes,' he agreed and didn't add anything, and it occurred to me that a mortuary was one place where the presence of a dead body was not necessarily a matter for comment.

Yet I couldn't countenance the thought that we might discuss a corpse without curiosity so I persisted, 'Not another murder, I hope?'

Billy scratched the back of his head and said after rather a long pause, 'Poisoning, at least that's what it's likely to be. Contaminated spirits. Common enough. We'll know soon enough. Perhaps you would like to finish your own chores before I begin mine.'

He had begun to walk back into the building and I followed.

'Are you on your own here?' I asked.

'I have an assistant but today he's visiting his family – outside the city.'

In the mortuary, Billy advanced to the table and drew back the shroud. I leant forward to see the woman's face.

She was about fifty, I thought. Billy concurred. I don't know whether I would have been more moved had she been young. It struck me as tragic anyway to reach this age bereft of any human solace other than a poisonous concoction designed to induce oblivion. The woman's lips were stretched because the skin on either side of her skull had begun to follow the dictates of gravity and move down towards the steel surface of the table. I could see the tips of uneven yellow teeth. Her pale blue eyes were open.

Billy took off his jacket, rolled up his sleeves and put on a large apron. I recoiled momentarily when I saw that the apron was bloodstained. He clenched his little clay pipe between his teeth.

'Mr Cameron,' he said. 'I'm going to investigate the contents of Maggie's stomach.' I wondered if the woman's name really was Maggie, or whether he was in the habit of giving his subjects nicknames. 'It's not the sort of thing that everyone likes to see, so if you'd care to be on your way I'll look forward to your company again in the morning.'

CHAPTER SIXTEEN

Back in my room, I laid the photographs on the table by the window. Then I took from my trunk the small valise in which I kept a magnifying glass, a book of tables that facilitated the calculation of actual distances within the constricted perspective of a photograph, and the wooden grid I'd had made to replace the greaseproof paper prototype. Beside this I placed a notebook and a pen with a fresh bottle of ink.

It was well after midnight before I finished.

People look at a photograph in the space of a second or two. The brain recognises what is familiar. Take, for example, a boating pond, with a small boy racing along the bank to meet a sailing boat heading across the water. This might be the *subject* of the photograph but the subject would not correspond completely to what is *contained* in the image. The camera doesn't discriminate or select. People admiring the composition – the pond, the boys, the little boat – might not see the faint excrescence of smoke in the background at the right of the picture, indicating a factory or a house behind the trees. They might fail to notice two figures, a man and a woman, obscured almost to the point of invisibility, making their way among the trees away from the pond; they might easily miss the lace piping on the edge of a black parasol that enters the composition in the bottom right foreground.

I examined the images and documented *everything* and then compared each detail to the details in the rest of the series. Annotating the first fifteen photographs filled almost twenty pages of the notebook.

The steady glow of the gas lamps in the street outside was broken into delicate and infinitely varied shards of shadow on the white walls. The shape of the desk on which the photographs lay was visible against the oblong of the window. I lay in bed and wondered what my father would have thought of this work.

I remembered how, when I was small, he showed me the intricate and elegant geometry of the new hotel on the Puerto Real.

Travelling across Cuba we were sometimes like two happy vagabonds, pretending that the ugliness around us wasn't there. I remembered the concentration and cleverness my father brought to photographic composition. His work really did have the stamp of a master. William Collins, Sons & Co agreed. I remembered how he used to enunciate the publisher's name, as though he and they were bound together in the creation of art.

Cuba now had different builders and they were energetically striving to remove the island's Spanish tint.

I rolled over in the bed and looked out of the other window. I had opened it a little to allow air to circulate. I gazed through the aperture at the June night. I remembered holding my father's lifeless body. It was as if I were still there, in front of that clumsy facade, which he had sought to render beautiful with his last photograph.

I thought of Eleanora and Paco. I could see their faces with a clarity that I had hoped would be chipped away with the passage of time. But it had not been chipped away.

My father would have allowed himself to be swindled out of his legacy. He would not have fought them for it. He would have persuaded himself – and he would have tried to persuade me – that the income we would derive from our portfolio once it had been published would be greater than whatever income might come from the estate that Eleanora and Paco were determined to have for themselves.

The estate was worth more than my father imagined – but that was, of course, beside the point.

He died so that others could have something that he did not covet. That seemed to me doubly unjust.

I dreamt of Paco's face. It was surprised, as though he had not expected to die. I dreamt of horses and cordite and dust, Eleanora lying on a bed of straw and piss, her dress up above her knees, which were pale and misshapen.

When I woke, it was because there was a sound like thunder, or perhaps it was more like the explosion of an artillery shell, or the rat-tat-tat of carbines in the street.

But it was none of these things. It was Gibson hammering at my door. I was late again.

* * *

156

'We agreed that you would be here at eight o'clock in the morning, punctually!' Mr Presser said when I was shown in.

I wondered if he neglected to address me by name because I was late or because I was foreign. Then I concluded that it was because I was without my patrons, the professor and the policeman. Mr Presser, I sensed, was a man who was apt to place people in a pecking order and deal with them accordingly.

I apologised for my lack of punctuality and waited for Mr Presser to escort me to the window. He would have preferred if I'd made my own way there.

After a second's hesitation he obliged me and I followed him to where the camera was set up. I extracted the plates from the previous day and inserted three new plates.

'I really am sorry, Mr Presser,' I said, easing the second plate into the groove behind the viewfinder. Changing the plates improved my mood. I had walked from the hotel to the bank still under the weight of dreams, and hurrying because I was late. I had arrived breathless and perspiring. Mr Presser was perfectly right to be annoyed. I had made an agreement and failed to honour it.

I watched him out of the corner of my eye and then I glanced at him, looking up from the camera.

He had had a second or two in which to decide whether or not to accept my apology. He seemed uncertain and then his face softened and he said, 'I hope you will keep to the times that we agreed, Mr Cameron.'

'I will certainly do that.'

I could not shake off the notion that Mr Presser lacked a centre of gravity. I wondered if bank managers see other people through the balance in their accounts.

'That's it,' I said.

He studied the camera, as though he expected it to be somehow different now that the plates had been changed and the timer had been reset. Then he studied me.

'I will be here punctually at eight tomorrow morning.'

'Eight,' he replied. 'Very well. I shall expect you at eight.'

Crossing the river, I looked out at a forest of masts and funnels. It was a warm summer morning, but the air was hard as crystal.

I walked through the empty lobby of the mortuary and into the dissecting room. There were no bodies on the tables. I crossed to the developing room and went inside.

Photographs were drying on the steel wire.

They depicted men and women in various states of coitus. The images on the line might have been arranged in such a way as to convey a story of sorts. A man removing his jacket, the woman on the other side of the bed already naked; then the man naked and so on. In some of the pictures there were men and women, in some there were only women, in others only men.

I heard a voice and I spun round to find Billy Fraser leering at me.

'Any of these to your liking?' he asked, blowing smoke from his clay pipe into the developing room.

I was for a moment speechless.

Billy shrugged. Standing close to him in the tiny room, inhaling pipe smoke, I suddenly grasped that this man was the exact opposite of Archibald Presser. Billy was assessing my reaction to his photographs with all the care and attention of a connoisseur. He was not concerned with my position in any pecking order; he did not care whether I was foreign or

158

home grown; he simply wanted to see how I responded to the pictures on the line.

I came very close to losing my temper. I pointed. My outstretched finger touched the filmy surface of one of the images. I pulled my hand away. 'Please remove these,' I said.

He stepped past me to the corner of the cubicle and began to take the photographs down.

'They're not *my* pictures, Señor Camarón,' he said, stressing his correct pronunciation of my name. 'They belong to the police. They were taken without the knowledge of the participants. One of the men is a judge and another is a member of the city council.'

'I don't understand.'

'The plates were seized from a blackmailer. The pictures are evidence, though I expect you'll understand just why we can all be fairly sure they'll never see the light of day.'

'You didn't *take* these pictures?'

'The man who took them is in gaol.' Billy leant against the developing table and puffed on his pipe. Then he said, 'I understand you were in Cuba.'

I nodded.

'You must have witnessed terrible things.' He waited and I nodded again.

'I have seen photographs,' he continued. 'Pictures of the dead.'

I waited again.

'I have seen photographs of the dead laid out as though for a portrait.' Billy puffed on his pipe as he spoke, so that a cloud enveloped both of us.

'Why do people think nothing of looking at *those* photographs?' He watched me carefully. Then he stepped out into the dissecting room. 'I'll let you get on, then,' he muttered as he left.

His question hovered in the atmosphere like tobacco smoke.

Billy was nowhere to be seen when I finished my work and left the building.

At the intersection before the bridge I waited on the pavement with a small flock of pedestrians watching the traffic policeman. As I stood on the kerb I became aware of a powerful smell. I thought at first that it was coming from the gutter. However, when the policeman blew his whistle and we began to cross the road the smell remained. I looked round and saw a small boy no more than eight or nine years old. He was gazing sideways at the masts on the river. I could see, even from four or five feet away, the lice scuttling in and out of the boy's unevenly cut fair hair. His face was streaked with dirt and his shirt and trousers could hardly be described as such, being a piece of cloth that was once a shirt but was now tied onto his thin body with string, and a piece of black textile, tied likewise around his waist, one leg of which reached above the knee, the other falling loosely about his ankle. His feet were bare.

When the boy turned his attention from the ships' masts he caught me scrutinising him. He gave me a frank look, as if to say that I might examine his appearance if I chose, but he reserved the right to challenge me for doing so. It was the expression of a species of humanity that has nothing to lose.

I was ashamed of my curiosity and at the same time ashamed of my helplessness. I reached into my pocket and found a penny, which I held out in my open palm. He snatched the penny.

He said something – I could not decipher what. He said it again. And again I was baffled. He spoke a third time and this time I recognised, or thought I recognised, that he was offering to carry my satchel or be of some similar assistance.

I scratched the back of my head, partly because I was ill at ease, partly because my gaze returned with fascinated horror to the animal life on the boy's scalp.

'No thank you,' I said.

I quickened my pace, but the boy kept up.

'Where are you going?' he asked.

'That doesn't concern you.'

My tone – like my fund of human compassion – was inadequate. Here was an individual who could not be snubbed.

'Where are *you* going?' I asked.

He shrugged. His bony shoulders shot up and then collapsed inside his ragged shirt.

'What's your name?' I asked.

'Tommy. What's yours?'

'Juan.'

His eyes opened wide and then they contracted a little as he considered the possibility that I was not telling him the truth.

'Honest?'

'Honest.'

He fell into step and marched beside me. The smell was no longer overpowering, either because the wind was benign or because my senses were becoming used to it.

We walked for half a block before Tommy said, 'Do you need baccy?'

I said I didn't.

'Do you have a family?' I asked.

He ignored me and carried on in silence. When I turned and started walking towards the hotel, he turned and continued walking beside me. I thought about passing my destination and making another attempt to shake him off. However, I didn't think I *could* shake him off, and as we continued to walk along the road together I didn't think I *should* shake him off.

I couldn't simply divest myself of my new companion as if he were a bug.

'I'm going in there,' I said when we were opposite the hotel.

'What's it like?' he asked.

I shrugged. 'Just like any other hotel, I suppose.'

He looked at me uncomprehendingly. 'Listen,' I said, 'I have to go to work now.' I fetched another penny from my trouser pocket and held it out.

He snatched the penny with a speed and decision that seemed to me to override any kind of camaraderie that I might have imagined had arisen between us.

'What sort of work?'

'Never you mind,' I said, as curtly as I could manage and with that I marched across the road. I didn't look round. I stepped into the hotel lobby. It wasn't till I had reached the reception desk that I looked around. To my enormous relief – accompanied by some shame – I saw that he had not followed me.

Behind the desk sat the girl who had been with Gibson the previous evening.

She stood up quickly. 'Can I get you anything, sir?'

There was something transparently good-humoured in her expression and in her voice, or perhaps I was just relieved to be in the company of a normal, pleasant human being after Presser and Billy and the ill-smelling Tommy.

The girl had reddish auburn hair, pale skin and freckles. She was not quite pretty but not plain either. Her eyes were blue.

I asked her if there was something to eat.

'Bread and ham?'

I agreed to that and asked where Gibson was.

'He hasn't been well.'

I thought she was going to elaborate, but she seemed to think better of it and nodded hopefully, favouring me with a smile.

I guessed that this was the first time she had stood in for him. She was nervous.

'What's your name?'

'Annie Belmont, sir.'

In my room I went to the window and looked out and my heart sank.

Tommy was across the road, standing, I thought, like someone prepared to stand for a very long time. I walked back out of the room and ran down the stairs.

'Annie!' I called through the door that led to the kitchen. I heard the sound of utensils being laid on a table and then the girl appeared again, drying her hands on a towel.

'Could you make *two* sandwiches?'

When she brought the food to my room, I took the tray from her at the door and said, 'Wait here.'

I put the tray on the table by the window and came back to her with one of the sandwiches.

'There's a little boy standing on the other side of the street,' I said. 'Please take this and give it to him.'

'I can't do that!' she said indignantly.

'Why not?'

'I would get into trouble.'

'What for?'

She thought for a few seconds. 'For encouraging vagrants.' She said this as though it was the answer to a catechism question that she had had difficulty remembering.

I took a sixpence from my trouser pocket and held it out.

She looked at the coin and then at me. She pursed her lips. 'I don't want to get into trouble, sir!'

'That little fellow hasn't had a proper meal for a long time. It's just a matter of Christian charity.'

'But if you give him something he'll never go away,' she said, not unreasonably.

'Perhaps not,' I replied, 'but would you please take it out to him.'

She allowed me to place the sixpence in her palm, and slipping the coin into the pocket of her apron she took the sandwich.

A few moments later I saw Annie come out of the hotel and cross the road. She handed Tommy the sandwich, leaning forward, sensibly and by no means subtly maintaining a certain physical remove from his infested head and clothes. He took the sandwich, looking at her with an expression that was at first mystified and then, eyes opening wide, comprehending. She said something else; I imagine telling him not to hang around expecting any more handouts. She turned and skipped back across the road.

I walked away from the window, resolving not to return until I had finished my examination of the photographs taken the previous day from Mr Presser's office.

I ate half of the sandwich and went back to the window.

Tommy wasn't there.

When I had finished eating, I laid the photographs on the desk, together with notebook and pen and ink.

These images were composed more densely than the pictures of Crown Street. The view from the hotel offered a sharply receding perspective, which meant that a majority of the figures were extremely small. I had used my magnifying glass a great deal. Now the task was different. The intersection outside the bank was more like a music-hall stage than a long tunnel. The dramatis personae were generally the same size. Some were of the same type as those photographed in the street: policemen, little girls with dolls and prams, men in bowler hats. Perhaps they were even the same people. That was something that I knew would make itself apparent over time. As one examined the figures again and again one became familiar with the individual traits of certain subjects, the different but recognisably characteristic ways in which a loafer would hold his cigarette when he was talking to others and when he was alone; the pose that a shopkeeper would strike when he was dealing with tradesmen – the same shopkeeper standing in various parts of the street and dressed differently according to the day of the week would be instantly tagged by the way he customarily folded his arms, held his head back and splayed his feet out, like a duck.

As I worked through the morning I began to become familiar with the characters. I never saw the dry-salter, or if I saw him I was unable to identify him as such, but I saw William Harrison, the chemist. He came in and out of his shop with regularity, and when he wasn't entering or exiting he was standing in front of the display window talking to passers-by. I guessed he was offering diagnoses. He would consult for free and make his money on the prescription. That was for many people a more attractive prospect than visiting the doctor, who would charge for the consultation with the apothecary's bill to be added afterwards.

Two policemen were on duty during the day. One was directing traffic, his arms akimbo like a sort of blue uniformed African dancer, when the camera began recording in the morning. He was relieved between a quarter past one and two in the afternoon. The afternoon policeman raised his arms more economically and in the photographs resembled a tin soldier, his hand signals like those of a military flag ensign.

There was a contrast in the two scenes that matched the description Macarthur had given on the first day. The square in front of the bank was 'respectable' and that part of the street that led up to it was not. Where it joined the square the street appeared to be at the very nadir of degradation and squalor. It improved, block by block, on the way south.

The denizens of the poorest and most desolate quarter, the three blocks before the square, could be seen in the square itself and in the better part of the street. There were little boys who looked as wretched and malodorous as Tommy and they loitered near the policemen and by the kerbside opposite the bank. I looked for Tommy but didn't see him in my first day's recording. I guessed that his regular beat was in the swathe of decaying tenements further to the east, near where I had first encountered him.

Here and there in the worst parts of the district could be seen a prosperous-looking matron or a smartly dressed man in a bowler hat. The two parts were distinct but they were not segregated. 'Respectable' citizens went about their business cheek by jowl with the workless and indigent. In one case I saw a man dressed in a clerical collar talking to a character who looked as though he was in an advanced state of drunkenness. The clergyman, in frock coat and top hat, remonstrated with the man, who stood bare-headed and collarless looking down at his untied boots while he was advised, presumably, of the evils of drink. On one side of this vignette of virtue confronting vice was a gaggle of children, most of them barefoot and dirty, and on the other was a kind of mirror gaggle of women, most of them in shawls and braided pigtails.

I considered the shape of human voices. When Macarthur spoke to me he was comprehensible, even though to my ears his accent was exotic, but when he spoke to Billy Fraser his pronunciation changed and I was barely able to follow what was said. Professor MacKay spoke English like an Old Testament prophet, slowly and clearly, but there was a sudden shift when he said something glib or amusing. *Couldn't* became *coodnie*, *do* became *dae* and there was a greater-than-usual sprinkling of *och*s and *aye*s.

I imagined the conversation between the drunk man and the minister and I knew that it would be conducted in a patois largely beyond me but eloquent and communicative to everyone in the little circle of drama that had been photographed two blocks from the square.

I saw both the minister and the drunk man again in a photograph taken later in the day. The drunkard appeared in five photographs altogether. After his encounter with the minister there was no sign of him for eight photographs. I wondered if he had found a place to sleep for a few hours. When he was next recorded, at a quarter to three, he was coming out of a public house, one foot in front of the other at an angle that indicated a jaunty step. I feared that the clergyman's earnest entreaties had not fallen on fertile ground. Three quarters of an hour later, the man was arguing with the driver of a coal cart. It was the sort of one-sided argument in which the drunk party becomes increasingly loud and inconsequential and the sober party assumes the function of an orchestra conductor, directing here and there with short sharp answers and hand gestures. The drunk man gesticulated and the carter divided his attention between the man and his horse, his whip suspended lazily from the front of his driving platform. The drunk man appeared again in the last photograph of the day, exhausted by his encounters with clergymen and carters and the demon drink, sitting on the pavement at the street corner two blocks from the bank, his head bent over almost to his chest, in a state of unconsciousness.

While this man spent his day trying and failing to make his world more bearable by dint of desperate argument and the consumption of whatever soporifics came to hand, the minister clearly depended more exclusively on argument. He was recorded twice in the afternoon and on both occasions he was talking. The first time, near the scene of his encounter with the drunk, he was chatting with two women who looked more like the minister than the poorer inhabitants of the area. They wore light-coloured dresses and carried straw bags. Both ladies faced the camera. One was slim and in her forties and her face was plain but intelligent, with dark eyebrows and a thin mouth. The other was twenty or so and very pretty; she had light hair that was loosely tied beneath her bonnet. She carried a violin case. She was smiling and, I could see from the shape of her mouth, she was about to respond to what the minister was saying. I might not have dwelt so long on this group of figures had I not sensed that something about the girl's posture was unusual. Then I saw that obscured from the camera by her body but visible just at the bottom of the far side of her skirt was a walking cane, and around the black leather on the boot of her right foot was the tip of a calliper.

The next time the minister was photographed was at a quarter past four. He was coming out of a close on the other side of Crown Street near the hotel and lifting his hat to a man who walked past the close carrying a suitcase. As always, the minister was speaking and, as always, it was possible to derive a remarkable amount of information from the moment recorded by the camera. The man had turned his head in the minister's direction but had continued to walk – perhaps he had slowed down – it was obvious that the two men knew each other, because the minister was smiling broadly. He wasn't simply greeting the man; he had said something amusing, perhaps in reference to the suitcase.

I was glad the minister had found a reason to be cheerful at the end of the day. I wondered if he knew how futile his efforts to talk sense into the drunkard had been. He must surely have known, and, if he did, then I saluted him for his pluckiness in the face of failure. Failure was impregnated in every tile and cobblestone of these streets.

By the early afternoon I had analysed the photographs thoroughly. I looked up from my notebook and rubbed my eyes. The timer and the camera exercised the little pirouette they performed every forty-five minutes and I heard the familiar whirr of an image being recorded. The rest of the day stretched out before me. I was ambivalent about leaving the camera unattended in the hotel, but less so than I would have been the day before. When you study a place you begin to identify currents and patterns that make sense of things. I have read that birds navigate by judging the warmth or coolness of the surrounding air. When I first arrived, I had thought of this as a seedy establishment in a bad neighbourhood, but now I understood that it was not seedy but, rather, 'economical' and that it was placed at the point where the poor part of the street met the better part.

Two constables strolled past on the other side of the road, like oriental pashas in stately progress. I decided to go out. When I stepped into the sunlight, I opted to walk north with as much reason as the day before I had opted to walk south. After crossing the river I followed a zigzag course through bustling side streets and past the main station till I came to the top of a steep street where there was a church with a tower. I continued west, down again into an expanse of tenements.

I thought of the girl in the photograph, the girl speaking to the minister. When we visited Robert and Effie McClellan on the journey to Santiago, Robert told us about a physician in Glasgow who was so utterly focused on the *science* of illness – on the organisms that can be seen beneath a microscope – that when his own child became ill with polio fever he failed to recognise the symptoms. 'Afterwards, he poured all his energy into studying the disease,' he said. 'I don't think he understood his family very well, but he became an authority on polio. I hear he's made great strides. They speak of a vaccine.'

'And the child?'

'Crippled, but otherwise a full recovery,' Robert said. He shook his head. 'Medicine cannot cure all the ills of humanity, though it can help along the way.' Then he added, 'But the best medicine is empathy, the best medicine is love.'

As I walked, I began to distinguish grades of poverty and prosperity. The plain black facades here had clean and curtained windows; the closes were tiled.

I passed a provisions store with the name *Thomas Lipton* painted above it with great flourish. A queue of women waited all the way out onto the pavement. Through the window I saw a man of about thirty with a huge handlebar moustache dispensing vegetables to a lady at the front of the queue. I could hear the echo of their exchange; he was bantering and the woman laughed and protested. Outside, two prams had been left in the care of a girl of about fourteen. I noticed that all of her attention was directed at one of the prams, while the other stood a little way away, apparently neglected. When I came closer I saw that the neglected pram was not being used to carry a living soul, but as a kind of supplementary carriage for vegetables.

After several blocks, the apartments began to be interspersed with low brick buildings that had shallow corrugated roofs. From these buildings came the sounds of hammering and drilling and grinding. Over the rooftops and at the ends of streets I saw the huge black cranes that lined the river. I followed an irregular path through the black canyons to the riverbank.

I was at the point where the principal activity on the river mutated from maritime trade to shipbuilding. All along the banks to my left were cranes; the surface of the water was almost invisible so dense was the traffic. To my right the cranes dwarfed the surrounding tenements. One crane was in motion, reaching its jagged arm out over the river above a massive expanse of iron that did not yet look like a ship's hull.

I had marked what I thought were tramlines running along the cobbles that separated the first line of tenements from a long high factory wall behind which the cranes operated. As I stood surveying the scene from a tenement corner, I saw that these were not tramlines but railway lines. A steam engine, creating its characteristic hiss and clatter, began puffing out of one of the yards pulling three open tenders on which had been placed the shaft and blades of a ship's propeller. The blades rose nearly to the height of the second-storey windows in the tenements past which the engine made its stately and impossibly noisy progress.

There were thousands of workers. Men moved quickly in both directions, coming from somewhere, going somewhere, without time to loiter in between. This crowd was dense and purposeful.

I walked for about two miles before I came to a break in the succession of yards. It was a very small break, where a tenement block encroached all the way to the waterfront. I followed a squat street to the bank of the river, noting that a large number of people were doing the same. When I reached the riverside I found a set of broad shallow steps leading down to a wooden platform just above the waterline. Two passenger ferries plied the river here, dragged across the water by steel chains that were submerged when the ferry reached either side, allowing other vessels to pass unhindered. A man in a black suit and a sailor's cap was issuing tickets. I bought a ticket and followed the line of people onto the vessel that had just docked.

From the level of the water, the size and scale of the activity on the river became fully visible. It was staggering. The river was obscured by the physical detritus of the business along both banks and the dense traffic in between. As we were hauled out into the middle of the current, I looked over the side and what I saw there was not water but a black viscous substance that glinted in the sunlight; it was so turgid and thick that the waves appeared almost sculpted; they rose lugubriously as ships passed on either side and seemed to maintain their shape for an impossibly long time. I mused upon this but not for long: the overpowering sensation experienced on this particular body of water was not the shape of the waves but the smell. It was not exclusively unpleasant, though it was definitely not wholesome. It was a combination of coal and oil and salt and the acrid, eye-watering emanation from steel welding. On top of this was the scent of wood, of manure and of tar.

It took us no more than two minutes to reach what I now considered 'my' side of the river.

An overweight and elderly woman, rather well dressed, was first in line to disembark. She had to be helped ashore by the ticket seller, a younger version of the one on the opposite bank, also dressed in black suit and naval cap.

'Come on there, missis,' he said, holding out his hand.

'Haud yer horses,' the woman replied.

'Gie 'er a haun!' someone shouted from the back.

'Ahm daen tha',' the ticket seller said defensively.

'Maybe you should *lift* her oot!' someone else suggested.

'Ah'll lift *you* oot first,' the woman said, turning to address whoever had spoken.

Everyone laughed and the ticket seller handed the woman down onto the wooden jetty, freeing up the line and allowing the other passengers to disembark.

I climbed up the steps and entered a street that was a replica of the one on the opposite bank. Inland from the riverside tenements I entered a district where new stone mansions had been built along broad leafy avenues. And then, as abruptly as it had begun, this bucolic oasis came to an end at a railway line. On the other side of the railway the red sandstone of the tenements was not yet soot-blackened; there were trees along the edges of the broad pavements. Through bay windows, it was possible to glimpse bookshelves and paintings. There were streets and streets of tenements like these all the way to the end of Crown Street.

I entered a public house. There were just a handful of men at the bar. I ordered a beer and had started to drink when I heard an altercation outside. The barman went out to investigate. He stood in the doorway, his aproned figure silhouetted in the sunlight. To my surprise when he came back inside he didn't go behind the counter but instead walked to where I was sitting and said, 'There's a message for you. You've to go right away to Simpson's Hotel.'

This was extraordinary.

I didn't see how anyone could possibly know that I was in this bar.

'It's urgent,' the man said. 'You've to go now.'

I stood and walked out, conscious that the barman and the others were taking a keen interest. I tried to look nonchalant.

Outside, I was greeted by a familiar and unpleasantly smelling figure, and any vestige of pretended nonchalance deserted me.

'Tommy! What are you doing here?'

'Sergeant Macarthur sent me.'

'How do you know Sergeant Macarthur?'

'I just know him.'

'How did you know I was here?'

'I saw you coming across the road.'

None of this was entirely satisfactory. I started to walk and Tommy started to walk beside me.

'You've to hurry,' he said, edging ahead of me.

'I'll go at my own pace,' I replied, trying to impose some control on my circumstances.

'No, you *have* to hurry,' he said.

'Why?'

'There's been another murder.'

CHAPTER SEVENTEEN

Macarthur was waiting in the lobby of the hotel.

'Where were you?' he asked.

'I understand there's been another murder,' I said.

'Yes, and we need your photographs. We need them *now*.'

'I'm not removing the plates till I've a full set for the whole day.'

'What the devil do you mean?'

I was irritated. 'I'm not going to stop the sequence of pictures. I need the whole set each day so that I can make a comprehensive comparison.'

'But the murderer has already struck!'

Macarthur spoke in the peremptory manner of a policeman at the scene of a crime, but there was something more. I sensed panic in his voice.

'What does it matter what you photograph now?' he snapped. 'We need the photographs you've already *taken* to see if you have a record of the murderer entering the building!'

'It's possible that I won't have a record, but it's also possible that something will happen in the coming hours that could have a bearing on the case.'

'What could possibly happen?'

'Well, for one thing, the murderer could return to the scene of the crime. Where did it happen?'

He hesitated before he said, 'Two doors down, the same close where Brendan Gillespie was murdered.'

'I would like to see the place.'

'You're not *investigating*!' he said, and of course he was right. 'I want the photographs.'

It was a simple matter to turn and walk out of the hotel. Tommy fell into step as I crossed the road and marched to the entrance where the murder had been committed.

When we reached the close, a uniformed constable blocked my way. I waited for Macarthur to catch up.

The constable looked at Macarthur and Macarthur, thwarted for now, nodded to indicate that I should be allowed to pass. Tommy knew better than to try and follow.

It was unclear to me why I had behaved as I had. Afterwards I tried to reconstruct my thoughts and I could find nothing to explain my sudden loss of confidence in Macarthur – except for that scintilla of panic that had attached itself to his voice.

'When did it happen?' I asked him as we walked into the darkness.

'The body was found about an hour ago.'

We moved to the bottom of the stairs. Another policeman stood guard at the narrow passageway that led to the backcourt.

He made way for us, and as he did I heard the sound of a carriage stopping in the street and the flutter of voices, instructions, greetings and explanations that accompany the arrival of a dignitary. Professor MacKay hurried into the close.

I had been surprised by Macarthur's agitation when we faced each other in the lobby of the hotel. I was surprised now by the professor's demeanour. He seemed to be in a state of shock. He was wide-eyed and his face was deathly pale.

'Where's the body?' he demanded, ignoring Macarthur and me.

'Here,' the constable said.

MacKay hurried on down the narrow passage.

There was a sickly smell in the enclosed space.

'Stand out of the light there!' he told the constable who was guarding the entrance from the backcourt. The policeman moved to one side. I saw that there was an audience of curious bystanders in the courtyard as there was in the street. I looked up: faces watched us from over the banister all the way up to the dirty glass cupola four floors above.

It took some time for my eyes to recover from the glare of the outside sunlight and become accustomed to the gloomy passageway. Once I was better used to the light I saw that the sickly smell was created in large part by an enormous amount of blood that had flooded the flagstones, creating puddles now beginning to congeal. I looked down and saw the sole of my right shoe squarely placed in a reservoir of red. I took a step backward and felt the ooze cling to my foot.

The body had been covered with some kind of canvas tarpaulin. 'Take it off,' MacKay ordered.

It wasn't clear whom he was instructing, but the policeman

behind me slipped past and removed the cover, lifting it in such a way that it would not drip blood and gore.

The corpse lay exposed.

My instinct was to take another step back, but I resisted.

We looked down on the mortal remains of a man who had been about twenty-five years old. The eyes had been closed.

I willed my consciousness away from revulsion and into a state of sober observation.

'Do we know who he is?' MacKay asked.

'Seamus Hanlon,' Macarthur said.

'Address?'

'The floor above.'

'Occupation?'

'Fitter.'

Hanlon was wearing canvas trousers that stretched, I thought at first, over his feet. Then I realised that he did not *have* feet, or arms. His face was as white as his shirt would have been had it not been covered in blood. He lay on his back, and yet there was room for a person to walk past him in the narrow passage; this was because the quadruple amputation had reduced that portion of the earth taken up by Seamus Hanlon.

MacKay bent down and lifted one protrusion and then another, peering at the points where the limbs had been hacked off. The word 'hacked' came into my mind, but when I steeled myself to look with the same care as the professor I noted that the gruesome work had been done not in a haphazard way but with precision. The arms had been surgically removed, leaving a cleanly chopped spaghetti of severed veins and ligaments.

The professor turned his attention to the legs. The incisions had been made around the knees.

'The killer was disturbed,' he said.

'How's that?' Macarthur asked.

'Look.'

Macarthur looked and so did I. The left tibia and foot had been removed with the same precision as the arms, and there was the same chopped spaghetti of arteries and ligament, but in the case of the right leg the amputation had been frenzied rather than deliberate. Here there was a melange. This really did look hacked.

MacKay turned his attention to Hanlon's head, moving it first to one side and then to the other. Rigor mortis had set in and the head moved in the neck socket rather as though it were attached to the torso by a rusty hinge. We could hear the scrape of cartilage as the neck was twisted.

MacKay opened first the right eye and then the left, closing each again. He tried to open the corpse's mouth but it was locked shut. He took what looked to me like a small chisel from his medical bag and inserted it between the teeth. Seeing this steel appliance placed against the bloodless lips, I was momentarily overcome by the image of an ancient mummy being violated by the tools of an archaeologist. We heard a crack as MacKay broke the jaw. He used his fingers to prise the teeth apart and peered into the dead man's mouth. For a moment he allowed his nostrils to linger over the aperture, and then he said, 'Well, he hadn't been drinking.'

The professor stood up straight again.

'Where's Fraser?' he demanded.

'He's been sent for,' Macarthur said.

MacKay nodded. He seemed only then to notice me. I was impressed by the change that came over him in the course of this brief examination. It was as if the minutiae of his work released him from some larger concern.

'Was your camera running?' he asked.

'I believe so.'

'When can we see the photographs?'

'I've already asked Mr Cameron to provide us with the pictures immediately,' Macarthur interjected.

MacKay glanced at Macarthur and then looked at me.

'I want to continue the sequence to the end. It's possible we may record something useful, even *after* the event. I don't intend to finish the exposures until seven o'clock. I'll develop the images immediately and make a detailed comparison. I can have that late this evening.'

MacKay considered this. Macarthur was about to speak, but MacKay raised his hand and the sergeant waited. MacKay looked down at the body again and then indicated to the policeman that he should place the tarpaulin over it.

'How late?'

I shrugged. 'Eleven o'clock.'

When we emerged from the close, the crowd had grown twice as large. Perhaps witnessing the removal of the body was a kind of exorcism. If not, then the people milling outside the close, smoking and talking to one another excitedly, were simply displaying a macabre and reprehensible curiosity.

The crowd was made up not only of immediate neighbours. There were 'respectable' types who had come hot foot from the other end of the street. There were women in shawls, women with prams, women with small children. Women appeared to make up the largest portion and they concentrated in the middle, with the men on the edges, smoking and silent.

'When are you going to catch him?' a small grey crone in a plaid shawl shouted at MacKay.

The constable turned and gave her a warning look but she ignored this and shouted over the constable's shoulder, 'Or are you just going to let him carry on? It's nothing to you when one of *us* dies!'

'That's enough!' the constable growled.

At that point the crowd's attention was drawn away from the angry woman.

A pale blue van drawn by two black ponies stopped in front of the close and Billy Fraser climbed down from the passenger seat. A man who looked about twice as tall as Billy descended from the driver's side and went to the back of the van to fetch a stretcher.

Billy hurried towards us.

'You have another one then?' he asked the professor.

'Aye.'

MacKay looked at Billy with an expression of distaste and suspicion. Billy shrugged in a way that seemed to indicate indifference. He walked on into the close. His assistant followed, carrying the folded stretcher. If he had reached up, the assistant could almost have touched the ceiling of the close with the tips of his fingers.

'I am going back to the hotel,' I told the professor, less to inform him of what I proposed to do than to utter a formula under which I could take my leave.

'Now the whole district knows that you're working with us,' Macarthur said sullenly.

I looked at the crowd. They displayed the attentiveness of people who have come to gawk and find themselves with nothing to gawk at except three men huddled on the other side of a police cordon.

'We will come to the hotel at eleven,' MacKay said.

Walking across the road, I became aware of a familiar odour.

'Is there something I can do for you?' Tommy asked.

'You can leave me alone.'

When I reached the hotel, the odour had diminished. I glanced around and saw Tommy still standing in the middle of the road.

I looked down at the pavement; then I looked at Tommy and waved to him irritably, indicating that he should approach.

He didn't move at first. When he decided to oblige me, he walked slowly, a scowl on his dirty face.

'Hurry up!' I shouted.

He quickened his pace a little.

I reached into my pocket and took out a penny.

'Go and get me a halfpenny worth of baccy,' I said. 'You can keep the change.'

'Sailor's or Farmer's?'

'Farmer's.'

He ran off.

I waited at the entrance.

The policeman outside the close fifty yards away began to discourage the crowd from loitering. Billy's van made a U-turn and headed back towards the northern side of the river. The gawkers slowly dispersed, spreading out in all directions. A small man, wearing a bowler hat and smoking a cream-coloured pipe, passed in front of the hotel, looking at me with curiosity. He was followed by a woman pushing a pram and then by two short women wearing shawls. The woman with the pram was dressed in mourning, with a black straw hat and a black veil over it; the pram too was black; one of the women in shawls had complained to Professor MacKay that the police weren't interested in finding the killer.

Tommy ran round the corner breathless, nearly colliding with the pram. He held out a small paper bag of tobacco and I took it from his grubby fingers.

'Tommy,' I said, 'do you go to school?'

He shook his head.

'Did you ever go to school?'

He looked down at the ground.

'Tell me,' I continued, assuming an inquisitorial sternness that I hoped would prompt him to answer.

He nodded his head very slightly.

'Where?'

He turned and pointed along the street that led from the other side of the main road. I looked.

'Where? At the church?'

He nodded again.

'Do you go to church?'

He shrugged.

'Tommy, do you know how many people have been murdered?'

'Five until today, now six.'

'Did they all go to that church?'

He nodded.

CHAPTER EIGHTEEN

When I brought the plates to the mortuary, Billy Fraser's assistant was cleaning the dissecting table nearest the door. Seamus Hanlon's body had been placed in one of the steel boxes.

Robert, the assistant, looked as if he could have lifted the dissecting table and put it up against the wall if he'd wanted to. His features were flat, his skin pockmarked, his eyes pale and his fair hair sparse.

'Billy's away,' he told me.

'I have pictures to develop.'

He looked at me closely. 'I know.'

I walked round him to the darkroom and began to work.

As each image revealed itself, I peered into it. Somewhere here was a demon that had claimed its latest victim.

But, of course, the process could not be so simple. The murderer would not stand out and identify himself even in my pristine pictures with their clear, close focus. When I placed the plates and images in the satchel and left the darkroom, though I had spent half an hour haphazardly searching the scenes in the photographs, I was no closer to understanding what had happened that afternoon than I had been when I stood with Macarthur and MacKay examining the horribly mutilated corpse.

I stepped out into the dissecting room and began to shiver. Mixed with the cold air was a scent of formaldehyde or something similarly acerbic. I put my hand up to my mouth. I looked around but could see little. The lamps had been extinguished and the only illumination was a weak light through the frosted glass of the door.

'Damn!' I whispered.

I stepped forward and then stopped. Obliged to rearrange the normal primacy of the senses, the mind acts quickly and, as it does this, it can become confused. I could see little and my sense of smell was assailed by the tart chemical odour of what I thought must be embalming fluid. In the seconds after I stepped out of the developing room, my ears took command and I thought I heard a scraping noise from one of the steel boxes.

This simply could not be.

I stopped and listened. I heard the scraping again.

'Robert!' I shouted into the darkness.

I shouted because I did not choose to cower in the dark. I shouted too because from time immemorial, human beings have banished demons with the power of declamation. I wanted to make my presence known in this place and challenge anyone or anything to show itself or flee.

There was another scraping. My head turned so quickly in the direction of the noise that my neck seemed to strain in its socket.

'Who's there?' I demanded.

This was a foolish question. The room was empty. It was a large square room and though it was almost completely unlit, there was enough illumination for me to see that there was nothing in front of the coffins or under the tables or above the cabinets. Everything was in plain view.

Again, I heard a scraping.

I took a step forward and turned to face the steel boxes. My chest rose. I do not know if I assumed this pose out of anger or out of fear or out of a combination of both. I glared at the boxes barely visible in the dark cold room and perhaps I would have addressed them a second time. Perhaps I would have demanded in the name of heaven that whatever lurked there show itself or depart – but I did not have time to speak because in those moments I heard a separate sound behind me, the sound of a giant crossing the room.

I spun round.

Robert carried a lighted taper in front of him and the flame cast a glow over his mouth and eyes.

Involuntarily, I took a step back towards the developing room. Robert reached up with the taper and a moment after this a spurt of light from the gas lamp on the wall penetrated the gloom and we could see one another properly.

'Why did you leave me in the dark?' I heard the sound of my voice and I was irritated because it betrayed a humiliating absence of calm.

'I didnae leave ye in the dark,' he said morosely. 'The lamp went oot. It does that noo an' then.'

'I heard a scraping!' I said, and again I was annoyed by the panic that seemed to have taken possession of my vocal cords.

Robert stared at me.

'I heard a scraping,' I said again. 'From here!' I pointed to the coffins.

He nodded and began to walk towards me. The toe of my shoe rose from the ground preparatory to taking another step backward, but I got command of myself and placed the toe back on the tiled floor.

'There,' I repeated, pointing at the boxes as Robert moved slowly forward.

When he rounded the last dissecting table he changed course and walked past me. He stopped in front of the place where I'd heard the scraping noise and lit a match and bent down. He looked even larger in this doubled-up posture than he did when he was standing straight. I reached the odd conclusion that Robert would have been too long and too broad for any of the steel coffins in front of which he was crouching.

'Aye,' he said, grazing the tips of his fingers across the surface of the tiles. 'Ye startled a rat.' He stood up and waved the match so that it went out. 'Y'er lucky it didnae go fer ye!'

I breathed deeply and nodded and resolved in a spirit of mortification never again to respond to unexpected circumstances with the flightiness of a nervous schoolgirl.

I was still annoyed with myself when I returned to the hotel. In my room I heard a soft tap on my bedroom door. When I opened the door I found Annie standing there. She examined me for a few seconds before extending her arms and a heavy tray, saying, 'Yer dinner, sir.'

She glanced over my shoulder towards the table, where I had laid out that day's photographs. I took the tray from her, though she protested that she should bring it inside.

I do not know how long it took me to finish the meal. I am not at all sure that I knew exactly what was *in* the meal, because as I ate I began to analyse everything the camera had recorded in Crown Street that day.

From the beginning I was systematic. I moved slowly, comparing each square in the developed pictures. I did not leap to the area around the close where the murder had been committed. I knew that I might just as likely find a clue elsewhere.

Perhaps in the future it will be possible to place cameras in city streets taking continuous photographs, but my method is not based on capturing everything that happens: it is based on patterns that might indicate what may have happened in the great stretches of time and activity that have *not* been recorded.

Several things had transpired near the close where Seamus Hanlon was dismembered. The minister I'd recorded the day before, remonstrating with the drunk, walked past the close twice. At a quarter to three, just before the body was found, a policeman entered the close. Earlier in the day, between eleven and a quarter to twelve, a short man with a bowler hat and a large moustache carried a long parcel wrapped in brown paper into the close.

Two closes down from the scene of the murder, next to a public house, a girl in a black shawl with gold braid stood, half on the pavement, half in the close, watching the opposite side of the road. She was pretty, perhaps about nineteen. I had seen her before and I could not think where. I might have passed her in Crown Street or she might have worked in one

189

of the shops where I had bought tobacco. I returned to the image several times, for no other reason than – having failed to glean anything useful from a comprehensive study of the photographs – I wanted at least to satisfy my curiosity about this one figure.

The street was filled. There were men in working clothes; there were women with prams; women with cloth bags in which they carried every conceivable kind of bundle; women gossiping, some of them clutching clay pipes between their teeth. Children played by the side of the road, some wearing little boots and white smocks and straw hats, and others, like Tommy, clad in whatever material they had been able to lay their hands on.

The victims were incomers. The poor Catholic Irish who inhabited these streets believed they were not protected by the law. The tens of thousands of them who were *in* the city were not yet *of* it. They were new and different and they were viewed with suspicion, often with dislike.

Yet I may have latched onto this only because I had nothing else to show for two days of labour. When my visitors arrived my photographs would not help them catch their man.

'Is this the extent of your information?' Professor MacKay asked.

'This is what I have been able to discover so far.'

Macarthur stood at the table where the photographs were laid out. 'Isn't there anyone who *looks* like our suspect?' he said.

'We don't know what our suspect looks like,' I replied.

'Clearly, it isn't the minister,' MacKay remarked, glancing at my notes and then looking again at the photographs in which the minister appeared, 'and why have you drawn attention to this man with the parcel? Surely he could simply be a resident who came home with a parcel wrapped up in brown paper. That doesn't amount to evidence of an intention to murder.'

'Of course it doesn't,' I said. 'I simply draw attention to the man because . . . he entered the close where the murder took place. It may be useful to find out who he is, and to enquire as to the nature of the parcel he was carrying. He may turn up in future photographs. For all I know he may be carrying more parcels.'

No matter how many times I attempt to explain that the object of my method is not to catch criminals in flagrante but to record the *environment* in which crimes have been committed and by means of this to extrapolate valuable information – no matter how often I explain this, people still assume that the object is to place the perpetrator in a photograph.

Macarthur shrugged. 'If we haven't caught our man when we were taking pictures all day, I can't say I really see the point.' He looked again at one of the photographs and then he picked it up and, speaking directly to me, said, 'Why didn't you mention this?'

'What?'

'Billy Fraser's here!'

He showed the photograph to Professor MacKay, who peered at it as he might have peered through the lens of a microscope.

'Is that Billy?' the professor asked me.

I took the photograph from him. *Damn!* It *was* Billy and I had missed him!

I'd been *meticulous*. I'd combed my photographs box by box. I could not fathom how I had missed this, except that I had worked in a state of growing unease as I realised I would have nothing useful to show my visitors when they came. And I had been preoccupied by the girl in the black shawl with gold braid.

How did I know the braid was gold? Because the same girl had been wearing the same shawl two nights before when she and her partner accosted Harrison and me outside the dining club. I remembered now. *That* was where I knew her from.

This niggling detail had distracted me from a figure of more obvious interest, walking north, between the close where the girl was standing and the close where Seamus Hanlon was murdered. Half of his body was obscured by a lady in a voluminous black coat and black hat. Billy looked even more diminutive walking in this woman's ambit, but the left part of his face, complete with pipe, was clearly visible. His left foot was thrown forward in what I recognised as his characteristic step, a short, rapid movement that compensated for his lack of stature and made him seem to be in a hurry even when he was walking at a normal pace.

'It's him,' I said.

It sounded like an admission.

'When was this photograph taken?' Macarthur demanded.

'Five o'clock,' I said.

'After the murder.' The professor spoke as though he had seen a ghost, in a voice just above a whisper. 'Just a little after . . . the same afternoon!'

This sudden change in his demeanour brought me back to a more customarily clear way of thinking.

Their train of thought was neither clinical nor empirical.

'What exactly is the significance of this?' I asked.

Macarthur looked at MacKay.

'The man has a history,' the professor said darkly.

'What sort of history?'

'We will need this photograph,' Macarthur said.

I was tired, and irritated by Macarthur's tone.

'You will have nothing until I have completed my experiment.'

The sergeant turned slightly to face me, and opened his mouth to respond. But the professor raised a hand. His features assembled themselves in a sort of practised impassiveness, yet the final impression was not entirely impassive: he was unable to eliminate an underlying agitation. There was a germ of uncertainty in the way he stood and the way he spoke.

'Very well,' he said with a tiny, almost imperceptible movement of his head. If I had had to determine the meaning of this gesture I would have said that it indicated a species of resignation.

He turned to me as he began to open the door. 'When you have finished, you will hand over all of your photographs to Sergeant Macarthur or to me.'

I woke the next morning just before seven. A tram was clattering by and the sound of its progress travelled up from the street, first from the south and then from right below my window, the noise diminishing as the tram moved north. There were other sounds too: a shutter being opened noisily, wound up by a rusty ratchet, horses whinnying.

A cool breeze came into the room. Even in this soot-sodden place there was a vein of blossoms and cut grass in the air.

I lay back and looked up at the ceiling, inhaling summer, listening to the morning. I thought of something so utterly removed from my immediate surroundings that it might have belonged to a different planet.

She had a musical way of speaking, musical like the infinitely beautiful melodies of Andalusia. Her voice was mystical and strong. Everything about her, from the wisps of hair that framed her face to the polished tips of her black city boots – everything about her was ravishing.

An hour later, when Macarthur's cab pulled up in front of the hotel, I climbed in beside the sergeant and he wished me a pleasant good morning.

'I believe your photographs can help,' he said when I had taken my seat. 'I was shaken yesterday and I apologise if my tone was abrupt.'

I greeted this sudden change warily. Of the three men whom I knew to be privy to my work in Glasgow, Macarthur was the one I trusted least.

I looked out of the window at the black facades.

'When we began this experiment,' he said, 'you warned Mr Presser that none of his staff should know that the camera was recording the square outside the bank.'

I nodded.

'That was good advice. If a handful knew in the morning then by the afternoon half the neighbourhood would know. And if people knew, they would behave differently. It's not just a matter of the murderer discovering that he could be photographed; the innocent too would behave differently and that would destroy the patterns you are trying to identify.'

I nodded again.

'Well, what I am going to tell you I should keep to myself and when I tell you I believe you'll understand why.'

The cab had begun to turn onto the square in front of the bank. We were held up at the crossing by a dairy cart that lumbered uncertainly against the run of traffic towards the centre of the square. Macarthur turned to face me. I felt obliged to hold his gaze.

'You have a photograph of Billy Fraser in Crown Street right around the time that Seamus Hanlon was murdered, and we have two witnesses that will testify that he was in the vicinity. We also have a witness who saw him running away from the scene after Edie Hamilton was attacked.'

He paused. The cab turned the corner and pulled up in front of the bank.

'We have placed you in close proximity to a man we now view with strong suspicion,' Macarthur continued. 'If you should choose to withdraw from this experiment, we would entirely understand.'

He opened the door and climbed out.

'I do not intend to withdraw,' I told Macarthur.

Mr Presser ushered us into his office. 'You are on time this morning!' he said. It was not clear whether he meant this remark to signal appreciation or surprise.

The sergeant and the bank manager remained near the door while I changed the plates. They spoke at a level that was just low enough to prevent me from hearing what they were saying. I caught the tail end of half a dozen words and I gathered that they were discussing a mutual acquaintance. I supposed that Mr Presser enjoyed the higher social standing of the two, yet they seemed to converse on an equal footing.

I finished and we took our leave having disturbed Mr Presser's office regime for no more than five minutes.

'Well,' Macarthur said as we walked down the steps from the bank, 'I expect you are bound for the mortuary.'

This might have qualified as black humour but neither of us smiled.

We began walking in the opposite direction.

Across the river I found Billy in the dissecting room bent over a cadaver on the far table. The cadaver was not human.

Billy glanced up.

I looked at the corpse.

'It ran amok at the Maryhill Barracks,' he said, looking first at the dog and then at me. 'They're afraid it may have been rabid. It bit two ensigns.'

'*Is* it rabid?'

He shook his head. 'Just hungry.'

I went into the developing room and began to work.

My murderer could have come from the south and he could have returned to the south after he dismembered Seamus Hanlon. He might never have walked in front of Mr Presser's bank.

I considered this as the familiar images of the policemen and loafers in the middle of the cross began to appear in the developing tray.

I worked quickly, only glancing very briefly at the pictures as I removed them from the tray and hung them up. When I emerged from the darkroom, Billy was still standing over the dead dog. I walked to the other side of the table, keeping my eye on Billy. I did not want to look at the mess of blood and tendrils that lay in front of him.

'You were in Crown Street yesterday afternoon,' I said.

He looked at me with an expression of weary displeasure.

'How do you know that, Mr Cameron?'

'Because you were photographed.'

'What of it?'

He didn't ask by whom he had been photographed. I had guessed by then, but now I was quite sure that he knew all about my pictures.

'What were you doing there?'

He gave me an obdurate look. I glanced down and saw the scalpel in his right hand embedded in a morass of tendon and cartilage. I looked quickly at his face again and held his gaze.

'That's none of your business, Mr Cameron. You attend to *your* business and I'll attend to mine.'

Leaving the mortuary by the back door, I plunged into the lane where the stallholders and their customers jostled one another. I found a stall selling old clothes and bought a pair of trousers and a shirt and a jacket and a pair of shoes and socks.

When I stopped at the crossing before the bridge, I saw Tommy waiting for me on the other side of the road.

'Did you catch the one that did it?' he asked when I crossed.

'No, but we will.'

Oddly, I believed this to be true.

'What's that?' he asked, pointing to the package of clothes under my arm.

'I'll tell you later.'

He fell into step beside me and we walked the rest of the way to the hotel in silence. When we got there, I told him to wait outside. I hurried up to my room and laid the new photographs on the table.

'Where are we going?' he asked when I rejoined him in the street.

I wondered whether to tell him the truth and decided not to. 'Wait and see.'

We walked two blocks to a large sandstone building I had spotted the first morning, when Macarthur and the professor took me on a guided tour of the murder scenes.

I made to climb up the steps and Tommy came to an abrupt stop on the pavement.

'Come on!' I said.

'Why?'

'Because you smell,' I said.

'Well, that's not my fault.'

'I know. That's why we're here. You don't *have* to smell.'

He thought for a moment and then, with the sober expression of a businessman who has decided, after due consideration, to make a substantial investment, he began to climb the stairs.

I placed three pennies on the wooden counter and stood to one side to let the attendant see Tommy. 'He's to be thoroughly washed,' I said.

'He with you?' the man asked suspiciously.

'Yes.'

'Anything goes missing, you'll be responsible?'

'I will,' I said. 'I'll wait for him here.'

'Wullie!' the attendant called. A moment later a squat middle-aged man in white clothes appeared in the lobby; he had the bearing of a soldier and the businesslike manner of a medical orderly.

'Take this one and give him the works,' the attendant said. 'He's with this gentleman.'

Wullie looked at me and then at Tommy and shrugged.

Before the two of them disappeared into the interior, from which could be heard the sounds of men and boys laughing and from which emanated a vapour of chlorine and salts, I handed Wullie the package of clothes I'd bought at the street market.

When Tommy emerged three quarters of an hour later he did not quite look like a new man but he did look different. In his rags he had had the appearance of a particularly noxious sprite, something not quite substantial though powerfully malodorous. Now he looked like a little boy.

'Good as new, sir,' Wullie announced, as though Tommy had been laundered and pressed.

Tommy glanced up at the man with an expression that seemed to me to convey a proper indignation at being presented like a basket of laundry.

I took him from the public bath to the public house, which, in his newly 'respectable' state, he was able to enter. The barman hardly glanced at Tommy as I led him to a corner of the room. He did not recognise him as the same boy who had arrived breathlessly the previous afternoon to summon me back to Crown Street. It was midmorning by now and the place was busy. I ordered two cheese and ham sandwiches for Tommy and a small glass of beer for each of us.

'How do they make it round?' Tommy asked.

He was holding his glass up and looking at it as at a thing of wonder. He appeared transfixed not by the colour or texture of the beer but by the shape and transparency of the receptacle in which it was served. I wondered if he had ever held a drinking glass in his hands before.

'I don't know.'

Perhaps by furnishing Tommy with clean clothes and a bath and a breakfast I had upset his universe.

'Where do you live?'

He shrugged.

'Who do you live with?'

'Depends.'

'What do you mean?'

He looked at me over the top of his glass. His expression was intensely unhappy. He turned his attention to his sandwiches, which he began eating in a systematic, preoccupied way.

'Thank you,' he said when he had finished. I gathered that this *thank you* was also designed as a kind of apology for his refusal to tell me more about his family or his circumstances.

When we came out into the street, Tommy blinked in the sunlight. His appearance seemed to change in unexpected ways. In the bar he had aped the manners of the men around him, but standing in the street now in his new clothes, he looked peculiarly vulnerable. In his rags he had been somehow *of* his environment. I hoped I had not done him a terrible disservice.

We began to walk in the direction of the hotel.

'Why don't you go to school?' I asked.

He glanced at me suspiciously.

'I want to visit your school,' I said. 'For my work.'

'What's your work?'

'I'm a photographer.'

'What's that?'

'I make photographs.'

'What's photographs?'

'You know, the pictures you see in the newspaper.'

'Do you work for the newspaper?'

'No.'

'Do you work for the police?'

'Sort of.'

'What do you mean?'

'Well, I'm helping them.'

'Why?'

'Because they want to find the murderer.'

I didn't like saying the word 'murderer' here. I felt inclined to glance around and make sure the person being referred to wasn't within earshot.

'They willnae catch him,' Tommy said dismissively.

'Why's that?'

'Because he can make himself disappear.'

'Nonsense,' I said. 'Now, let's go to the school.'

We approached from the opposite side of the road. The windows had been thrown open and we could hear the singsong recitation of multiplication tables and, from one classroom, the strains of what sounded like a hymn. This mingled with shouts of encouragement and complaint emanating from an organised game in the playground at the other end of the courtyard between the church and the school.

We had not reached the main school entrance, an arched double door set beneath a faux mediaeval architrave that looked rather out of place in the plain facade, when a man in a dark suit opened the door, moved forward onto the top step and shouted, 'Thomas Ogilvy, come here!'

The man shouted in a voice of innate authority yet his physical appearance was anything but magisterial. He was short and fat. We were twenty yards away and the aspect of the man's profile that caught and held the eye was his huge round stomach. It was encased in a black waistcoat from which hung a silver watch and chain.

As I was absorbing the singular manner and appearance of the man on the stairs and arriving at the conclusion that he was the headmaster, Tommy was, apparently, making a related but different series of assessments. His conclusions involved the urgent need to take evasive action. In the moments after he was summoned, Tommy turned and began to race hell for leather in the opposite direction. Watching him run like the wind and disappear around the first corner, it occurred to me that he never looked so much like the ragged urchin I had first encountered two mornings before than when he was in full flight from a perceived danger. The new clothes did not obscure the possibility of crisis that must have been ever-present in Tommy's world.

I scratched the back of my head and crossed the road.

'Good morning,' I said to the headmaster.

'Good morning.'

'I believe Tommy has been a pupil here.'

'May I know who you are?' he asked suspiciously.

I introduced myself and explained that I was working with the police. This did not appear to persuade the headmaster entirely of my bona fides.

'And what have you to do with Thomas Ogilvy?' he asked.

'He seems to have befriended me and I took the liberty of arranging for him to have a bath and a change of clothes. I was trying to find out why he does not come to school,' I added, 'just when you came out onto the steps.'

'But why have you taken an interest in him?' he persisted, slightly less blunt.

I raised my hands in a gesture of helplessness and said, 'I'm here for only a short time, but I'm not blind. I see how children like Tommy live. He attached himself to me and I responded in what I hope is a decent way.'

He scrutinised me closely and then he said, 'You are here to help solve the murders?'

I nodded.

'Then perhaps you will come inside.'

We walked through a broad entrance hall with a low ceiling. The interior of the building smelt of floor polish and sweat. There was a large crucifix at the end of the lobby and in the corner was an alabaster statue of the Virgin Mary in front of which fresh flowers had been arranged.

Perhaps the headmaster noticed me looking at this. 'May I ask where you are from?'

'Spain, by way of Cuba.'

'My goodness!' he said. Then he introduced himself. 'Gabriel Mahoney.'

Mahoney's office was a rather narrow room with an exceptionally high ceiling; the lower parts of the walls were panelled in cream-coloured wood and much of the floor space was taken up by a mahogany desk that was covered in books and papers.

The headmaster's manner became more agreeable the further we retreated into the interior of his school, so that by the time I was seated on the other side of his enormous desk he was gazing at me with an expression that was practically benign.

'Are you a policeman?' he asked.

'I'm a specialist in investigating homicides.'

'But why have you come from so far away? Don't we have specialists of this sort here in Glasgow?'

'I have a particular technical expertise. I was invited to contribute to the investigation.'

'And have you contributed?'

Before I could answer, he raised his voice and shouted, 'Elsie! Bring us a pot of tea!'

It occurred to me that he bore a striking resemblance to Professor MacKay. Not a physical resemblance but a similarity in manner. Both were direct and confident. And both worked behind huge mahogany desks that were deluged with paper.

Over tea and a piece of cake, which was served to me like a benediction by a thin and rather grim-looking woman who must have been at least twenty years older than the headmaster, we spoke about crime in general and the recent murders in particular.

Throughout, I avoided telling Mahoney the exact nature of my work.

'The first two murders didn't attract attention,' he said. 'It wasn't until the third that the horrible pattern became clear. Do you think the murderer is a butcher by trade, perhaps?'

'That would certainly be something that one might suppose,' I said.

He looked at me with a disappointed expression.

'You mean, you think our man might be a butcher?' he persisted.

'I suppose so.'

'Well, what have you found out by now?'

I raised my hands and shook my head. 'I can't talk about details, I'm afraid.'

'Och!' he said, glancing out the window. 'Here's what I believe. I believe the murderer *knows* us.'

'Us?'

'Can you credit that the police haven't been to see me! You'd think I might have an idea as to what's happening in my own community!'

'You mean the district?'

He looked at me patiently and said, 'You are a foreigner, Mr Cameron. What do foreigners do when they arrive somewhere new? They stick together.'

'You think the killer is Irish?'

'I think the killer *knows* this community.'

'Why?'

'Because each of the victims has had something in common.'

'And what is that?'

'They were all suffering from some sort of illness, the sort that, after last year, inspires a great deal of fear.'

I put down my cup.

'The plague!' he said, giving me a little indignant nod. His jowls quivered for a moment or two. 'Yes, sir! Here in the greatest power on earth! Plague!'

'And you believe these people were suffering from the disease?'

'They were all suffering from *some* sort of disease.'

'But why on earth would he cut off his victims' limbs?'

'Some variety of vile experiment?'

I had been in Madrid during an outbreak of cholera. I remembered the hysteria. Contagion is a universal threat. Panic causes people to react in bizarre and ugly ways.

'How do you know the victims were ill?' I asked.

'Because these are *my* people.'

'I'm not sure the police are aware that they all had illness in common,' I remarked indiscreetly.

'Of course they're not!' he replied, slamming his hand down on the desk. 'Because they haven't been to speak to *me*.'

When he had decided that we had nothing more to discuss on the subject of the murders, he changed tack and said, 'Do you think you can help me with Thomas Ogilvy?'

'I will certainly try.'

He gave me a sceptical look.

'You see, it's no good just giving him a new suit of clothes,' he continued. 'He has to be reeled in, and I'm not sure he hasn't got past that stage by now.'

'He wouldn't tell me where he lives.'

'Why did you want to know that?'

I shrugged. 'I suppose if I am to help him I should know something of his family circumstances.'

'He lives in a hovel near the river with a woman that I do not believe is his mother. She isn't fit to take care of him.'

I gave him a quizzical look.

'She hasn't been sober since she got off the Belfast boat.'

'Why did he run away just now?' I asked.

The headmaster sat back in his chair, so that his stomach seemed to rise up like the hide of a hippopotamus breaking through the surface of an African pond. He expelled a great sigh and threw out his hands before retracting them and allowing them to settle on his belly.

'The other children have been unkind. Tommy advertises his presence in the most unpleasant way before he actually appears, as I think you have noticed.'

'Well,' I said, 'I've had him scrubbed and turned out in new clothes. Couldn't that have been done before?'

'Oh, it *has* been done – repeatedly – but, Mr Cameron,

let's see how long the effects of your charitable endeavour will last. He will return tonight to sleep in a hole infested with rats and lice.'

'But can't something be done?'

'If something *could* be done it *would* have been done.'

'But he ran away just now,' I said. 'I believe he was frightened.'

'Tommy believes that if he comes back to school he might be sent to a home for vagrant boys – and that's certainly not a place where any right-thinking human being would like to be sent.'

'And will that be his fate?'

The headmaster raised his hands again and sighed once more and said, 'I honestly do not know.'

When I left the school there was no sign of Tommy. I walked back to the hotel and began to work on the photographs from Mr Presser's office.

I had removed my jacket and rolled up my sleeves. I opened the windows. The sound of trams and carts and singsong voices wafted into the room.

I looked at the first photograph briefly before dissecting it with my wooden frame. I saw a man of about twenty standing next to the policeman in the island in the middle of the intersection. He had the 'likely' look of an individual for whom each day brings new possibilities. He was smartly dressed, in a three-piece suit. I could see that his shoes were polished. He stood with his hands on his hips, pushing back the folds of his jacket. His expression was thoughtful, as though he were still trying to assess the significance of whatever it was he was looking at. The policeman standing next to him was gazing in a completely different direction, but I sensed that the two men had spoken to one another, even if only to exchange greetings. They stood in the companionable way of men who are accustomed to pass time in the same place. The young man wore a grey cap; he had a neatly trimmed moustache and small lively eyes that watched the world with shrewdness and optimism, waiting for the main chance. That at least is what I concluded as I marked him loafing in the centre of the photograph.

Now, after two days, I believed I understood more about this young man; I understood his familiarity with the terrible ugliness that existed just a block away; I understood that in the endless array of shipyards and factories spread out along the river, a man like this would never want for opportunity. He was at the centre of a thrusting, grasping, building, booming world. He had the capacity to prosper.

Why did he attract my attention? I suppose because he and any one of the men in the pictures could have been the killer. I was no closer to identifying a possible suspect. I was in the process of *failing*.

Yet I must persist.

I breathed the air that flowed like a river through the open window, and I began to examine each of the sections.

When I had finished I had established several things about the world below Mr Presser's office.

The first was that the policeman who surveyed his little kingdom, speaking to all sorts who passed by on the island in the middle of the traffic, was not always imperturbable. He became agitated at half past three, not because a member of the public had impinged upon his magisterial immobility but because two other policemen had engaged him in conversation.

More properly, I think, they had accosted him. One of the officers poked a finger into his fellow officer's chest. I could see the aggressive expression on the finger-poking officer's face. I could almost see the spittle that must have emanated from his mouth as he made his point. The first policeman's expression was one of indignation and denial.

William Harrison watched this altercation from his habitual stance outside his shop, though in the next picture, forty-five minutes later, he had abandoned his post. I wondered if this was connected to the argument between the constables. There was a black pram outside the chemist's shop so I thought it more likely that he had gone inside to serve the woman who belonged to the pram.

To my surprise – though why I should have been surprised, I could not really have said – I saw Gabriel Mahoney making his portly way round the opposite side of the intersection, past the dry-salter. He was smoking a white clay pipe and carrying a valise. I also spotted the clergyman, heading to the north side of the river after a day spent ministering to the poor.

There was no sign of Tommy in any of the photographs. It occurred to me that, forty-eight hours before, if my camera had captured Tommy running among the pedestrians, or flitting between trams and omnibuses and carts, I might have found the image arresting, perhaps even charming. I would have considered it picaresque.

At half past three I completed the last entry in my notebook and placed the photographs neatly in a file on the desk.

I took an omnibus to the West End.

Alan Fletcher had documented the scandal of the city's slums. He had produced a portrait of these places that could not be ignored. If the pen is mightier than the sword, then the camera is at least as mighty, I thought, watching the city pass before me from the top of the number 22 bus.

Five minutes earlier than the time appointed, I presented myself at the Fletchers' villa. I rang the bell and Jane came to the door. When I stepped inside, I stepped into an enchanted world. *Her* world.

CHAPTER NINETEEN

'I'm early,' I said, displaying my now customary and still disconcerting capacity to state the obvious.

'We'll let it pass!' She began to laugh.

I followed her into a large sitting room where the walls were covered in brilliantly coloured canvases.

'Perhaps I could bring you a glass of wine?'

'Thank you,' I said. 'You could.'

Whoever heard of anyone assent to the offer of a glass of wine with the words *you could*!

'Or perhaps something stronger, a brandy, or a whisky?' she suggested.

'No, really, wine would be very nice. Will you have some too?'

'Since it's a special occasion, I might!'

When the wine came, it was brought by a tall, stately gentleman.

'I'm Alan Fletcher,' he said. 'You must be Señor Camarón!'

After we had shaken hands and he had poured a glass for each of us, he asked me about my business in Glasgow.

'I'm helping the police with their enquiries.'

'Are you indeed!'

I began to explain.

'I *told* you what Juan was doing,' Jane said, coming into the room with two more glasses. She held them in front of her uncle and he filled them.

Alan Fletcher was dressed conventionally, in a light grey suit with a white shirt and a silver tie. But his manner was more bohemian than bourgeois. His iron grey moustache was flowing rather than clipped and his hair, swept back over his forehead, had been allowed to grow long.

'Do you use polysulphide?' he asked when I described the technique for making multiple exposures on a single plate.

'I have in the past, but as a rule I favour sodium sulphide.'

He considered this for a moment. 'I like a matt finish, don't like the jigsaw look of a fine finish.'

'In my case, detail is the essence,' I said.

Mary Fletcher came into the room. She was younger than her husband. She had been a great beauty once. Her expression was anxious but kind. Her long hair was tied with a lemon ribbon and her white summer dress was drawn in at the waist with a pale yellow waistband.

She gave me a tentative smile. Lifting the remaining glass of wine from the table beside the sofa, she sat down next to me.

'You're Professor MacKay's friend,' she began.

'Well, as a matter of fact we're not friends as such. I was proposed for the work I'm now doing and Professor MacKay is . . . well, he and Sergeant Macarthur . . .' I wasn't sure if they knew who Sergeant Macarthur was.

I felt myself sinking into a conversational morass.

'Professor MacKay is involved in Juan's murder case,' Jane said, rescuing me and making the murder case mine. 'The professor has become involved because of the pathology. They're trying to find motives in what remains of the bodies.'

Mary nodded and then, circumventing the prospect of a conversation about corpses, she said, 'MacKay's a conscientious man,' adding after a moment, 'and he's had his share of troubles.'

'Troubles?' Jane asked.

'His wife's brother died last year, in that terrible business. He was walking in the street when he was hit by a steam engine!'

'That man was a relative of Professor MacKay?' Jane asked.

Mary nodded. 'And they have their hands full with their daughter.' She put her hand up to her mouth and said, 'I am gossiping!'

'The daughter?' I asked.

'No, I've spoken out of turn!'

'Mary is too squeamish,' Alan said with an edge of sarcasm that sliced through the air. 'The girl has run off with a policeman.'

'Alan!'

'She's engaged, I believe, to the sergeant who is working with you,' Alan told me, ignoring his wife's indignation.

I remembered Macarthur's ambiguous presence at dinner with Harrison and MacKay, the way he took charge when the professor was too drunk to go home by himself.

'I suppose the family has come to terms with the match,' Mary said.

'But what's wrong with the match?' I asked, my curiosity easily sailing beyond whatever the bounds of propriety in this household might be.

'Well, to start with he's from a different background,' Alan said, 'and, if I'm not mistaken, a different persuasion too.'

I wasn't sure if Alan was amused because these issues seemed trivial to him or because the subject had upset his wife.

In any case, he changed the subject. 'I suppose detail *would* be the essence,' he said to me, 'if you're out to identify a murderer.'

'Oh dear!' Mary said. She glanced at me and then looked at her husband with an exasperated expression. 'Why are you talking about murder!'

One of the things I had found most remarkable about Effie and Robert McClellan when I met them in Cuba was the way in which they interacted with each other. They were so well matched that when I thought about them I thought about them both. They seemed like two parts of the same whole. I had not been with Mary and Alan Fletcher more than a few minutes before I reached the conclusion that they had not been blessed with this happy compatibility.

'But isn't it *boring*?' Alan asked, ignoring his wife. 'The same picture day after day?'

'It's *painstaking*,' I said. 'I'm identifying patterns. There are patterns that only reveal themselves slowly, and only reveal themselves in the kind of pictures that I make.'

'What sort of patterns?'

'Don't quiz him,' Mary said sharply.

'Perhaps he's onto something!' Alan replied, raising his shoulders and holding out his hands, palms up in a gesture of mock innocence.

214

'He *is* onto something,' Jane said, drawing Alan and Mary away from an awkward confrontation.

'What sort of patterns?' he repeated, facing me again. Mary looked at him with annoyance but then turned to me and waited to hear what I had to say.

'Every day, two policemen work for a very long shift at the junction between Crown Street and the river,' I began. 'The policemen are the focus of much that happens in the square. Everyone can see them and they can see everyone. Normally they're a sort of pillar of order in the middle of the traffic, but yesterday one of the policemen had an argument with two colleagues. In a strange way, the pillar seemed to collapse.'

I felt I had been obscure.

There was silence. Alan glanced at Jane and then said to me, 'So you don't expect to catch your man; you want to understand his world!'

'Let's go into the garden,' Jane said.

The garden stretched for twenty yards, making it deeper than it was broad. It was bordered by a high stone wall with a bevelled top. The stone was finely pointed and the undulations of the surface melded with beech trees and climbing plants. We sat in the middle of the lawn beneath a canvas awning of yellow and white stripes. A girl of about twenty, dressed in a light blouse and skirt and with her long hair over her shoulders, served lemonade. When the girl first appeared, Jane spoke to her in French.

'Agnès is visiting from Normandy,' Mary explained. Then she added unhappily, 'Alan is teaching her to paint.'

For several moments everyone looked at their lemonade.

'And if you understand your murderer's world,' Alan said, 'does that help you?'

215

'Perhaps it doesn't get as far as "understanding",' I said. 'It's more a matter of sensing a pulse, and when there's a change in the beat, then that may be the place to start looking for a way into the mystery.'

'*Sors-tu du gouffre noir ou descends-tu des astres?*' Alan said. '*Le Destin charmé suit tes jupons comme un chien; tu sèmes au hasard la joie et les désastres, et tu gouvernes tout et ne réponds de rien.*'

Mary made a sound with her tongue and her teeth to indicate irritation.

'Baudelaire,' Alan said by way of explanation. 'The passions have a habit of surfacing and they reveal themselves in surprising ways.'

'Sometimes it's not even passion: simply a deviation from the norm. Murder, after all, isn't an everyday event.'

'To solve a murder you must look for a motive, no?'

'I suspect that some murderers might be surprised by their own motives,' I said. 'A man might kill another man because he believes he's been cheated, but really the crime comes from a different place. Perhaps he kills because he's been rejected or humiliated, perhaps even in a trivial way – and his victim is simply the person who happened to be on hand at the right time.'

'Oh dear!' Mary said, and put her hand up to her mouth.

Alan took a sip of lemonade. 'Last year, we had plague here – an outbreak of bubonic plague.'

I was struck by how this epidemic had affected these people. They spoke of it with a kind of awe and, perversely, almost with a kind of pride. It was something that bound them together.

'More than a dozen died and most of them were in the district where these murders are taking place. Can you imagine! Plague! We have created a modern Hades; we have *re*created a mediaeval bedlam, where the most vile scourge of primitive society preys upon the poor. I think perhaps your killer has all manner of reasons to be angry.'

Jane sat very straight, her back not touching the back of the chair, her skin translucent in the sunlight refracted through the awning.

'My uncle believes that violence has been woven into our way of life,' she said. 'Even if we solve one despicable crime, there will be another to take its place.'

Mary stood up. 'It's very hot,' she said. 'I'm going inside.'

Alan stood too, still with his glass in his hand. 'Everything that we have,' he said, 'our lemonade, and our garden, and our money in the bank, it all comes from the great machine that *makes* things. It's the machine that shapes and distorts life – all our lives. Surely that's the evil.'

He followed his wife up to the house.

'I don't understand,' I said for a second time. I wondered at my utter lack of self-possession. I was silent for a moment and then I added, 'Your uncle's photographs have helped to change things for the better.'

'He no longer believes that. He has lost faith in progress. He believes the only response to atrocities like the ones you are investigating is to look away and contemplate things that are beautiful.'

We sat again in silence. Finally, I asked, 'Do *you* believe that?'

'Of course not! But the question is: what are we to do?'

I slipped my pocket watch from my waistcoat.

'When must you go back?' she asked.

The hour that followed was different from all the hours that went before.

I remember the intricate pattern of shadows on the surface of the garden wall. I remember knowing that if I should ever turn and face the shadows of my past I should do it now, because now I was in the presence of a kindred soul.

'In Cuba,' I said, 'there were some who believed that all of society's ills could be cured if the island broke away from Spain.'

'Did you think that?'

'No. I never imagined it would actually break away and I never thought that if that happened it would solve every problem. There were rich and poor in Cuba. There are rich and poor in every country – I didn't see how leaving Spain would alter that. It wasn't because of Spain that the poor in Cuba were poor. They haven't stopped being poor since the country broke away.'

'What was it like in Santiago?' she asked. 'We read about it in the newspapers. We were desperate to hear news, of course, because of Aunt Effie and Uncle Robert but I cannot imagine what it was really like to be in a city under siege.'

'We got there just before the Americans completed their encirclement.' I shook my head. 'I still cannot believe we chose that very time to go there, but then I still cannot believe we chose that very time to travel to Cuba in the first place. My father had an infinite store of optimism. When things went wrong he simply assumed they would come right in the end. That's the thinking that took us to Cuba.'

'I like this way of thinking!' she said. Then she asked again about Santiago.

'Towards the end it was very bad. There was no law, a free-for-all.'

Jane stood up and poured lemonade. I could smell canvas and grass. The lemonade swirled and tinkled in the glass.

'We stayed with a cousin of my father. A dispute had arisen over a legacy. This surprised my father. His title was clear. He was the sort of man who *would* be surprised by such things. All he really cared about was taking photographs.'

'Ah,' she said gently. 'So it runs in *your* family too.'

'He went out one morning. The cathedral had been damaged by artillery. He was close to the end of his work in Cuba, and he was afraid that the shelling would make it impossible to finish. I was unable to join him immediately.'

I took another sip of lemonade. 'I was delayed before I left the house. And then, after I'd gone out to join my father I was delayed again . . . there were difficulties. When I reached the square my father was dead. He had been shot through the heart. Soon after I arrived in the square, my father's cousin appeared and we took the body to be buried.'

'I'm very sorry,' she said softly and earnestly. I felt as though she had taken my hand.

I filled my pipe with some of the tobacco that Tommy had bought for me the day before.

'Paco kept repeating how sorry he was that he hadn't arrived earlier, that he hadn't been able to help my father.'

I lit the pipe and looked across the garden to the sunlit patterns on the wall.

'The last thing my father did before he was killed was to close the shutter of the side-strut Eclipse. I developed his photographs the next day. There were two images. Paco appeared in one of them, standing in a corner of the frame. He was next to a man with a rifle. In the second picture the man with the rifle had climbed onto a terrace by the cathedral and he was pointing his weapon at my father.'

CHAPTER TWENTY

I had begun to speak about Santiago and I wanted to finish my account. But at that moment Mary Fletcher hurried into the garden and interrupted us.

'You must speak to Agnès!' she told Jane. Then, distraught and in a breaking voice, she turned briefly to me and said, 'I'm sorry, Mr Cameron! I'm sorry to disturb you like this!'

In this way, we ended our afternoon in the garden. I took my leave quickly and awkwardly, Mary still hovering in the background to accompany Jane to whatever domestic crisis had occurred.

I travelled back on the top deck of an omnibus, looking out at the tenements and coming to terms with the fact that in some mysterious way my entire consciousness had shifted.

In my mind's eye, I re-examined each expression on Jane's face as I began to tell her everything that happened in Cuba.

I pored over this as if it were a photograph, repeated endlessly, each tiny frame compared against the others.

The air had become less balmy and the edge of a north-easterly breeze began to chill the afternoon as the bus approached the centre of town. I considered going down to the lower deck, but I was too preoccupied to move from my brooding perch on top. I had begun to develop a headache by the time we reached the river.

Leaving the bus at the top of Crown Street, I walked back to Harrison's shop.

The chemist was standing, as I knew from my photographs he liked to do, on the pavement outside. He held his hands behind his back, his expression genial and sad at the same time. He gave the impression of a man standing behind an invisible counter. His name was inscribed above the window behind him in solid block letters, and the pavement before him seemed to be a natural extension of his business premises.

'I'm in need of some aspirin powder,' I said.

'Mr Cameron!' He looked at me astutely. 'Where is the pain?'

'A headache. Nothing serious. I travelled on the top of the omnibus.'

'Ah,' he said, 'on summer evenings that's just the way!'

I followed him into the shop.

The interior was large. Two walls were entirely taken up with mahogany shelves on which were stacked every possible variety of remedy and potion and poultice. Harrison walked round the counter and back along the other side. I leant on the marble top and, to my surprise and initial consternation, Harrison leant over and brought his face close to mine so that our noses were almost touching.

'Mr Cameron,' he said, 'it won't do any harm if I take a wee look at the optical epithelium.'

I wondered if he used this medical terminology as a means of establishing his credentials as a physician, or perhaps he simply considered it a courtesy to explain himself with a certain amount of technical precision.

'If you'll permit me . . .' he said, raising his hand and placing his index finger and thumb above and below my right eye. He held the eye open and peered. When he was satisfied, he repeated this exercise with my left eye.

'Sometimes when the body ails, Mr Cameron, it has a strange way of telling us where the problem lies.'

He withdrew his hand and lowered his gaze a fraction. 'Mouth.'

I opened my mouth and he peered inside.

'Not a chill, Mr Cameron. You have reacted to our Glasgow air. The coal dust has tickled your throat, which is normal enough, and irritated the cornea, which is a little less so. The miasmas in these parts can be very unwelcoming.' He took a step back. 'I would recommend a course of guaic tincture. If that meets with your approval I'll have my sister make it up.'

I nodded and he walked to the end of the counter and spoke through an aperture in the wall.

A moment later, Jeanie Harrison appeared through a door at the very end of the room. She was carrying a large white sack, the sort that builders use to carry sand or cement. Though it looked heavy, Jeanie seemed to manage the weight with relative ease. She swung the sack round and placed it against the counter near her brother. She called across the room to me, 'Good evening, Mr Cameron, I'm sorry you're out of sorts. I'm afraid we won't have the compound until later this evening.'

'Shall I bring it round to the hotel?' William suggested.

'No, no, I'll be passing again. I'll drop in before ten.'

When I emerged from Harrison's shop, the shadows had begun to deepen. As I passed Mr Presser's bank and turned into Crown Street, I shivered.

The street stretched before me. I could just make out the white facade of Simpson's Hotel in the distance. Even though the tenements on either side of me were built no more than twenty years before, there was something *ancient* about this place. Perhaps it was the sense of fear – in my imagination and behind these walls – perhaps it was this that was old.

Bessie Armstrong and Hector MacKinnon had been found on the steps of the bank, and then Willie McGonagall, dismembered and abandoned in the courtyard behind Bailey's Bar. Further along, one on the same side as the bar and the other in the close opposite, Brendan Gillespie and Maggie McAllister; then the attempted murder of Edie Hamilton, and finally Seamus Hanlon, a block from my hotel.

I walked where the murderer walked. He had moved up and down this street carrying body parts and no one saw a thing. Even when the whole neighbourhood was electric with attention, he had gone unnoticed.

I *must* have captured him in a photograph.

Gibson looked up from behind the reception desk. He seemed to be better. There was some colour in his cheeks.

In my room I extracted the three plates from the camera and put them into my satchel and left again.

It was around half past eight when I arrived at the mortuary. The front door was locked.

I rang the bell and waited, surveying the street. A handful of carts trundled by, their drivers slouched forward lazily. There were few pedestrians, a handful of drunks. The drunkenness was of a catastrophic variety. I watched a man execute a crazy zigzag progress along the street, lifting his feet high as though climbing a steep hill, raving obscenities and daring horses and carts to run him over. No one came near. Drunkenness and poverty seemed to be tattooed into the city's skin.

'I didn't expect you quite so soon,' Billy said as he opened the heavy door of the mortuary.

I stepped past him into the lobby.

'I'm just finishing up,' he continued. 'I won't be more than a minute.'

We walked together into the dissection room.

'Oh!' I said.

I had feared that one of the tables might have been occupied. I had not imagined that all three would contain corpses and that two additional corpses would be laid out on the tiled floor.

Robert stood over one of the cadavers on the floor. It appeared to be that of a diminutive and very old woman. I could see quite clearly the thin white hair on her skull and the shrunken jaw. She was only partially covered by her shroud.

Robert glanced at me and then said to Billy, 'We've finished all the formaldehyde.'

'There's more in the developing room,' Billy replied, and his assistant moved away from the table; his apron was smeared with blood and gristle.

Billy turned to me and said, 'I have one more picture to

225

finish and then you may have the run of my facilities.'

He was looking at me to gauge my reaction to the plethora of death.

'There has been some sort of incident?' I asked, trying hard to speak casually.

'There has.'

'What happened?'

'A houseboat overturned near Glasgow Green.'

'And all these people drowned! Was no one able to help them?'

He shrugged. 'Maybe they weren't liked.'

Robert came out of the developing room carrying a large stone jar from which he had already removed the cork. Billy hurried around me in order to get to the door first.

'Wait just a moment. I'm finishing the last of the plates, the father of the family,' he said, walking ahead of me into the developing room.

When he said 'the father of the family', he glanced at the nearest dissection table, on which lay a male cadaver. The sight of a human body laid upon a stone slab like a meat carcass is innately jarring. But I composed my thoughts and looked from the body's feet to its shoulders.

At the neck some primitive instinct caused me to hesitate, but I forced myself to move on to the face, as though passing over an invisible barrier.

I gasped and took a step backward, very nearly standing on top of Billy.

'What's the matter?' he asked with a momentary edge of impatience.

'I know that man!' I whispered.

'How's that?'

'He's the landlord of the public house near my hotel!'

'Is that so?' Billy said without emotion. 'They said he was a barman but no one could tell me where.'

We heard the familiar tinkle of a timer bell. Billy opened the door of the developing room and said, 'I'll let you in in a moment.'

I walked to the table where the landlord lay. I had been in his bar. Yet this very fleeting connection impressed itself upon me. The corpse on the slab was not simply a corpse but a man I'd spoken to just a few hours before.

I looked down at the stretched white face, the moustache grizzled, the mouth set contentedly. Sometimes people remark on how peaceful the dead look. This man wore an expression of satisfaction, as though he had closed his public house at the end of a profitable day.

'There you are now, Mr Cameron,' Billy said.

I looked round quickly. Billy was right beside me.

'The room's ready.'

When I closed the door, I felt as though I was aboard an elaborate contraption – like Mr Wells' Time Machine – that could exist entirely separate from the world.

I took out the plates and placed them on the table and began to unscrew the frames. Billy had prepared the developing fluid. I sniffed the liquid in the dish and I could tell that he had added potassium, exactly replicating the solution I had prepared two days earlier. Billy was extraordinarily alert to the habits of others.

I dimmed the lamp and placed the paper in the solution. The familiar contours of Crown Street began to emerge. I looked up from the picture in the dish and stared ahead at the dark wall. I thought about the drowned family in the next room, and beside me in the darkness I felt the presence of a demon, a tangible despair.

I looked at the picture of the long deep street filled with wandering souls. I thought about my father. He might have been one of these, walking purposefully past the bar and the grocer's shop on his way to document a fine facade. My father believed in the goodness of men and women. I remembered his own goodness now, but the memory was bitter. He had been made a victim of spite and avarice and greed.

I lifted the first photograph out of the tray and I saw the figure of the minister walking into Crown Street.

'Do you know this man?' I asked Billy when I came out of the developing room. I showed him an image in which the minister was striding south.

By presenting this photograph for Billy's inspection, I dispensed with the last vestige of discretion about the purpose of my photography. Discretion had not by now delivered any benefits, as far as I could see.

Having made what might turn out to be a misguided commitment, I delved even deeper, and showed him another photograph, later in the sequence when the minister was returning in the opposite direction.

Billy showed no sign of surprise at being invited to inspect my work. I could not decide whether this was an indication of tact or contempt. Rather than expressing astonishment (that might have been feigned or genuine), he focused his energy on reacting to the content of the image.

'It's the minister,' he said.

'*Which* minister?'

He frowned and appeared to search his memory for a name

or some other piece of information that might be supplied, and I was reminded of Gibson when he had tried to extort money on my first afternoon at the hotel.

'I cannae mind.'

'All right!' I snapped, snatching the photograph back.

'Haud yer horses, Mr Cameron,' Billy said. 'I cannae mind his name but I'll tell ye where ye can find him.'

'And where would that be?'

'The Free Church in Rose Street.'

Outside, I walked along the northern bank of the river and crossed the bridge to the square, where not one but two policemen were on duty. Harrison's was the only shop still open. A bell tinkled as I entered.

Jeanie stood in the doorway that led to the room where the medicines were prepared. Instead of coming to greet me she disappeared into the interior. I heard the sound of voices from within and then she returned carrying a small white paper bag.

'Here it is, Mr Cameron. I do hope you will feel better soon.'

She handed me the bag and I asked how much I had to pay.

'William,' she shouted into the back shop, 'how much is Mr Cameron's mixture?'

He came out of the back room, drying his hands on a towel. 'That'll be thruppence ha'penny,' he said in the apologetic but firm tone that shopkeepers use, as though the matter of payment is an awkward obstacle that friends sometimes have to climb over.

Harrison was half a head shorter than his sister and perhaps five years younger. He had the curious air of a man who has, indefinably, managed to fail in life yet remain in possession of his livelihood; she was more self-possessed.

Outside, I was surprised at the number of people still about. There were groups of adults near the public houses; children, some of them very small, played or loitered at a distance from these groups, attached to them in some way; pedestrians passed in both directions and I wondered if there was a level of activity after dark that involved things best not done in the daylight. I did not see any streetwalkers. I *did* see men carrying sacks and boxes. Just a block from the hotel, I witnessed what looked like the entire contents of an apartment being removed to a waiting cart. This work was being done at speed by three men, who looked at me shiftily when they saw that I was watching them.

A man had murdered six people and amputated their limbs and no one on this busy street had seen anything.

I glanced over my shoulder. I had for several minutes been under the odd impression that not only was I taking a close interest in everything that was happening, but that someone was taking a close interest in me.

But, of course, no one near me looked like a killer.

'Mr Cameron, there is a message for you.'

Gibson handed me a note. His fingers were narrow and his fingernails were clean.

The writing was an unusual and intricate copperplate. The letter said, *Mr Cameron, I would be grateful if you would call on me when you are free to do so. I have something to tell you that may be of use in your investigation.* It was signed *Gabriel Mahoney.*

Gibson had come round from behind his desk. I wondered if he was trying to read the letter over my shoulder.

I crossed the lobby to the stairs.

The gas lamp on the first floor had gone out and I had to fumble in order to find the keyhole. Again I had the odd but unmistakable sensation of being watched. I looked along the corridor and saw only shadows.

Then, out of the darkness a figure advanced. I could not at first discern its actual size or shape, just the movement in the dark, rushing towards me.

I withdrew my fingers from the keyhole and took a step backward.

And at the same time I let out a relieved sigh. The figure hurrying along the corridor was familiar.

'What on earth are you doing here?' I asked.

Tommy had a more than usually solemn expression on his face. He put a finger to his lips and jerked his head towards the stairs. I gathered that he had sneaked into the hotel and intended to sneak out again. I had no doubt that he would be able to do this.

'I'm not going back to school,' he began.

'Why not?'

'They'll take me away.'

'Did they tell you that?'

He shrugged.

'The headmaster said you can come back and no one will take you away.'

This wasn't true, of course, but I had resolved to ensure that nothing would befall this little boy that was against his interest.

'What happened to your shirt?' I asked.

It was torn at the collar.

He looked down at the floorboards.

'Meet me at the bridge tomorrow morning at eight o'clock,' I said.

He nodded and began walking to the end of the corridor. I wondered if I should follow and see how he intended to exit the building. Then it occurred to me that he would know better than I how to do this and much else.

I reached down and turned the key. In my room I began to work.

All of them were there, the characters I had come to recognise: the policeman, the minister, the chemist, the publican, the carter, the dry-salter, the grocer, the men and women who carried things and pushed things and pulled things and dragged things up and down the street; there were individuals dressed in bright summer clothes and others who wore heavy cotton and wool, too poor to change according to the season; some were in mourning, wearing light materials but all in black, and there was a multiplicity of headwear – straw boaters and bowler hats, boys' caps and men's caps and top hats and white cotton caps and veils for women and girls.

Perhaps I should have bought Tommy a cap. As this thought crossed my mind, I was assailed by a sense of sudden and utter hopelessness and shame.

I could not *buy* this little boy out of his ugly world. I could not simply dress him up like other children and send him back to school, a visitor with pennies to spend.

But I *had* pennies to spend. I could do no harm, I told myself, by doing kindness.

My father would have reasoned like that.

I arranged the photographs in sequence and began to examine them by means of the wooden grid.

Four hours later I had compiled a dozen pages of notes. I closed the ledger, put the photographs carefully into the file, undressed and got into bed.

About three o'clock in the morning I was awakened by the sound of raised voices. I climbed out of bed and walked to the window, careful not to show myself, but observing the scene outside from an oblique angle.

Three men were arguing. They looked about to come to blows. One in the middle tried to keep the other two apart. To my utter astonishment I recognised the two antagonists. One was William Harrison and the other was Jack Macarthur.

Macarthur glanced up at the window and I pulled back abruptly. They were in the street for another minute before Harrison went north towards his shop and Macarthur and the other man walked south. I watched them until I could no longer see them. A drunk man collapsed a block away and became motionless, sitting on the pavement and leaning against a wall with his head on one side. I returned to bed, but for a long time I could not sleep.

CHAPTER TWENTY-ONE

I woke at half past six, dressed and went downstairs.

Gibson got up from the sofa in the lobby, where he had slept, and walked through to the kitchen. I sat at the marble-topped table and after a few seconds Gibson returned with a tray on which was a coffee pot, a cup and saucer and a ham sandwich.

He was pale and drawn. I told him he looked unwell. He shrugged. 'Summer cold. It will pass.'

After breakfast, I lit my pipe and gazed through the gloom. Days of photography had yielded little, and the experiment was placed in a different light by the encounter I had witnessed from my window in the middle of the night.

I left the hotel at a quarter past seven and walked the length of Crown Street, already echoing to the distinctive bells and screeches of trams and omnibuses. Mr Presser was hurrying up the steps when I turned the corner and approached the bank. He greeted me coolly.

I thought I should reassure him that his contribution was valuable and that we were undoubtedly edging closer to solving the murders.

Though we were *not* edging closer. We were standing still and I was simply being a nuisance to Mr Presser.

'Another fine morning,' I said.

'It is,' he replied, without enthusiasm. He unlocked the accordion gate and drew it back enough to allow both of us to pass through.

I followed him into the interior of the empty bank. The high windows to the side and above the main entrance spread a pale city light on the marble and mahogany. When we climbed, we made the wooden staircase creak. This unmelodious noise seemed to violate the sanctity of the place.

Mr Presser unlocked his own office and I followed him inside. Before, he had been nervous but curious. Now he was withdrawn. I sensed that his change of manner was decisive.

'I won't be able to allow you the premises beyond today, Mr Cameron,' he said.

He had agreed to take part in the experiment with remarkable ease. At the time, I had thought this a great stroke of luck, but by now I knew that it wasn't luck.

I was sufficiently composed to pretend that I was stunned.

'I see,' I said, making a face that indicated that I didn't see.

'It's not that I don't wish to help,' he added hurriedly.

He explained that there were certain rules that, as an employee of the bank, he must observe, and although he had made an exception because it was a police matter and a matter that involved the public good, he could not make this exception indefinitely and therefore he believed that it was reasonable and right to terminate the arrangement as we were approaching the end of the week, and so on and so on.

I scanned the pictures and plaques on his wall and the books and ornaments on his large desk until my eye caught what I was looking for – it was a small bronze plaque fixed on a wooden plinth. It bore a square and a compass.

Mr Presser had not lent me his window because he was a public-spirited sort. He had cooperated because he was asked to do so by Jack Macarthur, and possibly also by William Harrison, both of whom, I had little doubt, shared with Mr Presser an allegiance to this or that ancient order.

My grandfather was an apostle of progress, a respectable, powerful conspirator like these men.

My father did not want to change the world – his only aspiration was to photograph beautiful buildings.

My father's legacy to me was a life of truth. He was an honest man.

I felt a tangle of lies around me now.

I extracted the three plates and put them in my satchel and then inserted fresh plates, checking the scene in front of the viewfinder. Everything was as it ought to be.

'I am sorry you won't help me further, Mr Presser,' I said, stressing, I suppose, the first person singular. 'I will collect the remaining images this evening, as per our original agreement, and I will remove my equipment then.'

There was no point in appealing to his sense of duty. His sense of duty was bound up elsewhere.

I bade him good morning and hurried down and out onto the square. Harrison was not at his post outside his shop.

Billy Fraser greeted me in his sly, watchful way and I hurried on past him to the developing room.

I had just one more day. And I was no closer to finding anything of value.

I watched the images appear and settle on the paper. William Harrison standing in front of his shop between a pram and a newspaper rack that was attended by a small boy in bare feet, a different policeman on points duty, a rare view of the dry-salter peering from his doorway as if the supply of customers had mysteriously dried up and he was looking out to enquire what the problem might be. I could see the sun shining on him, the breeze ruffling his hair. He looked a worried and unhappy man. Mr Presser too made a rare appearance in two of the photographs, walking from the bank at half past six and then, in the next image, walking south from the river. I wondered what had prompted his return.

'Making any progress?' Billy asked when I came out of the room, the photographs safely in my satchel.

I didn't reply.

'Have you been to see the minister?'

'Not yet.'

'Give him my regards when you do.'

'Yesterday you couldn't remember his name!'

He shrugged. 'I *cannae* mind his name. That's true, but he kens me well enough – he tried once to bring me back to my prayers. I told him I was too far gone in the devil's ways to think about repenting.'

Tommy was waiting for me outside. His clean clothes had become dirtier but standing downwind of him I was pleased to note that his old and evil odour had not yet returned.

'Can you run round to Harrison's and buy me a shaving brush?' I said. I gave him a sixpence and added, 'Meet me at the school. I have another interview with the headmaster.'

He looked obdurate. 'I'm not meeting you *there*.'

'There will be a penny change for the shaving brush. Do you want it?'

He nodded.

'Then meet me at the school.'

I watched him skip away along the riverbank and then I walked into the worst stretch of slum tenements.

I did not want to go into Harrison's myself because I was unsure how to proceed. What could I confront Harrison or Macarthur about? I could accuse them of conspiracy but I didn't know what the conspiracy was.

Tommy was already outside the school when I got there, which meant he had been to the chemist and covered twice the distance I had covered, and in less time.

'The lady asked me who the brush was for and I told her it was for you and she said to tell you that if you need any more of the medicine she'll make it up for you.'

I took the brush and examined it. The hairs were packed tight together and when I grazed it across the palm of my hand I felt its fine springy texture. I put it in my pocket.

Tommy held up the penny change.

'For you,' I said. 'Now, are you going to come inside with me?'

He looked down at the ground.

'Listen, if you go to school today, I'll have errands for you

238

when you finish this afternoon. That way you'll earn some money. No school, no errands.'

He thought for several seconds, not looking up from the ground, and then he raised his head and gave a huge shrug and indicated by means of a grimace and a glance in the direction of the school that he would submit, at least for a day.

I presented myself and Tommy at Gabriel Mahoney's office, where the headmaster greeted Tommy in a manner that I thought was just about pitch perfect, conveying a certain avuncular reassurance that nothing evil was about to befall the little man. At the same time he urged Tommy to ignore any scuttlebutt from the dimmer scholars.

Tommy was taken away by a lady in the dark uniform of the school's auxiliary staff.

'Thank you for bringing him back, Mr Cameron,' Mahoney began.

'I wish I could do more.'

He gave me a frank look that seemed to say: *If you wish to do more then why don't you?*

'You said in your note that you had something to tell me.'

'I told you yesterday that all the victims had been ill.'

I nodded.

'I received another visitor soon after you left: the policeman in charge of the case.'

'Sergeant Macarthur?'

'The same.'

'What did he want?'

'He wanted to know what you had been doing in my school. I told him exactly what transpired, Mr Cameron. I believe in telling the truth.'

He looked at me closely, as if deciding whether to trust me or not. Then he leant forward and said, 'I told him what I told you – that all of the victims had been ill.'

'And what did he say to that?'

'He instructed me not to speak of it to anyone.'

Back in my room I worked on the photographs. The appearance of the dry-salter caught my attention for no other reason than that it was unusual. He wore an apron and white cap and held a string bag of what looked to me like figs, while in his other hand was a key, which he raised towards the keyhole in the outside shutter of his shop.

CHAPTER TWENTY-TWO

I heard a knock and recognised it as Gibson's, not Annie's. I was becoming a part of my surroundings.

'A visitor for you, Mr Cameron,' he said.

I had removed my collar. I struggled with the stud for several seconds before I was able to put on my tie and jacket and go downstairs.

The study of repetitive photography is a curiously limiting discipline. The technique is premised on making detailed comparisons of minute collections of photographic material. Alan Fletcher was not the first person to ask me if it was boring. Oddly, it is *absorbing*. The technique draws the mind and the imagination into a tiny sphere but within that sphere there are infinite permutations. I had been inhabiting this constricted but complex world for two hours when Gibson interrupted me and I came down to the lobby.

My mind would have taken wing in any case, but so recently released from the shackles of my peculiar craft, it soared.

I actually felt the beating of my heart.

Standing by the reception, her eyes lowered in a polite, prim pretence of studying one of the pot plants, was Jane Macgregor.

She looked up when I reached the bottom of the stairs. I crossed the lobby in three strides and, as though it was the most natural thing in the world, I took her hand. She allowed her hand to be thus taken and made no effort to remove it from mine. We stood like this for several seconds.

'I wanted to speak to you more,' she said. 'I wanted to talk to you and we were not able to continue yesterday. I felt very bad.'

'Oh,' I said, utterly confounded by even the possibility that she should have experienced any sort of agitation on my account. 'Please don't feel bad! I wanted to talk to you more too.'

Gibson had taken up his usual position behind the reception desk and was watching our encounter as though he had paid for front-row seats in the music hall. I drew Jane to the other side of the lobby.

'I came because I might possibly be of some assistance,' she said. Her expression and her demeanour changed. She stood a little apart from me, her hands by her side, and she made a tiny bow.

Though she was in mourning – black skirt, black blouse, short black jacket – her appearance was strikingly elegant.

'I do want you to help me!' I said. I glanced around. I disliked the fact that she had to spend any time at all in this dingy place. I had left my photographs on the table and my notebook open beside them. It was my habit to pack everything away carefully when I went out, but even to leave her for a few seconds unescorted here was intolerable, so I said, 'I was just about to go out. Come with me.'

'Where are we going?' she asked as we stepped into the street.

'I think you can help me. We're going to see a minister.'

I explained what Billy Fraser had told me. 'This is his parish,' I said. 'Perhaps you could introduce me?'

'What makes you think *I* know this minister?' She spoke pointedly but when I glanced at her I saw that she was amused.

'Well . . .' I began. 'I thought . . . perhaps . . . since . . .'

'Since my aunt and uncle are missionaries?'

'Well, yes, actually.'

She started to laugh. 'Juan, you think we are all the same!'

'What do you mean?'

'My aunt and uncle are *Church of Scotland* missionaries!'

I didn't follow. 'Yes, so I thought you might have a . . .'

'But this minister is *Free* Church.'

I still didn't follow.

'It's altogether different, and anyway, what makes you think that I could help? I didn't say what denomination, if any, *I* belong to.'

'No, no . . .'

'My Uncle Alan is a freethinker and my Aunt Mary is an Episcopalian.'

'Yes, of course . . .'

She touched me gently on the arm and smiled. 'I think perhaps you look on us as some sort of strange exotic breed, one much the same as another!'

'No, no!'

Then she took my arm. 'I'm teasing!' she said. 'Let's go and meet the minister.'

Her step was slightly shorter than mine. I walked more slowly. Her scent was not French but something bracing and fresh, like heather.

'What are we going to ask the minister?'

'I'm not very sure,' I said.

She stepped away from me and said in mock astonishment, 'Juan Camarón, you are a singularly unprepared sort of foreigner!'

The church was just a block away from Simpson's Hotel and less than a hundred yards from Tommy's school. The heavy front door was locked and bolted.

'He'll no be here till efter,' said a voice from somewhere above us.

I had the curious and momentary notion that we were being addressed by some sort of angel speaking in a strong Glasgow accent.

Jane turned and crossed the road and spoke to a woman who was leaning out of a third-storey window. Jane's accent changed. I understood her perfectly when she spoke to me, but now I could catch only every other word. I gathered that she was explaining that we had to see the minister. The woman replied in a relaxed manner, speaking at some length, the cadence of her voice rising and falling and echoing in the street, which was so quiet, compared to Crown Street, that, standing on the steps of the church, I could hear pigeons cooing in the eaves high above me.

'The minister is Mr Buchan,' she told me when she returned from speaking to the woman. 'We are likely to find him at home. It's a bit of a walk, or would you prefer to take a tram?'

'Let's walk,' I said.

She nodded and smiled and then, when we began to move

244

away from the church, she set a brisk pace. The buildings on either side were very black and plain. In Crown Street the tenements had different kinds of ornament, but here the facades were austere.

There were just a handful of carts and cabs, but there seemed to be children everywhere; they stopped and stared at us as we passed.

'Strangers stand out,' Jane said, smiling brightly at a pair of barefoot girls who looked up at us as if transfixed, and followed us with solemn faces.

We reached the end of the street, where there was a long brick wall with broken glass fixed into a seam of concrete on top.

'Is it a prison?' I asked.

Jane smiled. 'No! The engine works.' She glanced at me. 'Railway engines.'

'And the glass at the top of the wall is to prevent anyone from climbing in and stealing one of the engines!'

She laughed.

We passed a huge gate and I saw, as I had seen by the river, a railway line coming out of the factory space and along the cobbled road for several hundred yards before it crossed into a goods yard.

'There's no distinction between the factory and the town,' I said.

'The town *is* a factory.'

'Madrid is nothing like this.'

'Do you miss your home?'

'I'm not sure where home is. Sometimes I miss Granada, but I haven't lived there for a long time.'

'You only speak about your father.'

'My mother ran away when I was small.'

'Ran away?'

We had arrived at another junction, where the brick wall veered to our left and ahead of us was a long and bustling thoroughfare. Jane prevented me from stepping into the street and I saw that the other pedestrians were patiently waiting. Then I realised that the policeman on duty had not yet given the signal that we could cross.

'It's nothing like this in Madrid!' I said again. 'People cross wherever they will.'

'Aren't there a lot of accidents?'

'I suppose there should be, but I don't think there are. Perhaps we have angels watching over us!'

'That's where the man was killed,' she said, pointing to a spot where the railway tracks crossed the tramlines.

'What man?'

'The man I told you about. A year ago in March. He was crossing early in the morning at the junction over there and he tripped on the railway track in front of an engine. He lost his legs, and died before they could get him to hospital.'

I stared at the spot. Then we crossed.

'My aunt also spoke of this,' she reminded me. 'The man who died was related to your Professor MacKay.'

We walked on past the spot where the railway car had killed the grocer.

'Your aunt said that Sergeant Macarthur is engaged to Professor MacKay's daughter. What would be unsuitable about that?'

'Suitable,' she said. 'Unsuitable. Who's to say? Perhaps the MacKays were aiming higher than a police sergeant.'

'Your uncle mentioned a difference of persuasion.'

'Ah,' she said. 'The MacKays are Episcopalian; perhaps the policeman is not.'

The street we entered was as busy as Crown Street but newer. I had started to measure prosperity in terms of noise. The noisier a thoroughfare the more commercially buoyant it was. This one was exceptionally noisy.

We walked for half an hour and the traffic and crowds on the pavement did not diminish until, quite suddenly, the tenements ended, the road widened and began to rise steeply and on either side there were trees and open fields. We came to a plantation of small villas, each with a little garden. Jane asked a boy sitting on a milk cart for the road where we'd been told the minister's house was. He pointed and said something incomprehensible.

'We're nearly there,' Jane assured me brightly.

Soon afterwards we took a turn to the right and entered a broad leafy avenue.

'It's number 34,' Jane said, 'so it will be on the left.'

'How far do you think we've walked?'

'I didn't notice that,' she said. 'I was enjoying your company.'

The house was modest and neat and utterly removed from the frenetic activity of the factories and tenements we had passed.

Jane rang the bell and a girl in an apron and a broadcloth shirt and skirt came to the door. She said she would see if the minister was at home and soon afterwards the Reverend Buchan walked along the hall and looked at us enquiringly.

Jane introduced herself and mentioned a parish somewhere in the city and the names of two clergymen who were known to the minister. I was struck by the subtle change in her demeanour. It was not that she became obsequious or even childlike, but she seemed to assume a sort of girlish correctness. The minister began to nod more and more genially until he said, 'Please, you had better come in then.'

The lobby had the distinctive smell of a well-run household, a combination of flower blossoms and wax. The minister's study was on the ground floor behind the parlour. A large window looked onto a vegetable garden at the back.

There was a fireplace framed by brown china tiles, with a bowl of yellow and pale blue carnations in the middle of the empty grate. The minister invited us to take the armchairs on either side of the fireplace while he pulled his desk chair forward so as to sit between us.

'Mr Camarón is a photographer. He met my aunt and uncle in Cuba,' Jane explained.

'My goodness, you've come a long way!' he said.

The Reverend Buchan's sentences carried an inflection different from Jane's or Jack Macarthur's or Professor MacKay's.

'I was born in Glasgow' – I sensed that I should give a more detailed account of myself – 'but my family moved to Spain when I was very young. Shortly before the war, my father and I sailed for Cuba.'

'You're well travelled!' he said. Then he added, more casually, 'My oldest boy's off to Cape Town next month. He's a bit of a globetrotter too!'

'My cousin, Archie, knew Johnny at school,' Jane told the minister. She turned to me and said, 'It's the school just along from your hotel.'

I was confused. Unless I was very much mistaken, she could not have been speaking of the school to which I had persuaded Tommy to return.

'The one with the tower,' she said. 'You pass it on your way into the city.'

'Ah,' I said.

I had noticed the building, recessed from the street by a small courtyard and cordoned off by iron railings. It was older than Tommy's school and larger, yet the difference was not one of age or size. There was something else that I couldn't quite put my finger on, except that perhaps the school attended by the minister's son was more settled, less makeshift and embattled than the one where immigrants were resolutely sticking to their alien ways.

'You're at that new place in Crown Street?' the Reverend Buchan asked. 'Why on earth are you staying there?'

'That's why we're here to see you, minister,' Jane continued quickly. 'Juan's been invited to look into the murders.'

The minister pursed his lips and said, 'I see.'

'I am applying a new technique in solving crime,' I said. 'I'm not a policeman. I can say that I am not even working *for* the police but *with* the police . . .'

'What is it that you do exactly?' His tone was both sceptical and curious.

I saw no reason to be circumspect.

'I take photographs, the same photograph of the same scene at regular intervals again and again. Then I study the images and look for patterns. That's why I'm staying at Simpson's. My camera is taking photographs of Crown Street from the window of the hotel right now.'

'But you're *here*, not *there*?'

'I've invented a device that triggers the camera operation automatically.'

'But how on earth can taking photographs help you find out who's killing these people?'

'So far,' I said evenly, 'it hasn't.'

After a moment I continued, 'I have documented the activity that goes on around the places where the murders occurred and I've studied each of these areas in minute detail to identify any clues that might help the police catch their man. My method proved useful in the recent murder case in Rutherglen – the case of Arabella Threadmyre – and I was invited to apply it here in Glasgow. I've been working under the auspices of Professor MacKay, whom you may know . . .'

He nodded.

'I came to speak to you,' I continued, holding the minister's eye, 'because there is something out of kilter in the investigation. I have worked in good faith. Now' – I found it hard to settle on the right words – 'now . . . well, you have appeared in some of my photographs and I believe you may be able to offer me a different perspective.' I paused and then I added, 'I was told by Billy Fraser that you and he are acquainted.'

'How in heaven's name have you got yourself mixed up with Billy Fraser?' he asked, and I sensed that his guard was up again.

I explained the use of the developing room at the mortuary, where I'd been introduced by Professor MacKay and Sergeant Macarthur.

'I appear in some of your photographs?' he asked.

Before Jane came to the hotel I had already placed two photographs, one of the minister speaking to the two women and the other as he lifted his hat to greet the man with the suitcase, in the inside pocket of my jacket. I took them out and handed them to him.

He looked at the pictures for a full thirty seconds before murmuring, 'Extraordinary!'

He was scrutinising the images with fascination rather than with indignation. When he spoke, it was clear that notions of propriety or privacy had not occurred to him.

'Well,' he said, 'in your photographs have you any sign of the man you are looking for?'

I confessed that I had not. 'But more and more I am starting to believe that these events do not simply involve the madness of one individual but the complicity of others. If there is insanity, there is also in some way corruption.'

He looked at me appraisingly. 'Why do you think that?'

Why should I trust him any more than Macarthur or MacKay or even Billy Fraser?

Jane broke into the silence. 'The people who have been murdered,' she told the minister, 'are all from your area, but none of them, I think, are your parishioners.'

He nodded.

'All of the victims have been Irish,' she said.

'All but one,' he corrected, 'and he belongs to the same persuasion.'

'Some in the district believe the crimes haven't been solved because the victims aren't Protestant,' I said.

He shook his head slowly. 'I don't think that's true.'

He stood up and walked to the door. 'Let me get us a pot of tea,' he said by way of explanation. He stepped out into the corridor and we heard him calling cheerily, 'Meg! Could you bring us some tea and some of your ginger cake!'

He came in and sat down again.

'I don't think that's true,' he repeated. 'These people insist on being separate. They have their own schools, their own clubs, their own pubs, they keep to themselves – of course they're treated differently!'

He paused again. He was striving to be fair-minded. I felt that he almost wished to be contradicted.

'I don't believe the police are being less diligent because of that.' He shook his head thoughtfully. 'Maybe there are some who wouldn't attend properly to their duties because the victims are from the other side, but surely no one wants these killings to continue!

'If I may say so, Mr Camarón,' he continued, surprising me by the carefully correct way in which he pronounced my name, 'you are very young to be doing this kind of work. Have you much previous experience?'

'I was able to help find a killer in Rutherglen.'

He looked at me steadily. 'But a case like this? Where one killing follows another?'

'I have not had experience of precisely this kind of case.'

Meg came in with a tray. She laid out cups and saucers and milk and sugar, and a plate of ginger cake on the low table in front of the fireplace.

We had not eaten lunch and we had arrived at the minister's house after a long walk. I was hungry.

Perhaps the minister saw me eyeing the cake; in any case he stood up and lifted the plate and presented it first to Jane and then to me. His high clerical collar seemed to me to defy any reasonable notion of comfort; it grazed his Adam's apple.

He sat down again and when the girl returned with the teapot he asked her to pour.

'Mrs Buchan says I'm to remind you that you have the

works committee at three o'clock. I'm to show them into the parlour.' The girl was earnest, and her tone of voice suggested a certain scepticism, as though punctuality might not be among the Reverend Buchan's salient virtues.

'Have another piece of cake, Mr Camarón,' the minister said indulgently, noting that I had finished my first piece.

I reached out and scooped up a slice.

The Reverend Buchan sipped his tea, and looked at the fireplace over the top of his cup. 'You know,' he said, focusing his attention on the flowers in the grate, 'the first people to die last August, when we were visited by that pestilential sickness, were in Rose Street, just a few doors from my church.'

The long shadow of the plague year.

'A child and her grandmother. Others in the family were infected but they survived. The medical authorities established a pattern.' He looked at me. 'The sort of pattern you are looking for, Mr Camarón, in your photographs. And they discovered that the others who died had been connected with the same family in Rose Street, and the most recent connection was that they had come to one or other of the two wakes. They can be wild affairs, particularly among the Irish, and you will forgive me, Mr Camarón, that's not a prejudice but simply a statement of fact. They have their own ways. They have a great way of blurring the line between mourning and gaiety.'

I guessed that the Reverend Buchan would never be tempted to blur this particular line.

'Mourners took a drink at the wake and a bite to eat and that was enough to contract the pestilence,' he continued. 'So you see, this other killer – the plague – stuck to one community, and it wasn't the fault of the medical authorities.

I don't think it's the fault of the police, in the present case, that these people are victims.'

He took another sip of his tea and then he put the cup and saucer on the table.

'My father was killed during the war in Cuba,' I said. 'He had to be buried on the same day because of the danger of contagion.'

I may have said this because it was to the point. But I don't believe that was the reason.

'I'm sorry to hear that, Mr Camarón. Your father was in the military?'

I shook my head. 'He was a photographer. He was making a photograph of the cathedral in Santiago when he was shot.'

He looked at me in a kindly way and then, unexpectedly, he said, 'My little girl was five years old when she went to the Lord. She took sick with a fever.' He pursed his lips bleakly and added, almost in a whisper, 'Death is a part of life.'

The three of us sat in silence for several moments.

'Miss Macgregor,' the minister said gently, 'please have another piece of Meg's excellent ginger cake.'

Jane leant forward and placed a slice of cake on her plate. The Reverend Buchan looked at the flowers in the fireplace again.

'All of the victims in these killings were suffering from some sort of illness,' I said.

He nodded. 'I've heard that too, and I've heard the most fantastic tales about a crazed doctor seeking to prevent a new outbreak of disease, but really, doesn't that sound just like a penny shocker! Even a crazed doctor would devote his most demonic energies to having the closes and privies treated with formalin and lime. Killing victims and running off with their hands and feet doesn't recommend itself as an obvious antidote to contagion.'

'Perhaps we've been looking at this the wrong way?' Jane said.

The minister pursed his lips again. 'You wouldn't be the only ones. The police have been looking at it in the wrong way too.'

'How's that?' Jane asked.

'Well, if they'd been looking at it the *right* way they'd have solved the crime by now.' He smiled. 'That's the first thing.'

I could see how this man would win the trust of different kinds of people, from the most desperate denizens of Crown Street to the most 'respectable'. He had a capacity to engage very directly – with the person speaking and with the subject being discussed.

'The papers say the victims let the killer come into their homes,' he said.

'How do they know that?'

'You have to understand, Mr Cameron' – he reverted to the Scottish pronunciation and I took this as a compliment, an indication of acceptance – 'that in a close there is no privacy. Everyone knows everyone else's comings and goings.' And he added almost slyly, 'Rather as though they were being photographed by a hidden camera.'

'But nobody saw anything!' I said.

'They saw the one thing that you see very rarely in these parts,' he replied. 'They saw front doors left wide open.'

'But . . .'

'The killer was allowed in, but the bodies were found in the close, or at a short distance from the close, is that not so?'

I said it was so. Willie McGonagall had been found in the backcourt next to Bailey's Bar. The bodies of Bessie

Armstrong and Hector McKinnon had been left on the steps of the bank. Maggie McAllister and Brendan Gillespie had been found in the close. And Seamus Hanlon – I had witnessed the bleeding carcass, the peculiar odour of fresh blood – had also been left in the close.

'But why did he kill in public? He could have done this' – Jane stopped and then finished the sentence slowly, choosing her words with care – '*wicked* deed when he was inside – he would have had . . . privacy.'

'And why would his victims have come out into the close with him? Why would they leave their doors open?' I addressed the minister, and as I did so I wondered why I should imagine he might be able to provide a satisfactory answer.

He was thoughtful. 'Was there much blood at the scene?'

'In Hanlon's case . . .' My tone became indignant. Just the memory of what I had witnessed made me agitated.

The minister stopped me. 'But the others?'

I remembered what I'd been told. 'Where McGonagall's carcass was discovered, there was little blood. I do not know in the case of Maggie McAllister. Of the two who were abandoned on the steps of the bank . . .' I thought a little more. 'The manager was outraged. He said the bodies were bad for business, but he made no mention of blood.'

'So,' the minister concluded, 'the three who were taken elsewhere – perhaps they were first murdered and then carried to the place where they were abandoned.'

'But . . .' Once again I was going to ask why.

'Let's say they were all murdered outside their homes, perhaps all of them murdered in their own close. The neighbours noticed that doors had been left open, but didn't hear or see anything till after the victims had been killed. And then, of course, they were presented with the obscenity of a mutilated corpse . . .' His voice trailed away. 'Miss Macgregor,' he said, 'this is an awful business, perhaps we shouldn't speak of it.'

Jane replied in a tone that dismissed any notion of delicate sensibility. 'It is an awful business, minister, but that is why Juan must get to the heart of it.' She lifted her ginger cake but before she put it in her mouth she asked, 'Why would this creature dispatch his victims in the close?'

'Consider the quantity of blood . . .' the minister said.

I nodded perhaps rather too zealously. The quantity of blood in the case of Seamus Hanlon was seared in my memory.

'Consider the man responsible for these crimes. A monster, no doubt. Yet his actions follow a pattern, do they not?'

I believe I may have sat back in my chair rather abruptly. Patterns were my stock in trade.

'I have followed this case, as you can imagine, with as much trepidation – and as much attention – as my parishioners,' the Reverend Buchan continued. 'My people are in that neighbourhood too, and they have this maniac in their midst.' He took a sip of tea and then put the cup and saucer on the table. Again, I wondered at the unyielding deprivation of comfort that must accompany the wearing of a clerical collar. 'The first victim was a wee lassie, worked in a shop . . .'

'Maggie McAllister,' I said.

He nodded. 'It was the end of November.'

'And the next . . .' The minister looked at me, but I couldn't remember the name. 'In any case, it was Christmas Day – truly a case of sacrilege. And the one after that was the end of January, and so on – always the end of the month.'

I failed to see the significance of this.

'A pattern!' the minister prompted.

'But it doesn't explain . . .' I began.

'*Nothing* will explain!' he said rather sharply. 'But perhaps we can edge towards a kind of . . . understanding. We are dealing with a mind that's twisted – but perhaps it follows a kind of logic.'

He stopped speaking and neither Jane nor I broke the silence that followed.

The silence was interrupted by Meg. 'Shall I clear away the tea things?'

I hadn't noticed her coming into the room.

The Reverend Buchan didn't seem to have heard. He continued to look down at the table and then, 'Oh! Aye, Meg, if you would be so good.'

She placed a tray on the table and piled up the cups and saucers and the plate with one slice of ginger cake still on it.

The minister still looked down at the table and then his gaze seemed to fix on Meg and he said, in a tone that suggested he was somehow surprised by the absurdity of the words that followed, 'What if the killer didn't want to make a mess?'

Meg left the room. Jane and I shared a look of considerable bafflement.

'The man is a maniac,' the minister said. 'Wouldn't it just be in keeping with this sort of . . . madness . . . to take account of a thing like that?'

He looked up at the clock on the mantelpiece. And then, changing tack in a way that appeared entirely random but which, I gathered from his way of conducting a conversation, was likely to be part of a larger point, he asked, 'Has Billy Fraser appeared in any of your photographs?'

I hesitated.

The minister's tone acquired an edge. 'You have been keen to learn anything that I might know, Mr Cameron. I believe I'm entitled to ask the same.'

'Yes. Billy has appeared in one of the photographs.'

'And you identified him?'

This was uncanny.

'I have my own method of analysing the images. I work in a scientific, a systematic way . . . but in this case, Billy appeared . . . and I didn't at first identify him.'

'Who helped you?'

'Sergeant Macarthur.'

He nodded. 'Do you know the nature of Billy's engagement with the court?'

'His photography?'

He didn't nod or speak, but waited for me to answer. There was beneath his genial exterior an unmistakable toughness – which should not have surprised me: he ministered in a district steeped in degradation and violence; he could not have functioned there without reserves of shrewdness. In this respect, he bore a great similarity to Gabriel Mahoney, though the two were separated by a chasm of belief and tradition.

'I know that he develops photographs that have been used in cases of blackmail.'

'Blackmail?' He wrinkled his nose. 'Billy has been a scourge, a danger to women and a purveyor of vice!'

'But what does this have to . . .'

'I do not have the answer to that, but you must ask yourself why there might be an interest in finding Billy in one of your photographs. When a man's inclined towards violence and depravity he can be a threat, but he can also serve a purpose.'

As he said this, we heard the sound of the front doorbell and then the shuffling of footsteps and the exchange of greetings that indicated the arrival of the works committee and their conveyance to the parlour next door.

The minister stood up and so did we.

'The Americans have been quite adamant – they do not wish to colonise Cuba,' he remarked as we moved out to the hall.

'They wish to develop trade and industry,' I said, rather startled that he had suddenly introduced the topic, 'but that is what was being done when the island was still a part of Spain.' There was clearly no time for a substantive discussion.

'You do not approve?'

I thought for a moment and then I said, 'Poverty is the same under any flag.'

'You know,' he remarked thoughtfully, 'I'm inclined to agree with that.'

CHAPTER TWENTY-THREE

When we were outside, Jane said, 'Show me where the murders happened.'

'Certainly not! I'm not taking you there!'

She looked at me intently and said, 'Perhaps I have misunderstood you, Juan. When you first came to call on me and we ate lunch together you told me all about your work. I thought you cared about the great issues of our age.'

'I do!'

'And do you imagine that I *don't* care about these things?'

'Of course not!'

'Then why do you consider it unthinkable for me to visit the scenes where these abominable murders took place?'

I could not immediately conjure up an appropriate response.

'I'm not taking a *prurient* interest,' she added reasonably. 'I want to understand this gruesome puzzle as much as you do.'

'But it's dangerous . . .'

'Will you protect me?'

'You *know* I will.'

'Then I shall not feel that I am in danger.'

She began to walk back towards the main road and I followed. This was when it occurred to me that her mourning clothes were a kind of camouflage. Dressed as she was, she blended into the district where the minister lived and she would not be out of place in the worst stretches of Crown Street. Death is a part of life: mourning is at home on every street.

We took a tram back along the route we had walked, and further on to the crossing outside Mr Presser's bank. As we stepped down to the pavement I recognised the constable on duty. He must have changed shifts because the previous day he had been directing the morning traffic and had been relieved towards midday.

We reached the bank and I glanced at my watch. It was a few seconds to half past three. I shook my head and glanced up at the window of Mr Presser's office.

'What is it?' Jane asked.

I was at first unable to explain. I had the singular sensation of being spied upon by myself. I stopped walking and looked up at the bank and said, 'We are being photographed.'

Jane looked up too. Then she looked around. 'Everything that we can see?'

'Just about.'

'Oh, Juan,' she remarked in a steady, reassuring voice, 'you must surely find something that will carry you to the truth.'

We began to walk again but before we had taken half a dozen steps William Harrison came out of his shop and placed himself in our path.

'Mr Cameron, how are you today?'

'Much better, thank you.'

'No more headaches, I hope.'

'None, thank you.'

I did not yet know how I should proceed as far as Harrison was concerned. Whatever had prompted his argument with Macarthur in the small hours of the morning he would certainly not discuss with me. We eyed one another and for a moment the encounter seemed to balance uncertainly on an unspoken wariness. Then Jane and I began to walk on and Harrison said, 'Good afternoon to you both.'

I sensed him watching, and then I concluded that I was being quite irrational. He might just as easily have walked back into his shop.

I glanced behind me.

He was watching.

'Here on the steps,' I told Jane when we reached the front of the bank. 'Down there at the lower entrance,' I added when we were at the corner.

At both places she would have liked to stop, but conscious of Harrison's interest I kept moving.

In Crown Street the traffic was dense, the noise was indescribable and there was a cloud of dust.

'Over there,' I shouted, pointing through the rush of carts and trams, 'by the public house.'

'Come on, then,' she said, taking my hand. 'Let's go and see.'

She guided me through the blaring, grinding throng of machines and horses.

I would have allowed her to guide me blindfold across Santiago in the midst of mayhem.

'He chose this narrow alcove and no one could see what he was doing,' I told her when we were in the courtyard where Willie McGonagall had been found.

'Where did the victim live?'

We stepped back out of the alcove and into the courtyard and looked at the surrounding windows.

'One of these, perhaps?'

'Let's go in and ask,' she said.

'Where?'

'The public house.'

'*You* can't go in!'

She shrugged. 'No, I suppose not, but *you* can. I'll wait for you here.'

'Will you be all right?' I glanced nervously at the pavement on either side.

'Oh, I think I can fend off any unwanted attentions for as long as it takes you to ask where Willie McGonagall lived.'

The bar was a large room with an uneven stone floor, a handful of benches and two long, dirty-looking tables. The men who sat smoking were sullen, and suspicious.

I asked the barman if he could tell me where the man who had been murdered outside had lived.

He looked at me as though I had arrived from a distant planet and was addressing him in an alien and exotic tongue.

'The man who was murdered?' I persisted. 'Did he live near here?'

The barman glanced over my shoulder at the other men.

'Who are you?' he asked.

'I'm a visitor. I've heard about the case. I want to know where the victim lived.'

He looked at me obdurately.

'*I* can show you,' a voice beside me said.

I turned and saw a giant, bearded, wearing a bowler hat with a hole in it and trousers that were much too short. His boots were ancient and without laces.

I glanced at the barman, who stared back poker-faced.

I was sorry I'd agreed to Jane's suggestion.

'You know where he lived?' I asked.

'I'll show you,' he said again.

I shrugged and began to move away from the bar. The man followed me. I stepped out into the sunlight and found that Jane was not where I had left her. I hurried to the entrance that led into the backcourt. The man followed. Jane wasn't in the entrance or in the backcourt itself. I turned and began to move towards the street. The man blocked my way.

'What's your hurry?' he said.

He leered down at me with the malevolent amusement of an individual whose view of the world is predicated on being larger and stronger than most men. He was not, I think, particularly intelligent, but he was certainly dangerous.

'Let's see if there's any money in the visitor's pocket,' he said, stepping towards me and reaching for the inside of my jacket.

I learned to box in Granada, and then in Madrid, where my venerable Jesuit tutor taught me the novel art of judo.

As the giant extended his hand, fingers ready to clutch at the wallet he expected to find in my inside pocket, I took his hand and drew him forward as though we were stepping lightly onto a dance floor.

In physical combat the secret is speed not force – and as important as speed is the ability to dance. When you dance,

265

you anticipate the movements of your partner and you move accordingly. When you engage in combat, if you wish to prevail, you do the same. You anticipate the movements of your partner and you move accordingly. Thus, when my assailant stepped forward I led him in the same direction. We did this for two steps, me holding his hand. He disliked having his hand held, so he retracted it. When he retracted his hand I extended mine. He was confused and took a step backward; I took a step forward. We danced this jig for several seconds and then he grunted and punched me with his left hand. It was the poor punch of a man who rarely has to punch because he has the strength and confidence to reach out and take what he wants, intimidating his victims with his very ease and confidence. His fist swung through the air, not in a short, sharp jab, which I would in any case have had time to dodge, but in a great arc, which I had even *more* time to dodge. I took a half step towards him, noting as I did so that he smelt almost as bad as Tommy before his visit to the public baths. I only had to endure the unpleasant proximity of this odour for half a second or so, because, as he swung (his entire might behind the punch that was directed where my head had been but no longer was) I pushed him lightly on his left shoulder and he spun round so fast that he lost his balance and clattered heavily onto the cobblestones.

I walked quickly back out into the street and looked up and down. Jane was across the road, speaking to a woman standing by a pram.

I heard the sound of a large body picking up speed as it ran over the flagstones from the backcourt. The giant made no attempt to come by stealth. I heard the beginnings of a grunt and recognised the displacement of air indicating that an unlaced boot was being raised at considerable speed to meet my rear. I stepped to one side and reached out to help the boot continue its arc well beyond the level my assailant had intended. Up it went and on up into the air, only guided and encouraged by my hand, so that for the second time, my opponent fell backward and onto the hard surface of the earth, this time so forcefully that the back of his head hit the ground with an audible crack.

The barman and some others came out to inspect the giant lying on the ground, gazing up at the sky. I looked across the road. Jane and the woman, both dressed in black, were surrounded by a group of little girls playing with a skipping rope.

As I plunged into the traffic, I heard some of the men from the bar shouting after me. From the middle of the road, I saw the woman gesticulating. Jane was pointing in the direction of the river. The woman touched her arm, expressing friendly appreciation.

Just then, Jane caught sight of me. The woman left her. I stepped between a coal cart and an omnibus, hearing the sound of the omnibus driver swearing at his horses in the vicious tone of a man who spends his days in the company of a species he loathes.

'I missed you when I came out of the bar!' I said.

'That lady asked me for directions and I crossed the road so as to show her.'

'Where did she want to go?'

'She was looking for a place that sells hemp. I believe there's a shop beside the customs house.' Jane glanced across the road to the pavement in front of the bar and asked, 'What happened?'

She had been facing away from the road and I gathered that she had not witnessed my altercation with the giant, who was now being escorted towards the public house.

'I was interrupted,' I said. 'Let's try again.'

Jane took my hand as we crossed the street.

'Wait here,' I told her and I went back into the pub. Inside, I asked in a loud voice if anyone would be good enough to show me the living quarters of the victim who had been found in the courtyard.

The giant had been taken to the furthest corner, where he sat, dazed, between two men who scowled in my direction but clearly had no intention of doing more than that.

I added that there was a shilling for anyone who would oblige me.

The barman came from behind the bar and this time he accompanied me out into the street.

'This way, sir,' he said.

Jane took my arm and we followed the barman to the end of the block.

'It's the second close on the left, the ground floor,' the man said when we reached the corner of a side street. 'I don't know which door.'

His hand began to rise in a manner that invited a corresponding movement on my part. I reached into my jacket pocket and took out a shilling.

'Thank you, sir,' he said as though we had just completed the most affable and everyday transaction.

When we got to the close, Jane said, 'Let's go in.'

'Perhaps not.'

'Come on!' She went ahead of me.

The interior was dark. The lower part of the wall in the entrance was tiled.

There were three doors.

'What shall we say?' I asked.

None of the nameplates bore the name 'McGonagall'.

As I spoke, the door in the middle opened and a careworn face looked out. The face belonged to a woman who might have been twenty or forty. She waited for us to explain our presence.

'Hello,' Jane said. 'We are from the parish welfare committee. Is this where William McGonagall lived?'

The woman looked at us suspiciously and pointed to the door at the end of the corridor.

Jane began to walk towards it.

'There's nobody home,' the woman said. 'It was just him and his brother and the brother's gone back to Dublin.'

We thanked her and began to leave. I heard doors above us opening and glanced up to see faces looking down over the banister.

'There was no blood at the scene of the crime,' I said, looking up.

The faces that had peered from the upper floors darted back out of sight.

'He could have been killed here in the close, like the others.' We peered together into the darkness. 'But how could the body, or what was left of it, be moved' – I pointed from the close to the backcourt, where the alcove behind the bar was located – 'from here to there? No one saw anything!'

'There will be a back way,' she said.

Instead of continuing out to the street we doubled back past the stairs, where there was a rickety gate that led onto the backcourt. There were lines and lines of washing hanging out to dry. We skirted the laundry and followed the ground floor of the tenement till we came to a railing.

'There's a gate,' she said.

The gate was unlocked. Passing through it we reached another court and this one, by means of a narrow passageway, led into the courtyard behind the bar.

'Voila!' Jane said.

'But he couldn't have been dragged here without the killer being seen.'

'What if the body was *in* something?'

I disliked standing there. We were drawing attention to ourselves. I felt too that we were blundering forward with no particular method in our curiosity. We were like people looking at photographs and leaping to what they believe to be the most interesting parts.

'Let's see the other places,' I said.

We walked back out through the broad entrance beside the bar and re-entered Crown Street, even noisier than before as the traffic built up towards the evening rush.

We had just stepped back onto the pavement when we saw a familiar figure running towards us from the intersection.

'Did you really knock down Alex MacLean?' Tommy asked.

'Who told you that?'

'Everyone says you did! They say you knocked him over and then you pummelled him senseless!'

'I did nothing of the kind,' I told Tommy indignantly.

He gazed at Jane as though she was Princess Mary.

'Jane,' I said, 'allow me to introduce Master Thomas Ogilvy, my helper and confederate.'

Jane extended her hand and Tommy looked at it as though it was an exhibit in a museum. He glanced at me to see what he should do and I indicated by means of vigorous facial gestures and the rapid movement of my shoulder that he should take her hand and shake it. This he did, looking first at the ground and then up at Jane's face.

'How do you do?' Jane asked.

'Yes, missus,' Tommy replied. He took possession of his hand again.

'Tommy,' I said, 'we have some things to do. Meet me at the hotel in about an hour.'

We watched him run off.

'And where is the next port of call?' Jane asked.

'Number 24.'

She took my arm and we walked the three blocks to the close.

'Is your uncle a Mason?' I asked before we reached the third block.

She looked at me with a disappointed expression. 'What an extraordinary thing to ask!'

'I believe that Mr Presser in the bank is a Mason, and that Sergeant Macarthur is a Mason.'

'No, my uncle is not a Mason,' she said.

I glanced at her and noted her exasperation.

'I'm sorry,' I said.

She squeezed my arm. 'Don't be.'

We walked for a few moments in silence and then I told her about the incident outside my window during the night,

271

and about Mr Presser's sudden announcement that he would no longer be able to oblige me.

'But none of that amounts to a conspiracy,' she said reasonably.

We entered the close where Brendan Gillespie's body had been found.

'What was his job?' she asked.

'Lamplighter. Hector MacKinnon was a teacher, Bessie Armstrong was a laundress, Willie McGonagall was a carter and Maggie McAllister was a shop assistant.'

'They all had employment,' she said, 'they all had some sort of illness, and they all let the killer into their apartment.'

'And followed him out again,' I said.

He voice was suddenly exasperated. 'But why this ghastly ritual, cutting off the arms, cutting off the feet!'

I had to peer at her through the murky light at the end of the corridor. Perhaps the force of her words was magnified because I could barely see her.

One word settled in the very centre of my thoughts.

'Perhaps it really *was* a ritual,' I said.

We climbed the stairs to the landing, where there was a window that looked out onto a backcourt, this one like the other, filled with washing.

Jane could see me clearly now.

'A religious ritual?' she asked.

I shrugged. 'What sort of religion would hold with something as ghastly as that? But just consider – he could have done this . . . *wicked* thing behind closed doors. Instead, he had his victims come out, and he butchered them where he might be seen.' We stood as though in a darkness deepened by

272

the pervasive taint of evil. 'And can you imagine the effect on people when they saw those rivers of blood!'

'Then he took the bodies – some of the bodies – to a public place . . . the steps of the bank . . .' She looked at me with an expression that seemed to express the horror of a sudden insight.

I said what I believed Jane was thinking: 'A public sacrifice.'

She was silent.

'Well, it isn't any more fantastical than the notion that he didn't want to leave a mess in the house of his victims,' I said.

'But what about the place we have just been?' She was more matter-of-fact, as though our dramatic speculations were distasteful and perhaps quite foolish. 'Willie McGonagall's body was hidden.'

'Perhaps the killer was disturbed,' I said. 'Perhaps that's not where he planned to abandon the body. Perhaps he had selected a more public place – in front of Bailey's Bar, for example, instead of behind it?'

The nameplate on the door was Gillespie, but when we knocked no one was at home. I was relieved. Though I did not wish to admit this, to myself or to Jane, I did not want to confront grieving relatives.

However, a block and a half further on, at the close where the body of Maggie McAllister had been deposited, we found the bereaved family at home.

A small man opened the door of the dead woman's apartment. His expression was preoccupied and tired but not unkind. He waited politely while we explained our presence.

'We have just been to the Rose Street church,' Jane said, somewhat misleadingly. 'We are visiting in the neighbourhood . . . and there has been so much sadness over what happened . . . these terrible events . . . we wanted . . . to express our condolences . . . and to see if there is anything could be done.'

'Who is it?' a woman's voice asked from inside.

'People from the church,' he said.

'Bring them in.'

'Not *our* church.'

Moments later a woman's face appeared at the door, displacing her husband in the threshold.

Jane again expressed our condolences.

'You'll be from Arthur's church?' the woman said. She thought for a moment and then she added, 'You had better come in.'

The sitting room was small but tidy and clean. We sat together on the sofa while Mrs McAllister made tea and her husband told us what a fine daughter they had had and how well she had been doing in her work. There was a crucifix above the fireplace.

'Arthur was Maggie's intended?' Jane asked when Mrs McAllister had served tea and had sat down in the armchair opposite her husband.

'Well,' she said, an expression that mingled indignation and indulgence suffusing her round cheeks, 'that's maybe as he would have described it.'

'They couldn't have got married,' Mr McAllister explained. 'Neither family would have allowed it.'

In the course of three quarters of an hour, the McAllisters painted a portrait of their daughter. I had deep misgivings; we were there under false pretences. Yet I think they experienced a kind of relief talking about their girl.

'Had she been ill?' I asked.

Mr McAllister glanced at his wife and then he said, 'Nerves.'

Mrs McAllister shook her head and tears came into her eyes. 'If we'd let her follow her own path . . .'

'She wasn't able to sleep and she'd been off her food,' the father said. 'Well, you know what this area went through last summer. The least little sniffle and people think it's back again. We were terribly worried, but she had started to feel better and we thought we were over the worst.'

As we walked down the stairs and out into the street, Jane said, 'Who would have been admitted to that house?'

'What do you mean?'

'Maggie would have been careful whom she let in.'

'The killer,' I said, 'was "respectable".'

'Exactly.'

As we walked to the hotel, Tommy ran towards us, this time even more pell-mell than before.

'Mr Cameron!' he shrieked. 'There's been another murder!'

CHAPTER TWENTY-FOUR

In the lobby of Simpson's Hotel, a dozen people filled the space between the reception desk and the stairs. One of them was Jack Macarthur. A single figure huddled behind the desk. It was Professor MacKay.

Macarthur stepped from the midst of the crowd.

'Where have you been?'

He looked at me with irritation and then at Jane. It was none of this man's business where I'd been: I stepped past him to the counter. The constable, the same one who had been on duty when we examined the body of Seamus Hanlon the day before, recognised me and allowed me to enter the inner circle.

I looked down and saw the distinctive – and now inanimate – features of William Gibson.

The reception desk stood on the lip of a shallow undulation in the flagstones. It was not possible to see the flagstones at all since the entire volume of the undulation had been filled to the brim with blood, so that it looked like a translucent lake amid the browns and blacks and greys of its surroundings. In the middle of this lake lay Gibson's body, minus his limbs.

The professor looked up. 'You are here,' he said.

'When did this happen?'

'The girl was in the whole afternoon except for five minutes when she went for tobacco. When she came back, she found this.'

'Is she here?'

He nodded in the direction of the kitchen.

I made my way back through the crowd. Jane had taken a seat on the bench near the door. Tommy stood beside her, like a sentinel.

'I'm going to speak to the maid,' I told Jane. 'Let me see you to a cab first.'

She didn't reply. Instead, she stood up and walked across the lobby in the direction of the kitchen.

She waited for me by the door. I crossed the lobby and entered the room ahead of her.

Annie Belmont sat alone on a low basket chair beside a huge black grate. Her face was tear-stained but her expression was robust. Her cheeks were red and there were red rings around her pale blue eyes.

I am become death.

I believed, with a certainty so absolute that it actually slowed down the measure of my step, that I was responsible for this young woman's loss. I believed that if I had never come to this hotel, the killer would not have come here either.

'Annie,' I said softly, in a voice of profound guilt. I reached out and took her white hand.

I heard the scrape of a heavy wooden chair being pulled across the kitchen flags behind me and then a hand on my shoulder. Jane disengaged me from Annie and sat next to the girl and said, 'What did you see, Annie?'

Annie was gazing vacantly in front of her. She turned her head, but didn't look directly at Jane or at me. 'Oh!' she said. 'Such blood!' She stopped and shook her head and looked down at the stones before she whispered to Jane, as if this were a sort of shameful confession, 'I've never seen so much blood!'

'Was that how you found him?'

She nodded, playing with a grey handkerchief that was the same colour as her skirt and apron.

'William had been ill,' I told Jane.

'He had a chill, sore throat.' She looked straight ahead of her, speaking to no one in particular.

'Did he take medicine?' I asked.

She gave me a bitter glance and then she transferred her gaze to Jane.

'Just sixpence worth of tincture.'

Tears flowed down her freckled cheeks yet she didn't raise the grey handkerchief to dry her face. Her grey-clad body began to convulse as though she were on the verge of a fit.

Jane put her arm round Annie and then looked up at me and to my surprise said in a very terse voice, 'Mr Cameron, please leave us.'

I opened my mouth to protest, but Jane wasn't looking at me any more. She had turned all of her attention to Annie.

Back in the lobby, Macarthur strode towards me.

278

'If you haven't got him by now, you're not going to get him,' he said.

'Would that be such a bad thing?'

'What the devil do you mean?'

'I saw you last night arguing with Harrison and another man outside the hotel.'

'What has that to do with anything!'

His voice rose, but not, I thought, simply from indignation or annoyance. There was another quality to it, something I had not witnessed in Macarthur until this moment. It was uncertainty.

'I want to see your photographs,' Professor MacKay said, joining us from the other side of the lobby and breaking the impasse between us, consciously. 'Never mind the analysis, never mind the delay,' he added sourly.

There was no point in arguing.

'Please excuse me one moment.'

I hurried back into the kitchen, where Jane and Annie were now whispering to one another, their heads so close they might almost have been touching.

'I have to go,' I told Jane.

'Can you come and visit me later, when you have time?'

Before I went upstairs I took Tommy aside and told him to escort Miss Macgregor when she left the hotel and to find her a cab.

'Will you be coming back?' he asked, now fully engaged in the capacity of trusted assistant.

'I expect so.'

I travelled to the mortuary in a police cab with Macarthur and the professor. No one spoke.

When we arrived, Robert told us that Billy had been out all afternoon. The professor wanted to know where, and Robert said he didn't know.

'There's a body waiting for him at Simpson's Hotel,' the professor said. 'If he's not back within the hour, you'd better go and collect it yourself.'

I proceeded to the developing room. Robert raised a hand and said, 'Billy left instructions that no one's to go inside.'

'Well, we'll just have to make an exception then, won't we,' Macarthur growled, stepping forward to confront the giant, who looked at him resentfully, shrugged and said, 'It's locked.'

'Where's the key?' Macarthur demanded.

'Billy has it.'

Macarthur walked to the door of the developing room and tried the handle. It was locked.

'Break it open,' the professor ordered.

'You can't do that!' Robert protested.

'Do you have a hammer?' Macarthur asked him, nicely introducing an element of threat to the question.

Robert looked confused and then angry and said, 'There's a key in Billy's office, behind the calendar.'

Macarthur left and returned a few moments later with the key. He unlocked the developing room and indicated to me with a jerk of his head that I should enter and get on with what we had come here to do.

I stepped inside and closed the door.

Billy had left a dozen pictures hanging up to dry. When my eyes became accustomed to the blue light I saw that eight of the images were pornographic; the remaining four showed corpses. One of the corpses, Seamus Hanlon's, was without hands and feet.

I took the photographs down and placed them at the end of the table and set about developing the plates I had brought from the hotel.

I should have insisted on waiting.

I should have refused to be hurried.

A few hours more and I would have had a complete sequence. That was the only way my method could properly work. Now, we were simply casting about, as though the man we sought would oblige us by walking into the middle of a photograph.

I should have insisted on making my own notes, I thought bitterly as I worked. And as I worked I knew that we were not going to find what we were looking for because we were looking for the wrong thing.

That was why I had not uncovered anything useful! I had allowed my own prejudices, my own preconceptions, to dictate what it was I was going to see.

I too had been searching for a likely suspect, a man who looked as if he was about to butcher one of his neighbours, or a man with the diabolical menace on his face that showed he had just done the deed.

I studied the pictures as they dried. I looked at the tramcars and omnibuses and carts and cabs making their way south to the suburbs and north to the centre of the city. I looked at each and every driver and carter who was in my frame. I looked for anything out of character. I studied the pedestrians, the early morning men and women and boys and girls striding purposefully to the day's work, and later the loiterers and loafers, watching the world, waiting for something to happen.

I searched for a moment in the last nine hours when one of these little groups fixed their attention on anything that might point to the circumstances behind the latest gruesome act of butchery.

I examined the shopkeepers and the landlords and the others I had come to recognise. One man stood at the corner three blocks from the hotel from ten o'clock to four o'clock every day, a small, portly, prosperous-looking man in a bowler and a three-piece suit with a loud check: in some pictures there were boys around him; in others there were men. I had been curious about this man until I passed him the day before on my way back to the hotel and I saw that he was a bookmaker; the boys were his runners. He caught me scrutinising him and gave me the cheerful, calculating look of an individual whose fortune is built on assessing the weaknesses of others.

The bookmaker appeared in four of the photographs.

'Well?' Professor MacKay demanded when I came out of the developing room.

I laid the pictures on the nearest of the three dissection tables. The steel tabletop felt cold; there was a hole at one end, where blood and other fluids were drained off into a bucket placed below; the level of the table fell in a gentle gradient from left to right. I had to place the pictures carefully, as they were inclined to float over the smooth steel.

As I laid them out, I wondered if the odd circumstances of this examination were apt. Perhaps we really were dissecting moments in time with a realistic possibility of finding truth in the chaos of the past.

'Well, is he here?' the professor demanded.

'I haven't been able to identify him,' I said in an even tone.

They looked at the pictures haphazardly, saying nothing. The professor gave up after ten minutes, walking away from the table with a sigh.

Just then, Billy Fraser hurried in.

'I have laid your photographs to one side,' I told Billy. 'They have not been damaged.'

'What photographs?' the professor asked irritably.

'Pictures taken earlier here at the mortuary,' I lied.

Billy looked at me with veiled gratitude.

'Where have you been?' Macarthur demanded.

Billy glanced at the professor. 'On an errand,' he said.

'I asked you where!' Macarthur persisted. The timbre of his voice was drained of resonance or roundness: it was threatening.

'Smith & Co,' Billy said.

Now Macarthur glanced at the professor. 'You went by Crown Street?'

'What if I did?'

'Anyone at Smith & Co see you?'

'Go and ask them.'

'Sergeant Macarthur will do just that,' the professor told Billy. 'Now, you get on with your business.'

'The body in Simpson's?' Billy said.

All three of us stared at him.

'I heard about it on the way here.' He looked at us with an expression that mixed defiance with contempt. Then he hurried out into the hallway, where he began giving instructions to Robert.

Professor MacKay turned and spoke to me like a magistrate pronouncing sentence against a particularly obtuse offender.

'Señor Camarón, I am grateful that you have come all this way in order to lend your assistance, but I'm afraid you must accept that your method has not produced the results we had hoped for.'

A great contrast to the genial, collegial manner he had shown before. On the other hand, if my method didn't work . . . yet, his judgement was too summary. He was too quick to conclude that the method wouldn't work. He was hurrying – or being hurried. He made an effort to project his customary gravitas, but the gravitas was undermined by the very effort required to project it. 'This experiment is now terminated.'

Outside, the professor shook hands with me and nodded to Macarthur and was driven away in his brougham.

'Your welcome in this city will not last beyond tomorrow morning, Mr Camarón,' Macarthur said, inflecting my name in what I took as a heavily ironical and insulting way.

I had a history of resisting efforts to evict me from cities where my presence was an inconvenience.

'Good afternoon,' I said, speaking slowly enough to make him turn and face me.

Walking away with the raucous din of carts and tramcars drowning my steps, I felt his eyes boring into the point between my shoulder blades.

CHAPTER TWENTY-FIVE

Billy Fraser was waiting for me in the lobby of the hotel.

'Mr Cameron, you and I should have a talk,' he said.

His peculiar manner invested even his most workaday expressions with something unwholesome. If he had wished me a pleasant afternoon, I think it might have sounded like a threat.

'What do we have to talk about?'

'Not here. Let's go to your room.'

'We can talk here,' I said.

'Mr Cameron, when you have heard what I have to say you will understand why I must speak to you in confidence.'

Two men had been assigned to clean up the blood and gore from behind the reception desk. I gathered that they were loafers who had been hired for the job because they were available immediately and would work for drink money. A policeman stood at the front door; he had recognised me when I came in, but did not see fit to offer a greeting – I guessed that news of my dismissal had preceded me. And there were two newspapermen sitting on the bench next to the front door comparing notes. I had seen them earlier in the afternoon when Tommy had summoned us with news of Gibson's murder. They had been standing outside the hotel entrance asking the gaggle of onlookers if anyone had seen anything out of the ordinary. Now they were watching Billy and me.

Reluctantly I nodded to Billy, indicating that he could come up.

'Can we have a word, sir?' one of the newspapermen asked as we started to cross the lobby.

'Maybe later,' I said.

The man raised his hand and began to say something, but I continued walking and then climbed the stairs two at a time. Billy laboured behind.

A malevolent presence had attached itself to me. It wasn't Billy and it wasn't Macarthur. It wasn't the newspapermen with their brash curiosity.

It was the malaise whose cause I could not locate but whose consequences were evident in suspicion, corruption and murder.

Billy wore a cologne with a sharp seedy scent. It rose ahead of him on the stairs.

I unlocked the door and when we got inside I crossed the room and stood with my back to the window.

Billy closed the door and walked towards me.

'Mr Cameron, you were good enough not to describe to Professor MacKay or Sergeant Macarthur the nature of the photographs you found in my developing room.'

'The images you deal in are not my concern.'

'I come into contact with all sorts,' he said, looking on either side of me where the tripod legs jutted towards the wooden floor. 'That's the nature of my work, and, of course, many of the people I come into contact with are dead by the time I meet them.'

I waited.

'May I sit down?' he asked.

I pointed to the chair by the table and moved to the end of the bed and stood facing Billy, who sat on the side of the chair and twisted round to look at me.

'As you know, I've examined the corpses of all the victims.'

I waited.

'Mr Cameron, could I have a glass of water?'

I pointed to a jug on the dresser. He got up slowly and filled a glass with water from the jug. He took a long draught and returned to the seat and sat down again. This series of movements seemed to inject more of the sharp seedy scent into the room.

'All of the victims had taken laudanum,' he said.

'How can you tell?'

'It stays in the stomach a long time. Other things do too. If you extract just a portion of mucus from the stomach or intestines and you put it over a burner, the alcohol will separate from the rest, and if the alcohol is yellowish it means it has laudanum in it.'

'But you've included this in the reports you give to Professor MacKay and Sergeant Macarthur,' I said.

He ignored me and looked for the first time in the direction of the camera. 'Your photographs are taken at regular intervals.'

There was no point in dissembling now. And at the very moment that I thought this, I had a chilling realisation.

The killer had completed his evil business having secured entry to the homes of his victims. As my thoughts began to travel in anarchic lines, Billy stood up and began walking towards me.

'Yes,' I said, 'the pictures are taken at regular intervals.'

'By the volume of images you develop I would deduce that the intervals are one hour?'

He moved closer, glancing between me and the camera.

'Forty-five minutes,' I said.

He nodded thoughtfully and strolled past me to the alcove, where he looked down through the viewfinder. He stared into it for several seconds and then raised his head and looked at me and said, 'I have been sent on an errand, every day for the last three days.'

I don't suppose I could have imagined a comment more obscure.

'What do you mean?'

I was ashamed by the bewildered tone of my voice.

'Professor MacKay long ago entrusted me with the task of ensuring that his laboratory at the university is supplied with vanadium sulphate – it's used in the production of formaldehyde. I accepted this task when I was first given my place at the mortuary. Two days ago, the same afternoon that man was murdered across the road from here, the professor told me he had expended his supply unexpectedly and he needed a sample of vanadium sulphate as a matter of urgency.'

He gazed out the window, looking north and then turned and looked south.

'The factory that manufactures steam engines is just half a mile from here,' Billy said, peering through the window.

'I know it,' I said. 'I've passed it.' I spoke because I wanted to test my voice and instil in it and in my situation a measure of calm.

He looked at me thoughtfully. 'You have?' he said. 'You will not have known, perhaps, that between here and the factory are the premises of Walter Smith & Co, an industrial chemist. They produce vanadium sulphate as a by-product in the manufacture of steel alloy for engine parts. They are the only supplier of vanadium in the city.'

'Why are you telling me this?'

'Because Professor MacKay asked me the day before yesterday to collect vanadium from Walter Smith, but when I arrived I discovered that they were waiting for a consignment, and when I reported this to the professor he insisted that I call again yesterday and again today, till I could bring him this material.'

He looked at me sharply, as though he were explaining something, the import of which was transparently obvious but which I had failed to grasp.

'Mr Cameron,' he went on with exaggerated patience, 'I believe I may appear in your pictures. I believe I was *intended* to appear in them.'

Billy turned and looked into the viewfinder again. Then he raised his head and stared at me. I thought he was going to say something else, but instead, he moved out of the alcove and began to walk towards me.

I took a step backward. I tried to see if he had anything in his hand, some sort of device by which he could deliver a lethal dose of some chemical preparation before I would have an opportunity to fend him off, but his hands were empty and remained by his side.

I could not continue to retreat without losing all sense of dignity.

I tensed and stood. He came very close and said, 'Mr Cameron, do you think they have got rid of you because you haven't found the murderer?'

I could smell the sharp scent. I looked into Billy's eyes and saw a hard intelligence there. His gaze was the gaze of a man who has survived and intends to continue surviving, even if he has been banished to the periphery of his world.

He shook his head. 'No, Mr Cameron, they've got rid of you because you are very, very close.'

Before I knew it, he was moving past me to the door. I spun round and began to ask him what he meant by this, but he opened the door and said, 'If I'm damned I'll be damned for my own sins, not another's.'

I suddenly spoke with the same reckless indiscretion that had prompted me to protect Billy's photographs in the developing room an hour before.

'Do you know William Harrison?'

'The chemist?'

'Yes.'

He shrugged. 'He has a shop at the cross.'

'What's his relationship to Sergeant Macarthur?'

Billy looked blank.

'What's his connection to Professor MacKay?'

'They are brothers-in-law. Why?'

I shook my head. 'I don't know.'

'Then I will bid you good evening.'

This greeting seemed to me the most curiously unaffected thing that Billy had said to me since I first made his acquaintance.

CHAPTER TWENTY-SIX

When I went down to the lobby, the men who had been cleaning behind the reception desk had gone. I glanced in the direction of the kitchen. No sign of activity. Suddenly, I became conscious of movement behind me and then a voice calling my name.

It was the newspaperman. I guessed that he'd been snooping behind the reception desk.

'I said I wasn't going to talk to you.'

'You said you would talk to me later.'

'Well, then, later.'

'Later's now.'

'What do you want?'

'I want to know why you've been fired.'

'I haven't been fired.'

'I heard they paid you a lot of money and you haven't been able to get a picture of the murderer.'

'What's your name?'

'George Stephenson. The *Citizen*.' He reached into his jacket pocket and extracted a calling card, with his name and the address of the *Evening Citizen*. He presented this to me.

'I understand you are Italian, Signor Cameron. Or is it Cameroni?'

I was amused and relieved by this absurd confusion.

'I can't speak to you now,' I said. 'I'm late for an appointment. Can I call at your offices tomorrow?' I looked down at the address. It was near the Fletchers' gallery.

'Let me take just a few details for today's edition,' he said.

He was a big man, with a round face and a thick grey walrus moustache. His hair was steel grey, short and wiry. He did not display the grudging deference of a manual worker or the casual distance of a gentleman. He was somewhere in between, like me.

'I'm Spanish, not Italian,' I said. 'I'm a photographer. I've not completed my work yet and it is too early to tell whether or not I will succeed. I believe I may be able to give you more satisfactory information in the morning. Now, if you will excuse me.'

I had walked to the door as I spoke, and, when I finished, I stepped out into the street and began to run. The policeman was standing near the entrance. I raced past him and carried on for twenty yards, at which point I struck out into the traffic and jumped onto a tram that was heading towards the city centre.

I climbed to the top deck and sat down and caught my breath.

The sun illuminated everything. The canvas awnings in front of the shops were like ships' sails. I saw the dry-salter and the chemist and the traffic policeman. Small boys loitered and girls played with hoops on the corner of the crossing. Women walked to and fro, with bags and bundles, pulling tiny tots and pushing prams. It struck me that in these streets women, not men, were the beasts of burden.

I would return in two hours to collect the final day's photography from the window of Mr Presser's office.

The tram crossed the bridge and entered the first canyon of the city centre. Entrances to the buildings here were flanked by massive pillars, the windows above them decorated with heavy arches and architraves and pilasters, the facades designed to project solidity, strength, probity, ambition, solvency, power.

Beyond the centre I felt an almost tangible relief. My thoughts became less agitated. I smoked and looked out at new tenements along Great Western Road not yet blackened, not yet scarred by the patina of poverty. Neat, prosperous lines of sandstone were broken here and there by church steeples. After half a mile we crossed a bridge over a steep gulley and the main thoroughfare broadened, with long leafy service lanes on either side in front of townhouses.

I travelled across worlds. The avenues now around me were a thousand miles from Crown Street.

I climbed down to the bottom deck when I saw a church steeple that I'd set as my point of reference, and jumped off as the tram slowed. I had to cross the main road, climb a long hill and take a sharp left at a crossing where there was a cluster of shops. Opposite the shops was a gazebo in the Turkish fashion; an omnibus waited at its terminus nearby.

I breathed in the scent of roses and azaleas and laburnum trees. An omnibus toiled up the hill, displacing every other sound with its insistent monotone of metal and steam, but after it had passed, the music of the gardens returned; insects buzzed and skylarks whooped among larch and beech.

Three women sat under the gazebo. The oldest wore black from head to toe; her daughters were dressed in summer finery. The youngest had her hand on the handle of a black pram, which she rocked gently backward and forward. Their voices carried in the soft breeze. 'He won't surely want to go back to his old firm,' the woman in black said. '*He* will,' her daughter replied. The youngest girl murmured something to her child.

Agnès brought tea to the sitting room. Her chestnut hair was tied carelessly behind her head, kept in place by a leather clasp. Strands flew across her crown and she put her hand up from time to time to draw these back into some kind of order. She had been painting and there were flecks of blue and yellow on her cotton smock. She exchanged some words with Jane. I heard Mary's name spoken.

The French girl would have turned heads if she'd walked into any room; she was very pretty. Jane had a presence infinitely more alluring, though.

Perhaps every man who falls in love thinks like this.

They carried on talking. I heard Alan's name and then Mary's again. Agnès was agitated and unhappy. Jane, speaking in rapid and earnest French, was trying to reason with her.

To separate myself from this private exchange I concentrated on the large canvas above the fireplace. It depicted a group of women in white skirts and blouses and hats, holding parasols. They stood and sat beside a brightly coloured marquee that had been erected on a white beach and behind them were chalk cliffs. The scene was a jet of light; the figures were indistinct and yet the composition and colour, the flowing line of the drawing and the sea and sand and cliff conspired to invest them with a kind of *possibility*.

It was an escape from the squalor of the real world, the world where Jack Macarthur schemed, where Headmaster Mahoney and Minister Buchan struggled against a corrupting tide.

Even if escape were possible, was it right to run away?

Agnès began to cry. Her voice rose and then broke. Jane leant forward and dabbed the girl's face with a blue handkerchief and as she did this she whispered to her. Agnès began to nod, tentatively at first and then more resolutely. When Jane finished speaking, Agnès straightened up and hurried out of the room.

Jane came and sat beside me.

'She is in love with my uncle,' she said simply. 'Such things happen.' After a moment she added, 'I suspect that *he* is in love with her, though, and that's less easily addressed.'

She looked down at her hands.

'But this does not help us with the matter at hand,' she said in a brighter tone.

I told her what had happened after I left her. 'Do you remember when we passed the place where the man was killed last year, the steam engine cut off his legs?'

'Yes?'

'You said the victim was related to Professor MacKay.'

'Yes.'

'Did you know that William Harrison the chemist is related to Professor MacKay too?'

Jane raised her hands a little, palms up. 'How is this connected to what we're looking for?'

'I don't know, but till now *everything* has been connected.'

She nodded. 'The man who was killed at the crossing was Mrs MacKay's brother.'

'Jeanie Harrison's husband,' I said. 'But what does it mean!'

'It means,' she said sensibly, 'that these people are related. No more than that, perhaps.'

We were both silent for a moment and then Jane said, 'When Annie Belmont went out to buy tobacco, William was behind the reception desk. He had started to feel better, she said. When she returned, what was left of him lay on the flagstones. She's adamant that she was not away for more than five minutes. They didn't have William's usual blend at the tobacconist across the road and she had to walk further along Crown Street to one of the public houses.'

'North or south?'

Jane nodded, 'I thought of that too. She walked south. And, no, she didn't see anyone she recognised or anyone who looked suspicious. The killer simply vanished into thin air, together with William's arms and legs.'

We sat in silence for several moments and then I said, 'Edie Hamilton was attacked in the close, and the attempt was bungled.'

Jane poured milk into my tea.

'Billy Fraser said something strange to me when he left.' I spoke slowly. Ideas began to change places in my head. 'He said, "If I'm damned I'll be damned for my own sins, not another's."'

She poured milk into her own cup.

'Billy was seen near Edie's close soon after the attack,' I said.

'But you don't think he had anything to do with it.'

'I'm beginning to think that he *did* have something to do with that particular attack. The Reverend Buchan has a low opinion of Billy Fraser. He said he was a danger to women.'

'But he too seemed to believe that Billy is not the murderer.'

'Billy develops photographs in the normal course of his work. He takes pictures of the bodies that are brought to the mortuary,' I said. 'He also develops pictures that are sent to him by the police, pictures connected to blackmail.'

I would have been unable to complete my account of what I knew about Billy if we had not reached a plateau of common understanding. 'And he deals in another kind of photography,' I said. 'This morning in the developing room I found pictures of naked men and women. They were not photographs that had been made for blackmail. The people in the images *knew* they were being photographed. These pictures were made as a kind of entertainment.'

She didn't blush. She said, 'So, he's involved in crimes of some sort.'

'What if Billy *did* assault Edie Hamilton?'

'If he *did* assault Edie Hamilton . . .' she repeated softly and then went on speaking. 'But he isn't the murderer?'

I nodded. 'They *wanted* him to be photographed in Crown Street. He has a record of molesting women. That's what the Reverend Buchan meant . . .' I stopped and tried to recall the minister's words. 'He said a man who's a threat can also serve a purpose.'

'What purpose?'

'To hide the real murderer!'

I put down my cup.

'Who, then, is being protected?' she asked.

'Someone respectable, someone given access to respectable homes, someone with medical knowledge.' I paused. 'And someone who is driven by a fiendish compulsion to sever the limbs of his victims and carry them away.'

Jane's face became pale. 'His path goes from the bank right to your hotel,' she said.

Her eyes narrowed and she pursed her lips and then, to my complete surprise, she stood up and hurried out of the room. I found myself vacantly contemplating the women on the beach.

It was a large solid house where the sounds in one part were not easily heard in another. I knew that Agnès was at home. Alan and Mary might be out. I had not seen them.

Jane was gone a long time. I listened to the silence and looked at the painting.

When she returned she was holding a gun.

My face must have revealed an unedifying mixture of confusion and alarm.

She stood above me, clutching the weapon, and her expression was suddenly amused.

'I'm not going to shoot you, Juan!'

She sat down beside me.

'It's my father's service revolver!' She had a box of cartridges, which she laid on the sofa. 'I want you to take it with you.'

I didn't want to touch the gun or the cartridges.

'Take it,' she said again.

I shook my head.

'Why not?'

'I'm not a man for guns.'

She looked at the revolver and the cartridges. If I'd told her I didn't like the colour of her dress her expression might have been similar.

'I'd better put it back, then,' she said in a subdued tone. 'My aunt would have a heart attack if she knew it was in the house. I only kept it because it's hard to give away.' She glanced at me and added, 'As you have demonstrated.'

She returned a few minutes later.

I took out my pipe and filled it. When I felt in my pocket for matches, Jane fetched a flint from the fireside. She flicked the lever twice and with both hands held the heavy mechanism in front of me so that I could turn the pipe sideways and bring the flame onto the tobacco. I blew smoke into the room.

'I admired your aunt and uncle in Cuba,' I said, inhaling tobacco smoke. 'They are earnest as well as cheerful. I think people like that are very fortunate.'

Jane was sitting close beside me.

'They live on their own terms, in their own way, in the heart of a world that's different. They do not intend to change – they actually want the Cubans to be like them! Yet they are respected. I admire . . . I admire their courage.'

We looked at the women on the sunlit seashore.

'My father was killed at the very moment he completed his record of Spanish architecture in the West. He had never, I believe, hurt anyone – sometimes I think my mother ran away because she could not live with a man who would not *compete*, who simply carried on doing his own work doggedly and honestly.

'I wasn't with him when he died. I would have held him. I would have told him that his life had been of value, that he was loved, that he was a *good* man. But I was not beside him then.'

I felt her hand in mine.

'He was shot on the instructions of his cousin. Of this I

300

am quite certain. We buried my father in a cemetery on the edge of the city within sight of the siege lines. There were eucalyptus trees.

'The next day I developed his last photographs. And soon after that, Paco and Eleanora were killed. They passed me in the courtyard on their way to the stable, and I followed them there. I wanted to confront them . . . There was an explosion . . . smoke, dust. I was knocked to the ground. There was so much dust, so much smoke.

'Paco lay near the window. I walked over to him and looked down at his body and I was struck by how clean his clothes were. He was surrounded by mud and straw but his white shirt was spotless. His face looked peaceful. I didn't kneel down and feel his pulse. I *knew* he was dead. And Eleanora lay at a bad-tempered angle (that's what I thought then). She was on her side and her dress had been pulled up so that I could see her boots and her knees and she was covered in dirt.

'Her eyes were open and she was still breathing. I leant over her. Her eyes moved. She tried to speak. I ran to the door and shouted for help but no one answered. I would have carried her into the house. I kept shouting.

'When I went back into the stable, Eleanora was dead.'

Jane put her hands on my face and pressed her forehead against mine and we sat like this for a long time. I felt the great weight of death in Santiago begin to fall away from me.

CHAPTER TWENTY-SEVEN

Archibald Presser looked over my shoulder to right and left as he unlocked the accordion gate and let me into the bank. We climbed the stairs from the banking hall, creating a familiar creak.

When I had first met him, all of Mr Presser's nervous energy was funnelled into agreeing to an unusual proposal. MacKay and Macarthur and I had come to him for a favour and he had granted the favour. And afterwards I understood that the transaction was not as clear as I had naively believed. But what if Jane was right and I was looking for conspiracies that didn't exist?

Walking up the creaking stairs and entering his office, I found myself disliking the modest cut of Mr Presser's suit. It was the kind of suit that would be worn by a man who could identify the moving force in any proposition and make sure he was not standing in its way.

The camera, which had seemed such an exotic and intrusive addition to Mr Presser's office when we placed it here three days before, now looked rather small, rather redundant. I walked round the desk and unclipped the frame that held the plates.

'Despite the latest murders,' I said (in order to fill the silence in the room), 'people think it's something that will not happen to *them*.'

'There is a great deal of fear,' he acknowledged curtly.

Mr Presser was nervous, but was he afraid? He didn't seem to me to be afraid – even though two of the victims had been abandoned on the steps of his bank.

I began to consider why he would not be afraid.

The most obvious answer could not be borne out by common sense.

He didn't *look* the part.

But who looks the part?

I glanced at him as I removed the plates. He had locked the accordion gate and the main door downstairs after letting me in.

Someone respectable.

He took a step towards me.

'Can I help you with that?' he asked.

I had placed the plates in the satchel and had just begun to detach the camera from the tripod.

'It looks heavy,' he said.

'No. I can manage.'

He stopped where he was and continued to watch me as I detached the camera and placed it in its case, and then began to unscrew the frame from the tripod. The thread of the socket that held the frame seemed to have been damaged, because, though I turned it and turned it, it would not separate from the tripod.

'Here, let me!' Mr Presser came towards me with his hands stretched out.

I stepped aside and allowed him to manhandle the frame and pull it roughly from the tripod, twisting it and wrenching it away from the screw at the top.

The murderer had a trick of administering a narcotic so swiftly that the victim would be helpless in his presence.

Mr Presser turned and held out the frame.

I snatched it from him and put it in the bag and reached out and got hold of the tripod.

'Aren't you going to fold it up?' he asked.

'No need. I don't have far to go.'

'Don't be absurd!' He reached out to take the tripod from me.

I was holding the bag in my right hand and the tripod in my left. Every instinct in my body prompted me not to surrender the tripod.

And yet, that would be bizarre.

I felt him take it from me. He held it with some familiarity.

'I used to use one,' he explained. 'Not for a camera but for a machine press.'

'A machine press?'

'I was a scissors maker before I went into the banking line.' He spoke less curtly than before.

I must have shown my surprise because he added, now speaking with a strangely relaxed familiarity, 'People think that bank managers are born bank managers, but we have lives like others.'

He handed me the tripod, folded and easier to carry.

'Shall we?' he said.

He indicated that I should walk ahead of him. This I was reluctant to do, but I did not see that I had much choice. I walked briskly, and he walked briskly behind me. I got out the door and reached the head of the stairs.

'Just one moment,' he said.

I turned and saw that he was bending down to lock his office door.

I began to walk down the main stairs. They creaked.

'Please wait, Mr Cameron!'

I continued moving down the stairs; if he wanted to hurry after me he was free to do so.

Each step I took made a creak that echoed through the empty building.

'Mr Cameron,' he said, coming down the stairs two at a time, and seeming not to make them creak at all, 'it pains me that we should part on terms that are not entirely satisfactory.'

He had reached the step I was on. I took a step and he took a step in tandem. As we moved from the second to the first step and then onto the marble floor I thought that he moved closer to me, sidling alongside.

The murderer had not used force to bring his victims out in the open. He had walked close beside them, I thought.

We reached the door.

'Here we are,' I said, turning to face him. I had my hands full, the camera bag in one hand and the tripod in the other. Otherwise, I would have reached down and turned the handle of the door.

Mr Presser made no effort to do this. Instead, he glanced at the street outside, as if to check that I had not come in the company of another person.

A scissors maker. Someone skilled with a blade.

I placed the tripod and the bag in front of me, like a shield. I resolved to parry any thrust. He looked at me with apparent bafflement, a ruse I could well imagine would be in his arsenal of tricks to dupe the unsuspecting. Then he reached behind him and took something from beneath his jacket. I was ready to raise the tripod and hit him hard over the head with it.

He had removed a small set of keys. He selected one, reached down and unlocked the door and the gate.

'I am sorry I could not have been of greater service,' he said, looking at me with a sad, still baffled expression.

He drew back the gate so that I could go through.

'Thank you for the help you *have* been able to give, Mr Presser,' I said, trying to raise my voice above that of a whisper.

I hurried down the steps.

I had recovered some composure by the time I reached the mortuary. And, as composure returned, I was assailed by a proper sense of shame.

Mr Presser could not have been the killer. For one thing, I had a record of him entering the bank at the time Seamus Hanlon was murdered.

Yet I had been irrationally and extremely afraid. The killer's power was an enemy of reason.

Robert was in the dissection room. I did not see Billy, and I walked straight to the developing room without speaking.

Robert opened one of the drawers that served as temporary coffins and seemed to begin cleaning it. He watched me crossing the room, and he responded to my silence with a silence of his own.

In those few seconds I wished I was in a busy, sunlit *granadino* avenue.

Enveloped in the dark of the developing room, I began to work. The photographs that appeared in the sulphate solution were my final chance to seize the truth.

One by one they materialised. I placed each on the line and then divided my attention between the paper in the solution and the finished images drying in the eerie light.

The figures danced. They *danced* with the energy of random life, unbound by patterns, unbound by anything that would make them intelligible. They were *beyond* me. I had sought to impose my own understanding and this was to attempt something utterly impossible. Life cannot be reduced to a sequence of photographs.

I chastised myself for thinking like this.

I was *not* trying to impose a pattern. I was trying to *identify* whatever pattern might already exist.

I hadn't found what I was looking for, but it *must* be there – and the only way to reveal it was to complete the minute comparison of each image, frame by frame.

I waited until the last photograph was dry. The air around me was hot and dank, but I did not dare open the door until all were safely stowed away in the satchel.

When this was done I stepped into the cool dissection room. Robert had gone. I hurried round the tables and pushed the door open and moved into the gloomy corridor.

Shadows converged on one another on the edge of night.

When I identified the waiting figure, I knew it was the figure – beneath the surface of my conscious thoughts – I had always expected.

CHAPTER TWENTY-EIGHT

'Did you assault a man outside Bailey's Bar this afternoon?' Jack Macarthur demanded.

'He tried to rob me of my wallet. I didn't let him.'

'He says you took him out of the bar and beat him. He had to see the doctor he was so badly hurt.'

I looked at him steadily.

'We'll have to go to the station and talk about this,' he said.

A blue police van was waiting outside. Macarthur walked round to the back, where a policeman held the door open.

'I'll take that,' Macarthur said, extending his hand to relieve me of my satchel.

I gave it to him.

'Get in.'

I climbed into the back of the van and sat on the hard bench that stretched along one side of the interior. The door slammed and I heard the sound of bolts being drawn, one at the top of the door and the other at the side.

I was in complete darkness, but I was not alone. Almost as soon as I had sat down, even before the van lurched forward and began to trundle over the cobbles, I began to scratch myself. The van smelt of alcohol and vomit, and it was alive with bugs.

The journey lasted no more than ten minutes and when the van stopped and the bolts were drawn I needed no encouragement to climb out.

I was in a yard surrounded by high stone walls: a lamp cut through the twilight above the main entrance to a building on one side. The constable marched me to a door at the end of the building, which opened onto a long corridor lit by three lamps fixed halfway up the plaster wall. The lamps flickered when the door was opened. We walked along the corridor to a set of stone stairs, descended the stairs and walked the length of another corridor, this one tiled in the institutional manner of Gabriel Mahoney's school. I was pushed into a large room, at the centre of which was a small table with a chair on either side.

'Sit,' the policeman told me.

I sat on one of the chairs. It was fixed to the floor. The policeman went out again and locked the door. There was a lamp on the wall between two windows too high up for me to see out of. Apart from the chairs and table there was no other furniture.

I might sit here for hours, perhaps until morning, I knew. I knew, too, that there was no point in pacing round the room. It was already stuffy and I would simply begin to perspire.

Having considered this, I stood up and began to pace.

I had surrendered the photographs. This angered me. I had lost control over the one thing that was exclusively my own responsibility. I had seen the pictures but I hadn't yet subjected them to the careful study that made them useful.

I felt a fresh surge of resentment, directed at Macarthur but more violently and painfully directed at myself. Why had I given in so meekly?

This thought filled me with such disquiet that I sat down on the chair and then immediately stood up again and began to pace more quickly.

I was angry with my own behaviour. I had stumbled clumsily and stupidly into a conspiracy. And now I considered the further evil that could result from my amateurish bungling. Tommy had become my sidekick and he had been seen with me. Jane too had been seen with me.

I walked to the door and hammered it. My fists made a small quiet thud on the steel surface. I strode to the opposite wall below the gas lamp and hit the tiles there, but this just made my fingers smart.

Billy Fraser would be arrested, I thought. Perhaps he had already been arrested. He would be charged with murders I was now almost certain he did not commit.

I went back to the door and hammered it again.

To my astonishment, I felt the bolt being drawn and the door was opened.

I took several steps backward. Two figures came in. The second was Sergeant Macarthur. The first was Professor MacKay.

'Mr Cameron,' the professor said, 'what the devil have you got yourself mixed up in!'

'I beg your pardon?'

311

'You had better sit down.'

I glanced at Macarthur. He was looking purposefully at the gas jet high up on the wall behind me.

The professor walked over to the chair on the other side of the table and I took the seat opposite.

Macarthur placed my satchel in the middle of the table.

'Are the pictures still inside?' the professor asked him with conspicuous distaste.

'Yes.'

MacKay nodded and Macarthur extracted from my satchel a piece of cardboard in which were half a dozen pictures. He spread the pictures in front of me and I recognised Billy Fraser's handiwork. I might have seen the same images hanging up to dry in the developing room, or perhaps these were a different variety of the same species. In any case, they depicted men and women engaged in various kinds of sexual act.

'Did you take these photographs?' the professor asked in a voice that seemed to convey sorrow rather than anger.

'No.'

'Then why were they found in your bag?'

'Because someone put them there.'

'Don't be glib with me!' As he said this, the blood appeared to drain away from his face.

'I did not take those photographs.'

The professor stared at me and then he glanced at Macarthur and said, 'And the business with Alex MacLean.'

Macarthur shrugged. 'MacLean says that Cameron assaulted him. Cameron approached him in Bailey's Bar with some sort of proposal and MacLean declined and then a fight broke out. Other people witnessed it.'

'Is this true?' the professor said, turning to me.

I could not determine whether the professor was going through the motions of indignation, if this charade was something in which he was actively engaged or something by which he was being duped. Yet I could not believe he was a gullible man.

'Of course it isn't true!'

'There were witnesses, you say?' The professor turned to Macarthur.

'Half a dozen at least.'

MacKay turned to me again and said, 'What are we to make of all this?'

Before I could reply, he continued. 'This is business for the magistrate.' He glanced down at the photographs. 'And it's a dirty business indeed. I don't think you want us to take it that far, Mr Cameron, do you?'

I remained silent.

MacKay's face suddenly turned the colour of beetroot and he pounded the table so hard that two of the pictures rose and floated in a current of air from the desk to the floor. Macarthur picked them up.

The professor's histrionic display resolved my dilemma. He was not being duped, I decided. He was an active participant in the charade.

'Do you want to go before the magistrate?' he asked.

'I do not.'

'Here's what I'm going to do with you.'

The insolence of *with you* was very hard to bear.

'I'm going to give you an opportunity to go back where you came from. We'll have Alex MacLean's testimony notarised and we'll have your pictures' – he pointed to the photographs on the table between us – 'safe, so that if we ever hear so much as a peep out of you again, Mr Cameron, we will see to it that you are held accountable.'

I waited.

'You will stay here tonight,' he added. 'We will put you on the first train to London in the morning.'

'Professor MacKay,' I said, 'at your invitation . . . I became involved in this investigation. I felt a moral obligation to do so . . . an obligation to do good. This leaves me no choice.'

I paused. Neither of them chose to speak, and I sensed that the initiative was not fully in their grasp.

'I will select your original option,' I went on, 'and take my case to the magistrate. I will explain that I have nothing to do with these photographs and that far from instigating a brawl I was the innocent victim of an attempted robbery. If my case stands up, I will be exonerated. If it does not, I will make sure that the newspapers get to know about my association with you, how it was through your good office that I joined the police investigation, how you worked closely with me for several days. My reputation will already be destroyed; I will have nothing to lose. You, however, will lose a great deal.'

He looked at me, I thought, with the expression of a man trying to stop a runaway train.

'Alternatively, you will *not* have me locked up,' I continued. 'You will allow me to return to my hotel.'

'You won't bargain with me!' he growled.

'We could post an officer at Simpson's,' Macarthur said quickly.

The professor glanced at the sergeant and then at me. He stood up. '*You* guard him, then,' he snapped and hurried out.

At the entrance to the building, Macarthur refused to return the photographs he had taken from me. He simply stared me down and then he insisted that I step outside and get in the van. I said I would remain where I was until my property was restored. He considered this for a long moment. The constable took a step forward, clearly intending to push me out into the courtyard where the van waited, and just at that moment Macarthur changed tack. 'Wait,' he told the constable. He walked back along the corridor and entered one of the rooms. When he returned he had the photographs. He placed them in my satchel and handed it to me.

On the way to the hotel we travelled in the police van, but thankfully in the front, where there was room for Macarthur and me, as well as the officer who was to spend the night in the lobby. We travelled in silence. When I climbed down, Macarthur climbed down after me.

He followed me into the hotel and, after I had walked behind the empty reception desk and retrieved my key, he accompanied me to the top of the stairs.

'What do you want?' I demanded when we reached the door of my room.

'I want to make sure that you don't try to do any further mischief. The officer downstairs has instructions to prevent you from leaving the building. I will return tomorrow morning. We *will* put you on the London train.'

I unlocked the door and went inside.

The next several seconds imposed on my senses a greater degree of strain than the human psyche is, I believe, designed to absorb.

I was not alone.

The only illumination in the room came from the streetlamp fixed to the facade of the hotel two windows away. A faint light from this made it possible for me to see a figure move towards me from the window.

I had closed the door and the figure moved so quickly that I did not have time to open it again. I took a step backward and my back slammed into the wood in the centre of the door and I raised an arm to parry what I anticipated would be a blow.

But there was no blow. The figure stopped very close. I recognised a faint but familiar odour.

'Tommy!'

'Is that you, Mr Cameron?' he asked in a frightened voice.

'Who the devil did you think it was?'

I walked round him and took a match and lit the jet between the alcove and the writing table.

'How did you get in here?'

He looked mystified. Perhaps he wondered why I should care how he got in, or perhaps it seemed to him so obvious that he was surprised I should have asked. He nodded towards the window.

'It was open,' he said.

'But it's on the first floor!'

'There's a drainpipe.'

'Well, more to the point, why did you break into my room?'

'I didn't break in,' he said reasonably. 'The window was open.'

'Why are you here?' I asked sternly.

'I'm going to go back to school,' he said. 'Mr Mahoney told me they wouldn't take me away, and Miss O'Reilly, that's my teacher, she says I'm better at counting than the others.'

He waited. What he told me was so remote from my immediate concerns that I smiled.

'I'm pleased you're going back to school, Tommy.'

'But that's not why I came. I came because I know why they took you away in the police van.'

'How do you know they took me away in the police van?'

'I saw you. I was outside the mortuary waiting for you.'

'Why did they take me away?'

'Because Mr Harrison told them to.'

'Mr Harrison, the chemist?'

He nodded.

'How do you know that?'

'When you left the bank, Sergeant Macarthur came and spoke to Mr Presser.'

'You saw me leave the bank?'

'You told me to come and see you this evening so I thought I would get there early. I was going to cross the road and catch up with you but then I saw Sergeant Macarthur. He waited until you had walked past the dry-salter and then he came and spoke to Mr Presser so I decided to hear what they were saying.'

'How did you do that?'

'There's a stairway down to the basement below the bank. It starts in the street and then goes round the corner under the steps. It's locked but it's easy to climb over the gate. From the side of the steps I could hear what they said.'

'What did they say?'

'Sergeant Macarthur asked Mr Presser if you had taken away your camera and the photographs. He said that you had. Then Mr Harrison came and he told them they shouldn't have let you take the photographs and that Sergeant Macarthur was to do something about it. I had to wait till they went away before I ran after you. You'd gone into the mortuary when I got there. I couldn't go in because Sergeant Macarthur was already there.'

It was about half past ten. I sat on the bed and drummed my fingers on my knees.

'There's a constable in the lobby,' I said. 'He's there to make sure that I don't go anywhere.'

Tommy nodded.

'Can you go out and come in again without being seen?'

He looked at me as though I had asked a particularly vacuous question.

'I'm going to give you money for a cab,' I said. 'I want you to go to the other side of town and deliver a letter. Will you do that for me?'

He nodded vigorously.

I got up and went to the desk and wrote down everything that had transpired in the last two hours, together with Tommy's testimony. I asked Jane to contact George Stephenson at the *Evening Citizen* and tell him to come to the hotel. Publicity, I thought, would give me a bargaining chip, at the very least.

'How are you going to get out?' I asked Tommy as I opened the door and looked onto the landing. There appeared to be no one there.

He pointed to the end of the corridor, where he had disappeared the night before. I peered into the darkness. Then I closed the door and followed him to a narrow window covered with canvas. It began about two feet up the wall and continued for what I judged to be about half of Tommy's height. A grown man could not have wriggled through it. For

Tommy, however, this was the work of a moment. He pushed back the canvas flap and seemed to slither upwards. I saw his head disappear and then his torso, then his legs and feet. I leant forward and, on tiptoe, I was just able to make out the stone walls and windows of a backcourt. A noxious odour emanated through the flap and I guessed that Tommy was descending, by means of another drainpipe, I presumed, onto the area reserved for refuse.

Further on, I saw the passageway that led from the courtyard to the main road. Tommy stopped there and looked briefly back and waved his hand, like a horseman riding off to bring reinforcements to a beleaguered garrison.

In my room I laid out the photographs that Macarthur had returned to me.

One was missing.

I looked up from the table and out to the street. I saw the policeman walking up and down. There was a fresh breeze. The policeman's helmet was pulled down over his head and his tunic was fastened up to the neck.

One photograph was missing.

So, I *had* recorded something significant.

The quarter to three photograph was gone. The one taken moments before William Gibson's murder.

My usual suspects, then, the figures who appeared in the remaining pictures, could be ruled out.

I set about annotating the figures in the photographs. I listed the policemen, three of them, and the boys who frequented the traffic island, the loafers there too, including the likely lad with the expectant expression on his face; there were Mr Presser and the dry-salter and Mr Harrison, and there were the bookmaker and his runners; the men who frequented Bailey's Bar featured prominently, though I noted that Alex MacLean, the man I'd twice thrown onto the cobbles, was not among them. I did not think that this was because of his putative injuries but because he would lie low for a day or two out of shame. Maggie McAllister's parents appeared in the photographs and so did the Reverend Buchan and a dozen shopkeepers; there were carters, including the coalman, who had appeared in photographs in previous days, and I even recognised the drivers of tramcars and omnibuses.

Yet I could not dredge up from the depths of my consciousness the figure who must appear in the missing photograph but was absent from the ones that had been left.

I thought and paced and thought and paced again. Then, when I had spent an hour sifting through the photographs from the previous three days, I saw what had been in front of me all the time. I saw what I had been unable to see.

The camera does not *see*; it simply records. It records shapes that appear before it and we impose on those shapes a meaning that corresponds to our thinking.

And the harder we try to understand, the more we impose patterns of meaning.

She was there.

I found the photographs taken in Crown Street at a quarter to three, immediately before Seamus Hanlon's murder, and then, before and after that, on the cross. Then I scanned the photograph on the day of William Gibson's murder.

She was in three pictures, in Crown Street and then at the cross, before and after Seamus Hanlon's murder. The photograph taken from Mr Presser's window just before Gibson's murder had been removed. She wasn't in any of the other photographs of the square that day.

I walked away from the table as though the murderer herself were in the room beside me.

Back at the table, I looked down at the images again. I knew this was my killer.

She walked through the crowds incongruous and at one with her surroundings.

I began to study the other photographs, and I must confess that I did not do this in a systematic and scientific manner. I pulled the pictures from their folders, rifling through them in a frenzied effort to learn more about this single figure.

She had been in Crown Street the day before, in the afternoon, and the day before that in the morning. In the morning she was photographed walking to the cross, in the afternoon she was on the other side of the street walking south, and the day before that she was in the cross again, walking in front of the bank, past the space where she had left the dismembered remains of Bessie Armstrong and Hector MacKinnon months before. In the afternoon of the previous day she had been walking north towards the bridge that led over the river, the route I took to reach the mortuary.

The figure was tall, almost stately, dressed in black. In one photograph her right leg was raised to step from the pavement, the left foot pushed forward. She wore black boots of the sort that make it possible to walk through the mud and detritus of city streets. In two images, she had her back to the camera. In the rest, she looked to one side – as a person might do when they know they are being photographed but do not wish to be recognised.

I looked down at the images and then through the window where the policeman had been pacing. There was no sign of him now. The street was deserted.

And then I heard a knock at the door.

Tommy would have knocked with intent. That was his way. This knock was soft and speculative.

'Who's there?'

No answer.

I bent down and looked through the keyhole.

An eye looked back at me.

I heard a scurrying in the corridor and then nothing.

I unlocked the door and stepped out.

'Who's there?'

I could hear nothing from along the corridor and nothing from the floor above or the floor below.

I went down the stairs. On the landing, the floorboards creaked. I looked behind me, back up to my room, where the door stood open; yellow light from the jet above the desk cast a pall over the corridor.

There was no one in the downstairs lobby. I walked over the flagstones and heard the sound of my footsteps. I stepped out into the night air, cooler now. The street was empty. No sign of the constable. Back in the hotel I strode over to the reception.

I looked behind the desk. I tried to resist fear.

All I saw were newly scrubbed flagstones. There was no trace of anything in the lobby or of anyone.

'Annie!' I called, moving towards the kitchen.

Far away on the corner where the bookmaker habitually stood, two drunk men sang a raucous chorus, the mordant tuneless notes of which disturbed the sleeping street.

'Annie!' I called again, entering the kitchen.

The long table in the middle of the room had been cleared, all the jars and bowls that held cooking ingredients neatly stacked at the opposite end from the fire. The chair by the fire was empty but for two knitting needles and a ball of wool. But when I scanned the room I saw an object that made me curse under my breath and look suddenly behind me.

By the wall of the kitchen, nearest to the entrance from the lobby, stood a large black pram.

I stepped towards it. The hood was up, and a canvas cover stretched over the top. Gingerly I reached down and unclipped one corner of the canvas cover and then the other. I peeled the canvas back and looked inside.

Surgical instruments.

Instruments with which to dissect a cadaver, instruments with which to sever the feet and arms from a corpse.

I heard a noise in the lobby. I spun round.

I listened.

The sound was not repeated. I walked back to the door, circumventing the pram and keeping close to the wall. I strained to hear the least thing. My own breathing seemed to me like an infernal din.

I looked out.

Nothing.

I stepped forward.

The wooden beam beneath the doorway creaked.

I shook myself and took a more forthright step. I was determined not to creep like a frightened mouse. The lobby was deserted.

Then, from the top of the stairs I heard footsteps. I ran to the first stair and bounded up. I was looking ahead, directly through the open door into my bedroom. The light flickered as though the jet had been touched by a breeze from the window, or because someone was walking past it. I could not remember if it had flickered before. I stood transfixed and waiting for an indication of where the presence was, in my room or in the gloom at the end of the corridor.

To my left, all I saw was darkness. I heard the sound of the canvas flap through which Tommy had climbed. It scraped against the plaster wall in the breeze.

The breeze was everywhere, tinkling the lamps on the wall opposite the reception desk, ruffling the curtains of the window in my room.

I could not stand there forever. I believed the presence knew where I was.

So, I darted to the side of the door and pressed my back flat against the wall and tried to peer, first through the darkness to the end of the corridor and then through the long narrow slit between the open door and the lintel.

My eyes struggled to penetrate the gloom, and through the aperture I could see only a part of the window above the desk.

Resolving that I must do or die, I launched myself into my own bedroom, frantically looking right and left. I opened my mouth to cry out, but some primordial cautionary instinct made me stay silent.

I saw no one, and no sign that anyone had been there.

I exhaled as though I had been holding my breath for a very long time and then I fell on my knees and looked beneath the bed. Nothing.

I got up and reached out and opened the door of the wardrobe. Empty.

As I stared into the wardrobe, I heard someone walking on the floor above. I dashed out and ran up the stairs to the landing, where the stairway doubled back. I turned and looked up and saw the hem of a black dress and the heel of a booted foot disappear from view.

She ran along the corridor and I reached the top of the stairs. When I got there she was gone.

I heard something behind me and for an instant I believed I was trapped – the woman in black was not alone; she had an accomplice, and the accomplice stood behind me ready to throttle me or drive a knife between my shoulder blades.

I turned – prepared to struggle but conscious that I might already be too late.

The alcove was empty, the wallpaper mildewed and the plaster beneath it bulging with damp.

Again I focused on the corridor.

There were two doors on the right and one on the left. I moved forward very slowly, trying hard not to make the floorboards creak. From downstairs, I heard only the breeze as it flitted through the empty hotel, making wood tap upon plaster and metal tap upon wood.

I put my hand on the handle of the first door and turned it and pushed it open.

The room was in darkness; a pale diffuse light from the gas lamp on the facade, below the line of these windows, allowed me to discern a bed and a table and chair and a wardrobe.

I did not go inside but moved along the corridor to the next room. I reached down and tried the handle and found that it responded to my touch; the hasp came back into the lock and I pushed the door forward and exposed what lay inside.

Less light here. I stopped at the threshold and waited.

A second of silence and then my ears were assailed by a scream.

I stood overwhelmed by events that seemed to happen before I could fully absorb that they had happened.

The door on the other side of the corridor flew open and the woman from the photographs ran out and made for the stairs. It was not until this that I understood that the scream did not come from the room where I stood or even from the same floor. It came from the ground floor.

I seemed in my own mind to be fixed to the doorway. It was with an effort of will that I wrenched myself out of this immobile stance and raced back along the corridor behind the figure in black.

As I got to the head of the stairs she was already halfway to the landing, and to my horror I saw, transfixed on the landing, looking up with an expression of terrified fascination, little Tommy.

He faced the harridan who descended towards him. She raised a long knife ready to strike.

'No!' I shouted.

It was as if I had wakened the dead.

But the woman did not alter course. She hurtled towards Tommy and I saw the knife begin its downward arc.

Tommy saw this too, and when he grasped what was going to happen he acted with greater speed and presence of mind than I had so far shown in these macabre circumstances. He acted as he would have acted if a constable had been sent to apprehend him and bring him to school against his will. He seemed to oscillate his body so that I saw it one moment facing me and facing the murderous onslaught of the woman in black, knife now descending – and then it was no longer facing me. Tommy sprang sideways down the stairs. He seemed to slither out of the woman's path.

She did not stop. The speed and force of her movements revealed a mechanical determination. I witnessed a psyche consumed by an atavistic impulse to kill.

I leapt from the fourth step above the landing and threw myself at the woman's shoulders.

I glimpsed livid skin beneath the veil as I got the full weight of my own shoulder into her back. I felt a tissue of skin and fat beneath the fabric of her mourning weeds and then muscle, and when I felt the muscle I realised that I would have barely the force that was necessary to topple her. I continued to move forward. I felt her fall and hit the masonry at the side of the landing, and then I found that while I'd succeeded in giving Tommy an opportunity to escape and had made the woman lose her balance and hit the wall, it was I and not she who now fell to the ground.

She uttered an exclamation.

I tried to roll over and regain my feet but I was spread-eagled on the carpeted landing. I smelt dust and when I looked up I saw through the veil the hard, frenzied eyes of a killing machine. I saw the knife rise up above me; it was not like a kitchen knife or even a butcher's blade; it was long and razor sharp, the sort of instrument a surgeon would use to sever cartilage. It came towards me.

Time stopped.

My last thought was that I had broken my shoulder, either

when I crashed into the woman or when I hit the floor. I was ashamed that I had executed this manoeuvre so clumsily, and out of the corner of my eye I saw Tommy standing at the bottom of the stairs watching everything and I hated that he should see this, and hated more that when I was gone he would be unprotected, from this woman and from all the violence of the world.

And then, the point of the surgeon's knife not more than a handful of inches from my face, I heard the same scream I'd heard before, the strained sound of a voice that I recognised. It was closer now; it was close to Tommy, close to me and my killer and it was followed – not followed, it was *accompanied* by another sound, so hard and loud that it seemed to impose itself on everything, even on the downward arc of the stiletto.

The point stopped and stayed above me for a moment and I watched the contorted face of the woman beneath her mourning veil suddenly relax, as though a great burden had been removed from her soul, and instead of standing over me, arm jack-knifed in a hacking motion, she tottered and the knife fell beside my head and the woman fell head over heels onto the stairs below, only the hem of her dress touching me as it was pulled after her.

I looked round and saw Jane standing next to Tommy, her father's service revolver in her hand.

I leapt to my feet, feeling a jagged pain in my shoulder.

The woman lay with her head almost at the bottom of the stairs, her feet above her on the upper stairs, on her back. In the seconds that it took me to stand and move forward to where she lay, blood spurted up from her chest like a fountain and then fell away as though the pump beneath the fountain had abruptly lost its power. It made a spray of red across the carpet and the wooden boards on either side of the stairs. The lifeless body appeared to be borne on this red carpet. The eyes were open.

I looked at the face of Jeanie Harrison.

I stepped down to where Jane stood and took the gun from her. She released her grip on it willingly.

'Are you all right?' she whispered.

I nodded.

'We were almost too late!' she said. The realisation of this seemed to have a sudden and profound impact, because she staggered backward and sat on a chair in the alcove. Tommy ran towards her and began to whisper childish expostulations, urging her not to be upset, telling her that they had come in time and that the woman who had died was a bad woman who wouldn't kill anyone any more.

He was like a little prophet, speaking with clarity and truth.

We heard footsteps race across the lobby and up the stairs.

William Harrison and Jack Macarthur both stopped when they saw me with a gun in my hand.

'Your sister is dead,' I told Harrison.

He looked as if he had been turned to stone. He was utterly still and the blood drained from his face, and his eyes seemed to be fixed on me as though his thoughts could not in ten thousand years encompass and absorb what I had said.

I didn't look at Macarthur. I determined to send him tumbling down the stairs if he attempted to disarm me. He was unsure about what to do.

Harrison stared at me for a long moment and then, as though nothing of consequence could happen now, one foot shambled onto the step above the other and he began to climb the stairs.

The man who covered the last few steps and sat beside the body was utterly diminished. This was not the lodge master who pulled invisible strings to shield his pathologically unhinged sibling from the consequences of her crimes.

He seemed deluged by sadness. Gently he reached out and before he closed his sister's eyes he whispered some endearment that could only have been heard by her.

I turned on Macarthur and said, 'You sent the constable away.'

I advanced down the stairs.

'You relieved the constable because you believed that this business could be finished here tonight.'

I advanced another step and Macarthur tensed, ready to defend himself.

'You believed that I would be murdered.'

I raised the hand in which I was holding Jane's revolver. I did not intend to point the gun at Macarthur. I did not intend to shoot him, even if he had tried to strike me, as I had reason to believe he might.

But Macarthur thought this was my intent, and anticipating his own demise he appeared to give way to some kind of inner collapse.

'It wasn't my idea!' he said, almost like a schoolboy admitting the truth in the seconds before bursting into uncontrollable tears.

'Then whose?'

'It was the professor! *He* said you were a meddler!'

'I don't believe you!'

'It's true! I didn't want to. I knew you would see your way through!'

'Tommy!' I shouted, still with my eyes on Macarthur. 'Go and find the constable, the one who was here or any other one. Tell him to come at once.'

Tommy clattered past me and then past Macarthur (whom he favoured with a sour look) and raced on down the stairs and across the lobby and out of the hotel.

I began to feel the effects of my injured shoulder. I was weary, too weary to maintain the anger that I felt towards the sergeant, or even the primal fear that the dead woman on the stairs had induced in me when she lived. I was too weary to try and comprehend the weird tenderness of William Harrison, who had sought by any means to protect his sister.

Macarthur, by contrast, appeared to recover his self-possession. I watched this almost as if it were taking place in the bright light of a photographic studio. His face had been expressionless before, except for a kind of contraction around the eyes that made me think he was about to cry. Now, his mouth set in a spiteful shape and his eyes assumed a calculating hardness that was the precursor to a more determined and decisive course of action than he had been able to manage until then.

He stepped up to the landing and darted past me to where the body lay and in a moment he had the knife in his hand and he wielded it like a man who had suddenly turned the tables.

But he simply could not undo the lies by which he had paved his own way to perdition.

Facing me with the knife in his hand, he could not think of an appropriate form of words with which to express what must have been conflicting thoughts.

Finally he settled on, 'Give me the gun.'

The weariness that had engulfed me became my protector, because I was too tired to comply and too tired to explain my lack of compliance.

I did nothing.

Then I heard a voice beside me.

'Put it down.'

I glanced round and saw Jane, sitting on the chair, looking at the sergeant very calmly. 'It's over,' she said.

He seemed confounded. He sat down on the stairs and let the knife drop onto the wood beside him.

The weapon had barely settled on the stair before we witnessed a familiar figure climbing up from the lobby.

James MacKay looked at me with a combination of astonishment and horror.

'You are all right!' he said, not solicitously but with surprise.

He climbed the remaining steps and turned to see the body of Jeanie Harrison, her brother sitting next to it still in a state of shocked stillness.

'You would have had me murdered,' I said to the professor's back.

He gazed for several seconds in front of him and then he turned slowly. His face was ashen.

'I believe I would,' he said in a tone that conveyed genuine awe.

And then a great commotion, with the unmistakable sound of constabulary boots on the flagstones in the lobby and on the wooden stairs.

'What's going on?' the constable who was supposed to have been guarding me demanded.

Barely a minute later, George Stephenson of the *Evening Citizen* arrived.

CHAPTER TWENTY-NINE

William Harrison had spent two years studying medicine before abandoning his studies to take over the shop on the death of his father. Jeanie completed her nurse's training and joined William in the shop. William never married. His sister wed a local grocer, Dickson McCartney, in 1888. The match produced no children but the couple were devoted to each other.

During the plague outbreak, the Harrisons' shop was a calm centre in the middle of a civic storm. William and Jeanie upheld sensible tenets of public health amid a welter of hysteria and hare-brained misconceptions. They correctly diagnosed diphtheria, consumption, scarlet fever, pneumonia and the common cold in patients who feared that they had been afflicted by plague, and they were assiduous in prescribing medicines at affordable prices. William and Jeanie treated patients in their homes and won respect and trust among people from all communities in the district.

But Jeanie was by then inhabiting a world at one remove from reality.

That spring, walking to work before dawn, Dickson McCartney was killed by a runaway railway tender, at the junction near the end of Crown Street. His right leg was sheared off and his right arm was so badly mangled at the elbow that it was effectively amputated. He died from loss of blood.

Two days after the funeral, Jeanie walked in the very early morning to the place where her husband had met his horrible end. She stood in the middle of the road and looked down at the offending rails. She might have stood there for longer but the policeman on duty recognised her. Gently, he weaned her away from her macabre vigil and shepherded her to the pavement. She stood beside the constable while he flagged a passing cab. He was struck by her manner, which was distracted but composed. He engaged her in conversation and he felt that there was something not quite right in her responses, as though outwardly she was calm but inside there was a struggle of some sort. Discreetly he reported this to William Harrison when, later the same week, he had occasion to meet the chemist at a function organised by the police benevolent association.

Jeanie returned to the shop and set about her work as though she had not been suddenly widowed under the most gruesome of circumstances. The very calmness with which she concentrated on preparing medicines and visiting the sick first alerted her brother to the devastation that had begun to work its way across his sister's psyche.

The pram made its appearance in November and was explained as a convenient means of carriage for multiple bottles and vials containing medications necessitated by the expanding number of patients Jeanie had begun to visit.

William speculated that his sister, knowing that she would never have children, had entered into a kind of imaginary motherhood. He was perfectly sure that something was badly wrong with Jeanie's mind, but he did not know how to respond.

He knew that Jeanie had taken medicines to Maggie McAllister and Brendan Gillespie. Yet he refused to countenance the possibility that his sister's madness had become murderous. He *could* not believe this. He resisted the inclination to spy on her. To do so would have been to convict her.

Coincidences, absences, hurried resumptions of work after periods outside the shop, inexplicable changes of mood – all these intensified during the first three months of 1899 and William still refused to notice.

When William McGonagall, Bessie Armstrong and Hector MacKinnon were butchered, William Harrison intensified his mentality of denial. Yet the truth was evident. Jeanie returned from her daytime and nocturnal outings in unnaturally high spirits. Very early one morning he found her cleaning the pram in the backcourt and she chased him away with an oath, his sister who in the course of a lifetime had never uttered a profanity.

He knew that Jeanie had begun to punish humankind for the inhuman tragedy that had been visited upon her husband.

He could not be the instrument through which his sister would dangle at the end of a hangman's rope. What she had done was an unspeakable, an unfathomable aberration.

And then the killings stopped.

William began to see a possibility of saving Jeanie. He made arrangements to sell the shop and he prepared, through a school friend now well established as a lawyer in Durbanville, to purchase a vineyard on the Western Cape. In that remote place he would endeavour to steer his sister's overwrought mind out of the murderous cul-de-sac into which it had stumbled.

But although Jeanie had stopped murdering, the police had not stopped investigating. It was not true that the authorities were sanguine about the killings because the victims belonged to a separate community. The same authorities who had been rocked by the outbreak of plague were rocked by the murderous mayhem wrought by a phantom. As long as the killer remained free, the hysterical fear of new killings would not be assuaged.

Jeanie Harrison would have been caught eventually; even in a rural corner of South Africa she could not have been safe forever. William knew this. So, in addition to preparing his sister's escape, he prepared a 'solution' to the murders.

William had influence in the City Chambers, where he had held municipal office, and he was active in the sort of fraternal societies where he and people like him organised activities to promote progress and serve the common good. Jack Macarthur was a very junior member of one of these societies.

Macarthur might have resisted the proposition that Harrison put to him – even though to do so would have been to place himself outside a circle of influence and preferment that could transform a promising career. Macarthur might have resisted but he was struggling with his own knotty ethical and legal problem and it was, like Harrison's predicament, a problem that had been caused not by his own weakness but by the weakness of someone close to him.

Macarthur's engagement to Alison MacKay represented a significant step up the social ladder, but the romance between the daughter of a celebrated professor and the lowly police sergeant owed nothing to social climbing on Macarthur's part and everything to true and blossoming affection between himself and his fiancée. This was the backdrop against which Macarthur uncovered a shocking truth about his prospective father-in-law.

It was Professor MacKay's habit to dine at one of the clubs along the river and then, alone or in the company of a few close companions, he would visit establishments of a different order nearby to drink and carouse. Several times he was secretly photographed enjoying the favours of women whose conduct showed not only a deep fund of sexual invention but also a disciplined attention to the hidden camera so as to ensure the professor's maximum humiliation.

And these were the photographs that found their way to Billy Fraser, who began extorting money and favour from MacKay.

I was one of these favours.

When Billy, whose work with the police gave him privileged access to official whispers, learned that a photographer was to be brought from outside Glasgow, he insisted that his developing room be placed at my disposal, accompanied by the payment of a fee. It was one of many arrangements by which Billy was systematically exploiting his hold over the professor.

In this case, however, MacKay was more than willing to agree, because I had been enlisted not to catch the killer, but to make Billy Fraser the real killer's scapegoat. That was why Alfred Garvey called on me at Edward Morton's house after Arabella Threadmyre's arrest. My involvement was to have helped Garvey's fellow lodge member, Jack Macarthur.

Billy was believed to have assaulted several women in the neighbourhood south of the river. That I would use his premises suited the purpose of the scheme, because I would more easily identify Billy in the photographs.

It was simple enough to connect Billy to the murders because he was sighted leaving the scene of the attack on Edie Hamilton. It was straightforward to place him in the photographs because he was sent by Professor MacKay to buy vanadium, another sinecure that Billy had extorted from the professor, charging twice the cost of the vanadium to the public purse, in addition to an exorbitant carriage fee.

Billy believed he was using the professor. Only afterwards did he realise that it was he who was being used.

I photographed Billy in Crown Street and, if he had not begun to suspect a plot, I might have photographed him speaking to the prostitute sent to wait for him there by Jack Macarthur. She had been paid to lure Billy into the close, where she would have broken off the encounter and accused him of trying to molest her. The same girl I had recognised from the evening when I dined with the professor and the sergeant and the chemist.

But by then he was on his guard.

An alleged assault, with accompanying photographs (the sequence of which could easily have been adjusted for the purposes of misleading a court) and a witness, would have rendered Billy ripe for the plucking. He could have been hanged for his own crimes and those of Jeanie Harrison. The real killer would be spirited away to South Africa to live peaceably, guarded by her brother so that she posed no further danger to the community. Professor MacKay, a pioneer in the battle against physical affliction, could focus again on his research unmolested by the venal attentions of a common blackmailer.

But none of this came to pass.

Because Jeanie Harrison had started to kill again.

This was not part of the plan hatched at the fraternal association to which Jack Macarthur and William Harrison – and Archibald Presser – belonged. It was not part of the plan in which Professor MacKay had become a willing accomplice.

Instead of images that would incriminate Billy Fraser, I had created images that would incriminate Jeanie Harrison. That was why MacKay had been so stunned and Macarthur had been so difficult when I was summoned after the murder of Seamus Hanlon.

It is unreasonable to posit that Jeanie *wanted* to be caught, and yet, everything that she did after the death of her husband was unreasonable. Perhaps she sought some sort of violent denouement to an interior drama that she desperately wished to end.

She knew why I had been brought to the city and ensconced in Simpson's Hotel. She was one of the best-informed people in the district. She knew the illnesses and the fears, the difficulties and hopes of many, many households between the river and the park.

The plot to frame Billy Fraser and extricate Jeanie Harrison became more desperate, and as I began to delve beyond the photographs I'd been commissioned to produce, I contributed unknowingly to the frenetic pace of events.

Billy Fraser could *still* have been framed even after the murder of Seamus Hanlon. But the stakes had risen significantly. For one thing, the conspirators became in the space of an afternoon not simply guilty of perverting the course of justice – they became accessories to murder. Hanlon would not have died if Jeanie Harrison had been turned over to the authorities months earlier. And Billy had grasped that he was no longer the puppet master; instead, he was being dangled by a rope that would very soon metamorphose into hangman's hemp.

Perhaps Jeanie went after me because by doing so she would definitely undermine her brother's heroic effort to save her. Perhaps she didn't *want* to be saved. Or perhaps she was beyond such calculations by the time she came to Simpson's Hotel and in my absence murdered William Gibson.

Previously, her modus operandi had been simple and businesslike. She would arrive at the victim's lodging bearing the prescription that had been sought and then she would administer an opiate, after which she used some pretext to have her victim follow her to the bottom of the stairs. There, using her nurse's training, she performed the ghastly amputations, wheeled the bodies outside and discarded the torso and head. The limbs she transported further away, to her allotment near the Queen's Park. When the site was investigated, twenty-eight limbs were found buried beneath the rows of basil, ginger, thistle and foxglove. Seamus Hanlon's right leg, dense in viscous matter due to the imperfect amputation, had been subject to rapid fermentation that caused a noticeable efflorescence in the foxglove planted on top of it. In Gibson's case she did not have time to remove the body and must have had only seconds in which to slip away from the lobby before Annie Belmont returned from buying tobacco.

And as I stumbled towards the truth, assisted by the Reverend Buchan's shrewd insight and Billy Fraser's equally shrewd sense of self-preservation, I emerged as an obstacle in the final desperate attempt by the conspirators to carry out their original plan.

The iron logic of their pragmatism turned them – perhaps inevitably – into murderers. Macarthur proposed a desperate remedy and MacKay agreed. I was allowed to return to the hotel. The policeman was sent away, and William Harrison watched his sister slip out of the shop at midnight and turn the corner into Crown Street and he did nothing to stand in her way.

CHAPTER THIRTY

Shortly before I was to leave Glasgow and travel to the Isle of Bute to complete my business with Tristan MacKenzie, the solicitor, I visited the Reverend Buchan at his church in Rose Street. He was arranging hymnals in the vestibule.

'Señor Camarón,' he said. 'It's kind of you to call.'

He spoke in a tone that I would have described simply as 'agreeable' if I had not known a little more about him. It was confident and gentle and, I think, not dictated by convention or circumstance. He was a man who approached his world with very definite convictions, and foremost among these was the belief – in the face of compelling evidence to the contrary – that human beings are more than the sum of their parts, that gentleness is not simply a virtue but a necessity.

This is what I thought as I followed him into the large gloomy church and we took a seat on one of the pews near the back.

He was without his jacket and I noticed that the threads on the seam of his shirt near the elbow of the left arm were starting to unravel. He looked comfortable in his grey waistcoat, yet his clerical collar seemed to me every bit as impossibly constricting as it had seemed when I first met him.

'You were right,' I said. 'The murders had nothing to do with the religion of the victims.'

He nodded sadly. 'Jeanie and William didn't think that way – they tended to their business and to their patients without distinguishing among them. It just happened that in those streets the people Jeanie took medicine to belonged to that persuasion.'

'And you were right about Billy Fraser,' I said.

This time he shook his head ruefully. 'He was not the murderer but he will at least stand trial now for the crimes he *has* committed.'

Billy had been charged with several counts of assault and with a whole series of crimes connected to blackmail.

'But you know, I have been thinking a great deal about this terrible business,' he said, 'and there is an oddness at its centre.'

We were sitting slightly sideways in order to speak. The minister seemed to perch on the pew in a sort of professionally expert manner. I quickly found the arrangement awkward and uncomfortable, and although we spoke in the subdued tones that seem appropriate in a sacred place, our whispers echoed around the big empty building.

He looked down and then looked away from me, apparently wondering whether he should continue.

'William Harrison, you see, wasn't a *bad* man,' he said at last. 'I am prepared to believe that he did what he did because he wanted somehow to deliver his sister from the consequences of her terrible deeds. James MacKay too had what might be viewed as a higher motive since he was related to Jeanie. He had his own reasons for wishing to see the back of Billy Fraser, of course, but Fraser is certainly no loss to the community. Jack Macarthur wanted to protect his fiancée's father and he put his own future in jeopardy because of that. Poor Jeanie Harrison was unhinged: she did those terrible things in some way because of the profound feelings she had for her husband.

'All of them,' he concluded, looking at me with an expression of absolute bafflement, 'acted out of a sense of righteousness, even love.'

'Only Billy Fraser seems to have had base motives, and he alone is likely to escape the hangman.'

The minister sighed. 'I have tried and failed to decipher real justice in this business.'

'Minister,' I said, 'when I first came to visit you, I showed you two photographs that had been taken in Crown Street. In one, you were speaking to a man who was very clearly drunk. In another, you were speaking to two women. One of the women was in her forties. The other figure in the photograph was a girl of about twenty. She carried a violin and walked with a stick; she had a calliper on her right leg.'

He nodded. 'You do not know who she is?'

I did not.

'Alison MacKay,' he said. 'The professor's daughter.'

He saw my surprise. 'Alison comes regularly to the mission in Crown Street. She teaches music to the poorest children.'

'*Your* mission?'

He looked at me patiently. 'The MacKays are Episcopalian,'

he explained. 'The Episcopalians have their own mission.'

After a moment he said, 'I do not know if she will continue now that her circumstances have changed. Yet she has done a great deal of good.'

'Her disability?'

'Polio. They say her father has made great strides in understanding the disease.' He added thoughtfully, 'That will end now, of course.'

Later, as he walked me out to the front door of his church, the Reverend Buchan said, 'And you, Mr Cameron' – he reverted to the Scottish pronunciation in a way that I now recognised as a courtesy – 'what are you going to do now? Will you continue with your photography?'

I shook my head and said, 'Not this kind. It isn't possible to photograph the human soul.'

He smiled for the first time in our conversation, as though I had hit on something he had been searching for.

'Just so,' he said. 'Just so, Mr Cameron.'

After leaving Rose Street I went to see Gabriel Mahoney.

'Mr Cameron,' he said. 'You have fairly set the cat among the pigeons!'

He believed I had succeeded *because* I was an outsider. 'You saw us as we really are,' he said, 'not as we like to *think* we are. And Tommy has been lauded by his schoolmates as one of the heroes of the drama,' he added with satisfaction.

'I would like to do what I can to be of some assistance to him.'

Mr Mahoney was hard-headed and unsentimental. At his direction I made available a small sum that could be used to facilitate Tommy's progress through school, principally by making provision for his room and board in a 'respectable' household and so as to preclude any possibility that he would ever be committed to an institution.

'Would you like to come and speak to him?' Mr Mahoney asked.

We walked from the headmaster's office into a large atrium and then up two flights of stairs till we came to a tiled corridor, on either side of which were classrooms.

'It's this one,' Mr Mahoney said, reaching down to open the door.

I placed a hand on his arm and indicated that we should not enter after all. Through the window I had spied Tommy sitting in the middle of the room, looking ahead at the teacher and the board, surrounded by other children – no different from any of them.

'Let's not disturb them,' I said.

Mr Mahoney nodded.

'Very well then, Mr Cameron.'

Together we moved along the corridor and down the stairs.

I walked back along Crown Street. It was just before noon and the pavement bustled. I passed the school where the Reverend Buchan's son and Jane's cousin had been educated. It was where the respectable met the disreputable part of the street. It was, like the Reverend Buchan and Mr Mahoney, completely woven into the fabric of this district. Yet it was distinguished from the surrounding squalor: it was distinguished not by power or privilege but by optimism, by a belief that goodness can prevail.

Outside the school, two women had stopped to gossip. As they chatted in their singsong dialect they leant on the long high handles of their prams. It was near here that Jeanie Harrison had stopped and spoken to Jane, asking her for directions to a hemp shop on the other side of the river. Jeanie was pushing her pram from Simpson's Hotel, where she had just murdered William Gibson.

I crossed the river, inhaling the distinctive aroma of tar and salt and smoke, and walked through the centre of town to the Fletchers' gallery. The doorbell tinkled as I entered. Jane was sitting behind the desk.

We walked down Buchanan Street. My father might have hurried out into the middle of the traffic to get a better vantage point from which to admire some of the elegant facades here. I think he would have photographed them with real joy, because they seemed to me to be some of the finest buildings that can be made with steel and stone and confidence.

When we reached the river, we walked for a little along the northern bank, past a block of low warehouses, and Jane led me onto a bridge that was too narrow for vehicles. Halfway across she stopped and we looked at the river. The noise of the city was a distant hum of klaxons and engines and whistles and wheels on cobblestones. Closer, we could hear men shouting to one another from cutters and skiffs.

'You were exposed to the most awful danger,' I said, 'and because of me.'

Jane looked across the water. 'We are exposed to the most awful danger when we're born. There is danger. There is joy too.'

We watched the river in silence until I said, 'There's a new kind of photography – moving pictures. I'd like to try that.'

I told her about a picture house where I'd seen images of General Shafter's troops coming ashore at Daiquirí. 'It was as though you were actually there watching it happen!'

'And can you acquire the necessary equipment to make these moving pictures?' she asked, adding sensibly, 'I imagine it's expensive.'

'I have enough to buy a moving picture camera, but I'll need an assistant.'

'Someone with experience of photography?'

'Yes.'

She shook her head and said, 'I don't know anyone with those skills who would be prepared to be your assistant.' She continued to look out at the river.

I glanced at her. She was very earnest and beautiful.

'But if you were seeking a partner . . .' she added.

'You mean a business partner?'

'Certainly.'

I must have looked crestfallen.

'I'll marry you too, if you ask me to,' she said.

ACKNOWLEDGEMENTS

I would like to thank the many friends who have indulged my curiosity about odd corners of history while researching this novel. Huge appreciation also goes to my agent, Bill Goodall, and my editor at Allison & Busby, Kelly Smith. Above all, I am indebted to my daughter Katarina and my wife Marija, without whom writing novels would be no fun at all.

KEVIN SULLIVAN was born in Glasgow. His career in journalism has placed him on the frontline of defining historical moments, from documenting events at Tiananmen Square to driving over a landmine while reporting in Sarajevo. His work has taken him to Singapore, Japan, Bosnia and Spain, and his experiences influence his writing.

sullivan.ba　　@Kev1nSull1van